CODY

Thank you for reading!

Lots of love from
Glenys Drive,

—Jesse

Jesse Severson

Dedication

To the best parents a boy could have.

Author's Note: The following interviews took place in 2018.

Chapter One

Sheriff George Cremble

I couldn't believe it when you called me. God's honest truth.

It's been so long.

Twenty-five years since Sam Jenkins was killed – 1993. So long ago you hope folks forget 'bout it, but you ain't forget something like that. Regardless, I'd be surprised if anybody 'round here wants to go back and relive it. Maybe twenty years since I heard anyone say a word 'bout it.

Or maybe they just ain't talk 'bout it in front of me.

Maybe behind closed doors, people are talking up a storm and gossiping and all that nonsense. Saying how Sheriff Cremble never did find Sam Jenkins's killer – because they ain't know the truth. I suppose this deal you're working on will probably cause people to curse my name.

"*Damn you,* Sheriff Cremble," they'll say. "Can you believe what that *damn* Sheriff Cremble did to protect that Cody Jenkins boy? He let that boy kill his own daddy."

Some of 'em are gonna say I brought shame to this great little town of Well Springs, Texas. That I deserve to get strung up. And you know what I fear the most? Maybe they're right.

**

I miss that sheriff seat from time to time, but it ain't fit for an eighty-one-year-old fool like myself. Kyle's been doing a good job, though – Sheriff Dunham, I should say. Keeping everything on the up and up here in Well Springs and Ford County. I still poke my old nose in the office from time to time. Especially since Maggie passed two years back. I can't keep myself away from the fire, I suppose. It ain't a power thing, neither.

I've always wanted to do right for this town. I love Well Springs with all my heart and all my soul. I wanted to keep everything nice and smooth. Most of all, I wanted to break the curse, you know? Folks always told me to break that Cremble Curse – that's what they called it.

The Cremble Curse.

My granddaddy, Wesley, he was named sheriff of Ford County – Well Springs being the county seat – before Christmas in 1918. He was only twenty years of age. A babe. I couldn't imagine. He came back from The Great War, they called it. I remember I was a little boy looking at one of them German crosses that he kept in a glass container on his desk at home. I never understood it at the time. Why keep something from the bad men?

That's the way I seen it.

I used to ask him questions about the war. Every little boy loves thinking about war. Being a hero and so forth. He never really liked to talk about it. He never gave me no details about stories from the battlefield – shooting up this or storming that.

"Well, Georgie," he would say. "We was over there doing our best to make sure the Kaiser didn't get what he wanted, because that Kaiser was no good."

He just left it at that.

I didn't realize until I was much older, but they ain't kill the Kaiser back then. He survived the war. Hell, he didn't die until the war with

8

Hitler. My granddaddy and his buddies never did give the Kaiser what-for.

Instead, the Kaiser left town. Spent the rest of his life in Denmark or Holland or one of them countries over there. Just funny, I suppose: a man behind so much death and misery spent the rest of his life in some country home. Where's the fair in that?

From what my daddy told me, my granddaddy was the only one in town to go over there. Well Springs was even smaller back then, but can you imagine? The only one in town? But I think what he seen back in Europe did a number on him. He'd never admit it, of course, but I think it did. My daddy told me Wesley used to scream like hell in the middle of the night. Scare the daylights out of everyone. They called it "shell shock."

I don't know.

Wesley Cremble was the sheriff in Well Springs for two-and-a-half decades. He was the law in town. Most people mind their manners in this town, though. Always have. This is a God-fearing town.

It was after school in 1943 and I ain't remember why, but I was walking down Main Street near the police station, so I decided to stop in and give Sheriff Cremble a quick visit. I turned onto Third Street – the police station is the second building on your left – and I seen all these people running in and outta the station. Yelling and screaming. It shoulda scared me off and sent me running back home.

But I ran toward the station, instead.

The front door was open, probably from all them people running in and out. Screaming about Sheriff Cremble. It was a small station at the time and his desk was inside to the right. When I got to the door, I looked in and I saw the back of him sitting in his chair. Well, *sitting* ain't the right word. His neck was resting on the back of his chair and his arms was draped off the sides. Just hanging there. Lifeless. Legs straight outward in a diagonal line.

I never seen his face, though. Somebody swooped me up and carried me out.

And that, as they say, was that. He was forty-five. A young man. We found out later it was something with his heart or liver. Wasn't no funny business. Natural causes, they say.

It didn't take but a week before the town came together and made my daddy, William, the sheriff. Made sense, I suppose. It ain't like he was coming in off the street. My granddaddy had taken him in and made him a deputy. The law was a family business in this town, he'd say. William had been in that station and seen how his daddy ran things. William Cremble was twenty-six when he became sheriff in Well Springs. Older than his daddy was when he had taken over, but still a boy.

I was about six or so when my daddy became Sheriff and I ain't know nothing else but the law. Was born into it. Had it in my blood, my daddy used to say. Regardless, the other children joked that it musta been easy being the Sheriff's boy growing up. That I coulda got away with anything.

"Georgie, no matter how much Cain you raise, your daddy would never put you behind no bars," they'd say.

Maybe they was right. Maybe I coulda thrown a rock or two or stuck a chocolate bar in my pocket. But God bless him, my daddy was a good man. Kind, too. So kind. He was always thoughtful with people. Let them have their say before he'd decide to take them in or not. Never berated nobody. Always found the *humanity* in people.

I never wanted to disappoint such a man.

He made me a deputy at the end of the 1950s. I was around twenty-one or twenty-two. When I started out, he taught me how to be fair. How to hear somebody out, but be willing to lay the hammer when I needed. That's probably the most important part of the job, he'd say. I followed that man around like a daggum puppy dog for the first few years. He gave me more leash as I got older. Let me follow on calls and do my own patrols. I remember my first solo, I pulled over Harriet Stills driving down Ninth Street going fifteen over. Had to pull her over.

She started crying and I started laughing, which got her laughing. I think I let her go with a warning. That's why I loved being a deputy, you know? Got to be the law without being in *charge* of it all. Depending on the day, I would do my own thing or I'd ride along with Sheriff Cremble. We always had nice conversations, updating him about Maggie and the girls.

I was with him when it all happened – don't know if you heard the story yet. Terrible. I remember the date.

March 23, 1973.

He got a call about a childhood friend. Thompson. Charles Thompson. They had growed up together, but Charles went down one path while my daddy went down the other. Charles had some demons, to be fair. He fought Hitler over there and always loved to mock my daddy that he stayed home in Texas during the war. Charles was always a pain in the neck to my daddy. It was always something with him. Drinking. Hitting on his poor wife. Her name was Susan or Susanne.

Sad thing was when he wasn't on God-knows-what, Charles was one of the most charming men you'd ever meet. Funny as hell, too. Even times when my daddy had to bring him in, Charles always had him hurting a rib from a joke he'd tell from the backseat.

But when we got the call that day, my daddy told me I'd better come along. It sounded like a bad one. We pulled up to the house and he was walking a little faster than usual to the door. Didn't even bother to knock this time. Turned the knob and walked right in, hollering out Charles's name. We got into the living room and his wife was in the corner sitting up against the wall and her face looked beat pretty bad. There was a bunch of smoke pipes and God-knows-what on the table. Charles was screaming about the Viet Cong. Saying they ruined the name Charlie for him. If he didn't look so serious, knowing Charles, you'd swear he was doing his jokes. He was wearing his old Army uniform – at least the top part. He had on his jacket and hat, but was in his undies and socks.

Lord, he wouldn't stop screaming. His face was as red as a cherry. He was calling my daddy every name in the book. Calling him a coward. Calling him soft. Saying, "When we was taking down Hitler, where was you, Mr. William Cremble? *Sheriff* William Cremble?"

To my daddy's credit, he took it all in stride. I wanted to turn Charles's red face blue, but my daddy just calmly stood there asking what was bothering him. Why was he beating on his wife? What had he taken?

Charles ain't answer. He kept screaming about how the government was controlling his mind or some nonsense. Saying we can't stop them. Saying we needed to wipe out every damn Viet Cong. I tried to walk over to his wife, but he screamed to stay back. I told him I needed to make sure that she was all right. He called me something foul and said if I took another step he'd kill me. Well, my daddy ain't like that too much. He told Charles to watch his mouth. Charles screamed back a four-letter word. I told him I needed to see if she was all right and then everything happened so fast.

I took a few steps toward her and Charles reached back and grabbed an old sword he kept mounted on this deal on his wall and he started to charge me. Sword loaded up behind his head and screaming. Before I had time to reach for my gun, I heard a couple of gunshots and Charles flew down to the ground. Sword went flying. He ain't move at all on the ground. I looked down and Charles had a giant wound on his temple. Blood flowing everywhere and Charles's wife screaming so loud I think the Viet Cong coulda heard her. Daddy damn near took the top of Charles's head clean off. I looked over and my daddy had dropped the gun and fell into one of the chairs. He couldn't believe he done it, neither. Killed a friend.

That's all I really wanna say about that night. Week later he quit. Said he couldn't do it no more. Hell of a thing.

**

Maybe I'm lucky I wasn't the one to pull the trigger. Or maybe I'd have kept my daddy from quitting if I was the one to kill Charles – if I was a little faster with the trigger. Maybe I'd be the one hanging it up and finding something else to do with my time.

There was a lot of hurtful rumors going around after that incident with Charles. People saying my daddy was seeing her on the side or some nonsense. There was lots of talk about who would take over as Sheriff. Maybe it was time for somebody other than a Cremble to take over. That's when people started saying it was cursed. That seat. Or maybe it was only cursed for Crembles. That was the joke at the time.

The Cremble Curse.

Honest to God, I never even told nobody I wanted the job – because I didn't. I took a little bit of a leave, maybe a week or two, and then when I got back, I got a letter in the mail talking about a town vote that I needed to attend. Said it was important and it was addressed directly to me.

If I remember right, I dressed in regular clothes to the meeting and sat near the back. Maggie came with me but I wouldn't let the girls come. I ain't know what to expect. Everyone was real nice, asking about my daddy and what-have-you. Ethel Pearson made me a pie, I recall. She was always making pies so it weren't nothing special, but it meant a lot. It was something good, you know? I needed something good. They invited my daddy, but he ain't wanna come. Can't say I blame the man.

After a little bit, Jimmy Davis, he was the head of the county commission, called things to order and announced the results for the

13

new sheriff. He said the vote was a landslide and that I would take over as the newest acting sheriff if I were to accept. Apparently, the county wanted to keep it in the family, as they say. Truthfully, I didn't expect that. I figured they was done with Crembles dying and killing in office.

But I was wrong.

Maggie, she started crying and hugging and kissing me. People was cheering and clapping. It meant a lot. I saw it more as a statement on my daddy. They knew he was a good man put in a bad spot. During all the cheering and hollering, Maggie pushed me off the chair and toward the stage. I went up and shook Jimmy's hand and he said something to me that I'll never forget.

"George," he said. "We couldn't ask for a better man to replace an even better man."

Boy, that one meant something special. I don't know about the first part, but I sure as hell agree with the last part. The crowd was cheering for me to make a speech and Jimmy smiled and motioned toward the microphone. I ain't wanna do it. Truly. But the job is a job of courage. It wouldn't make for great optics, so they say, if the man in charge of courage in town was too scared to talk into a microphone.

"I wanna thank y'all," I said. "I wanna thank y'all not only for your confidence in me for this position, but for all the nice gestures during these trying times. I need to let y'all know I appreciate it. I know I ain't alone in saying Sheriff Cremble is a good man and I know he'd be happy to know that the job is getting handed down to me. I know that Sheriff Cremble would be – well, I suppose I'm Sheriff Cremble now, huh?"

It weren't meant to be a joke, but it gave the crowd a big chuckle. I don't really remember much about the rest of my speech. The crowd gave me another round of applause, Jimmy ushered me off to the side, and I went back to my seat. Maggie was smiling and crying, and rubbed my back when I sat down.

"Sheriff Cremble," she said.

It was another week or two before I had the swearing in and it became official. It was open to the public, but nobody showed up. Just family. I wasn't hurt by that or nothing. I was ready for all the fuss to be over. I wanted to get going with my new position. My daddy showed up to the ceremony but didn't say much. He wasn't saying much of nothing at that time.

The day before I got sworn in, though, we had a nice dinner at my folks' house. Real nice dinner. Alotta love in that house. After dinner, when the ladies was taking the dishes, me and my daddy was sitting there with our drinks.

He said one thing to me.

"Whenever you are in doubt, George, do what you believe is right and true," he said. "Never lose track of what you believe is right."

I ain't say nothing back. We just looked at each other. He nodded, raised his glass slightly, and then took a drink.

**

Before the night with Cody, I only used my gun twice that I can remember. Well Springs ain't a violent place. First time was a Friday night, around fall of '85. Donnie from the Armadillo Bar called me and said that some fella from outta town was drunk and causing all kinds of trouble. Trying to pick a fight with a few of the fellas and was trying to stick his hand up Louise's blouse. She was a bartender over there at the time. Nice lady. Well-built.

So I drive over there and walk in and it don't take me more than a moment to figure out the situation. This young fella was cussin' up a storm. Calvin George and Nick Morse was each holding one of his arms as he was flailing and kicking and spitting everywhere.

"Hate to trouble you, Sheriff," Donnie said from behind the bar.

15

"Hey Donnie," I said, walking over to him. "Hell of a game Zach had tonight."

"Thank you, Sheriff. I think they got a shot at winning conference this year. How's Maggie doing?"

"Oh, it's always something but she's still with me. Louise, how are you doing, darling?"

"Sheriff, you get this pervert outta here!" she said, pointing at the man.

"Louise, you wanna get a shot in before I take him away?" I said. "Seems like Calvin and Nick got him teed up for you."

Now I was joking around, but she stormed over and slapped the smarts outta this yahoo. He called her something foul and spit toward her. That was enough. I went over and grabbed the man behind the arm and pulled him off to the side after Calvin and Nick let him go.

"Listen here, stranger," I said, real stern-like. "I don't know who you are or what brought you to Well Springs. I don't care. I ain't gonna let you treat these good people like this. Now, you can either apologize and be on your way or I can take you in."

I assumed he would make nice and that would be that. I assumed wrong. This man up and drove his forehead right into my nose. Didn't break it, thank God. But it knocked me back and got me dizzy – nose starting to bleed everywhere – and next thing I know, he's sprinting out the door. The others in the bar made their way after him, but I told them to get back and I went running and stumbling outside. I saw him turn on his truck, rush it into reverse and swipe the side of Nick's truck as he pulled out onto the road.

I don't know what got into me. He was speeding away and I ran into the middle of the road, took out my gun, and fired a few shots at his back tires. Ha. What was I doing? Wanted to be John Wayne, I suppose. I ain't hit nothing, of course, and he kept on driving. Never saw that man again. Calvin, Nick, Louise, and Donnie came out into the street and was giving me a look. They couldn't believe I fired my gun, neither. I remember looking down at my hand and it was shaking a bit.

"You get him?" Donnie said, coming a little further into the middle of the road.

"No, Donnie. I wasn't trying to get him. Just wanted to give him a scare. Don't think he'll be coming back."

"Damn kid never did pay," Donnie said.

There was a bit of silence and then we all started laughing. Lord, that was funny for some reason. Really took away the tension.

A few years later, around '89 or '90, Miss Benton called me up. Bless her heart. She was something else. Lucille Benton. It was the middle of the day and I was about to run and get some lunch when Deputy Jackson came telling me that Miss Benton wanted to speak to me. She was a nice lady, but she was up there in years. Around late eighties at the time and I believe she made it to ninety-seven. She called the station and wasn't gonna let Deputy Jackson deal with her. She wanted me and she dug her heels in.

"Miss Benton, to what do I owe the pleasure?" I said, picking up the phone.

"Sheriff Cremble? Is that you?" she said.

"In the flesh. What can I do for you, Miss Benton?"

"Sheriff Cremble, you need to come over right away."

"What's wrong, dear?"

"You need to come over right now. I'm on Ninth Street. Yellow house."

"I know where you live, Miss Benton. Are you okay?"

"You need to come over here now."

She hung up, so what could I do? I headed over there. When I got to her house, she was standing out on the street in her robe – waving and screaming and so forth.

"Miss Benton, now what the heck is going on?" I said to her.

She was hollering about how her cat, Lamb, had jumped up into the oak tree in her yard and wouldn't come down. I shoulda expected something like this.

"Miss Benton, you called the sheriff of Well Springs, who could be fighting any number of crimes, to come get Lamb outta your tree?"

"Sheriff Cremble, we know that there ain't no crimes being committed right now. Secondly, I do believe my tax dollars help pay your checks."

"What taxes you paying, Miss Benton?"

"I don't believe that's any of your business, Sheriff. Now, you gonna get Lamb down for me? Or are you suggesting an old lady climb up that oak tree?"

"You ain't gotta climb nothing, dear. Can you step back for me?"

I don't remember why, but that day I musta been in a real spirit. I wasn't ready to go twelve rounds with some old lady about a cat. I took my gun out and shot a couple of rounds up in the air, to spook little Lamb down. Miss Benton was mad as hell, but it worked. Lamb hopped off that tree back onto the ground and ran back to her.

That would be the extent of my gun use on the job. Twice. Never needed it otherwise. Like I said, things always been pretty calm for the most part around here.

That's what made that night with Cody something else. Never could believe something like that could happen here. As time passed, though, I realized maybe I shouldn't have been so confused by it. Maybe it was a matter of time before something happened to Sam Jenkins.

I just never thought it would be his boy Cody who done it.

Sam Jenkins' death shocked the community. But the community ain't see the *shocking* part. Being in that room was the shocking part. The smell. The blood. My God. It was primal. Animal kind of stuff. Or the scene of a lover's quarrel gone wrong. Real rage.

I hope I done the right thing in the aftermath of everything. It's one of those deals, you know – you can't anticipate what you're gonna do until it happens. I ain't ask for it to happen, but that's part of the job. Being Sheriff.

It ain't all sipping coffee.

I think I done the right thing. I really do. But maybe I always tried to convince myself I done the right thing. There was nights that I lay awake, tossing and turning with doubt. The boy murdered his daddy. Murder is against the law last time I checked and I helped cover it up. And Sam being killed created a dark cloud over Well Springs. Made it the place where neighbors couldn't trust neighbors no more. There was the chance we'd never recover. The town would die in terror of some killer on the loose that never existed.

I feared it. Lord, I feared it.

But I believed what I done was right and true. I never wanted to lose track of what I felt was right.

Chapter Two

Debra Jenkins

My earliest memory of Sam was from first grade.

Well, I was in first grade. He would have been in fourth or fifth. It was recess on a nice day – springtime – and I remember drawing something. Maybe I was writing something. Regardless, I was by myself off to the side. Suddenly, this second grader – Kenny Dowlinson – came over and smacked the paper out of my hands. I was so scared. I started crying and Kenny was being all tough and bravado and saying this is what a man does. A tough man.

I was in first grade! I was like six. I was crying because I was afraid and Kenny wouldn't leave. I remember seeing Sam's shadow. I was looking down at the ground hoping Kenny would go away and I saw Sam's shadow sweeping over.

Sam pushed Kenny really hard and he flew to the ground and *he* started crying. It was a whole thing. I remember Mrs. Middleton came running over and screaming. At the time, it felt like the biggest moment in the world, but looking back it was silly. One kid pushed another kid because that kid was bugging someone. That's it.

But Sam got into big trouble because Kenny's parents were sort of bigwigs in town. They were in real estate and owned a few properties. Nothing major, but enough to have some pull in Well Springs.

Kenny never did bother me again, though. I wonder what he's up to nowadays. He joined the service last I heard and never came back to town. But that's my first memory of Sam: him coming to help me.

**

People always think they are so original and funny.

I understand part of being a kid is having classmates tease you — about your weight or your clothes or your name or whatever. It's part of childhood. But with a name like mine, people always thought they were so cute by making a joke about Little Debbie. *Hey Little Debbie, you got any cupcakes? Hey Little Debbie, you bring oatmeal cream pies for the rest of the class? Where's your little hat, Little Debbie?*

So stupid.

It's why I got into trouble in school for the first time. It was fifth or sixth grade and we were in the middle of class and Dave Finn wouldn't let up. He was bugging me and bugging me all day. It started at morning recess and I thought he'd let it go, but after lunch he was still relentless. We sat near the back of the class, and Dave was whispering something about Little Debbie and I snapped.

"Dave, will you *please* shut up, you asshole!"

The whole class went silent. Mrs. Jefferson was writing something on the board and she turned around and stared right at me.

"Debra Adams!" she cried out.

"I'm sorry, Mrs. Jefferson, Dave just won't leav-"

"Principal's office. Now!"

21

I forget if they called my parents or not. They must not have – my parents are pretty religious, so I would have got into even bigger trouble. But I sheepishly walked into the main office. The secretary told me to take a seat in one of the chairs off to the side. Sam was already sitting in one of the other chairs – his head resting against the wall and his hands interlocked on his lap. He would have been a freshman or sophomore. Being a small town and all, the elementary, middle, and high schools were all in one building. I walked over to sit down and I noticed the skin on the knuckles of his right hand had torn off. Dried blood was painted across the back of his hand.

When I sat down, he turned his head and asked me what I was in for. *What are you in for?* Like we were in prison or something.

"I called somebody a bad word," I said.

"What'd you call them?"

I looked at him and shook my head.

"C'mon, what'd you call them? A big doo-doo head?"

"I called them an asshole," I whispered.

"Whoa!" Sam laughed. "Wow, we got ourselves a certified little *bad ass* here."

It made me smile and he noticed I was looking at his knuckles.

"Oh, this?" he said, gingerly lifting up his hand. "What do you think happened?"

"I don't know."

"C'mon, what do you think happened? I won't be mad."

"How am I supposed to know?"

"Take a guess."

"You hit somebody?"

"Maybe," he said with a smile. "He deserved it though."

"Who was it?"

"Mark Thomas. I don't know if you know him. He's a junior."

"Is he the one with the earrings?"

That made Sam laugh again and he nodded. I told him that Mark seemed like an asshole. He told me I had some mouth on me and maybe we'd be friends someday. He got called to the back to see the principal.

"What was your name again?" he said as he got up.

"Debra."

"Debra. Nice talking with you, Debra. See you around."

"See you around."

The version I heard later was that Mark and Sam were arguing about something and Mark made some comment about how Sam's dad was a run-down alcoholic and his mom was nothing but a blitzed-out pill head that'll give it up for nothing. That kinda stuff. Sam snapped and landed a few punches and broke Mark's nose. Probably would have killed him if the people around didn't get Sam off him.

After all of that, Sam didn't get expelled or even suspended. He could always sweet talk his way out of trouble. He said he felt he needed to defend his mother because at that point in her life, nobody else would. Who would defend her if not her own son? That he would never abandon his mother by allowing somebody to drag her down like that. Sam got maybe a few days of detention. That's it. He caved somebody's face in and essentially got away with it. Funny how that works.

Sometimes I wonder about how different *my* life would have been if he had killed Mark that day.

**

I wasn't really in anything in high school. I didn't do sports or band or drama or any of that. I went to school and hung out with my friends. That was it. Sam played for the Well Springs football team – he was a senior when I was a freshman. He was a jock but he wasn't dumb. He was actually pretty smart, to tell you the truth. He could have gone to a real college.

23

But he was always a good football player. He broke somebody's leg in a game – against Kerrville. I didn't go to the game. The next week, though, everyone at school was talking about it and he was strutting around the hall. I thought the whole thing was pretty gross. Why would you be proud you broke somebody's leg?

He graduated from Well Springs High and went off to play football for the junior college a few towns over. I guess *went off* is the wrong term. He stayed in Well Springs and lived with his parents. Not exactly frat parties and all-nighters.

Well Springs High had a good team my senior year in 1983 – three years after Sam graduated – and we had just beat Mayfield in the homecoming game. I remember everyone in town was excited and I got invited to a party that night. It was at Andrew O'Daniel's house. I don't even remember why I was invited or why I even went. I'm pretty sure I went with my friend Lisa.

I remember David Beniot and Robert Struck offering me a drink as we walked in. David was sweet. He was a lineman. Bigger guy. He ended up being an electrician. Family man with kids and everything. Really happy for him. They ended up settling in the Houston area. I don't think Robert played much on the football team. But he was nice, too. They wanted me to be comfortable. So stupid, but I drank a few beers pretty fast. People were already drunk when I got there, so I was trying to catch up. I remember we were all in the living room and I was sitting on the couch in the middle seat – next to Lisa and somebody else.

Well, Sam was at the party to celebrate because he was still friends with some of the guys on the team. He was drinking straight from some bottle. Everybody loved him, though. He was having everybody laughing and in a good mood. He made a joke and everyone around him started laughing. He looked around and we made eye contact. I'll admit it: he was really attractive. He was a good looking, strong guy who seemed like he was a lot of fun. I smiled at him and he smiled back.

Later in the night – much later – we were both in the kitchen and he asked me if I wanted to take a shot. He said he would help me with it.

"And how do you help somebody take a shot?" I said.

"Here, watch this."

He poured out a shot on the kitchen table and lifted it up. He grabbed me by the hip and pulled me close to him.

"We're going to take this shot together. You put your lips on that side, I'll put my lips on this side. Easy peasy."

I mean, it's the stupidest thing in the world, looking back. Taking a shot together? A bunch of it would spill. But I was seventeen and dumb. So dumb. Well, he lifted up the glass and pushed our cheeks together and I opened my mouth. At the last minute he tossed all the shot into his mouth and then kissed me.

It startled me, but he was this college athlete and I enjoyed it. The attention and the affection. The kissing, though, turned into making out. It all happened so fast because I was pretty drunk. We were kissing in the kitchen and the next thing I remember, we were in some bedroom with the door shut.

He picked me up and carried me to the bed. Once I landed on the bed, he rolled us over so he was on the bottom. He clumsily took off his shirt and undid his belt. I didn't know what to do, so I took off my shirt. He reached around me and I could feel him fumble with the hooks of my bra. Part of me was hoping he wouldn't figure it out and give up and we would just laugh and it would kill the moment. After a few seconds, though, I felt my bra came off and his eyes got big.

I could have asked if he had a condom. He didn't, of course. To be fair, I didn't have one, either.

**

25

There were rumors I was bulimic.

The throwing up.

When I walked down the halls, people looked at me and whispered. When I saw they were looking at me, they'd turn away really quick. I was getting really emotional and snapping at my friends for stupid stuff. The worst was the day in Mrs. Bryant's first period class. The whole sickness thing already got to me earlier in the morning when I woke up. I threw up before school. At this point, I thought I had some weird bug that wouldn't go away. I was sitting on the far-left side of the classroom, my head resting up against the wall, when Mrs. Bryant asked a question. Nobody answered.

"Anybody? Debra?" she said, turning toward me.

Just the worst. I told her I didn't know.

"Well, guess," she said.

"No."

It was rude, but I wasn't feeling good. The rest of the class let out a sound of shock and I felt bad, in hindsight, that it probably embarrassed Mrs. Bryant. She told me that I was being really disrespectful. I called her a bad word and that escalated everything. I'm pretty sure it got me suspended for a couple of days. My parents, being as religious as they are, were not happy.

Then the sickness really got bad.

I left class to go to the restroom and the wave of nausea got stronger the closer I got. I thought I could make it, but I threw up through my hands all over the restroom floor. So embarrassing. I went into the stall and was sick for a while – curled around the toilet. I was crying. It felt so claustrophobic. I could hear people coming in, commenting about how disgusting the floor was and leaving.

Nobody asked if I was okay.

That's what started the rumors about me being bulimic. I was in there for close to an hour. Just crying and crying. It was partly because of how awful I felt, but mostly I was crying because it started to register that I might be pregnant.

**

There's only one pharmacy in Well Springs and I didn't want to take any chances. You never know who would see me and who'd they tell.

Oh, I saw Debbie Adams at the pharmacy and guess what she was buying? A pregnancy test! Can you believe it?

Instead, I drove out to Beaufield, which is a good hour-and-a-half away. That was one of the longest drives of my life. I remember I drove in silence. Total silence. Praying and praying that I wasn't pregnant. There were these series of billboards along the way — promoting a nursery and daycare in the nearby town of Harris. Probably was an omen, I guess. I got to the pharmacy and I sat in the parking lot for thirty minutes. Hands on the steering wheel. I hadn't seen anybody go in for a while, and I wanted to get it over with.

I walked around inside for a little while. A nice older man asked if he could help me find anything and I told him, *No, thank you*. Finally, I came across the tests. There were three of them. I didn't know the differences, so I bought the cheapest one. I thought about stealing it, because I didn't even want some stranger knowing I'm buying it. But what kind of lesson would that have taught?

Cody, I shoplifted to find out that you were going to exist.

I decided to buy it and the cashier ended up being that nice older man who tried to help me earlier. He looked at the box, looked at me, and shook his head slightly before telling me the total. I'll never forget that — him shaking his head. After I paid, I went to my car and cried some more. I didn't want to bring the box home and have somebody find it in the garbage or something, so I went to a fast food place in Beaufield and

27

went to the restroom. The directions were a little confusing, but I assumed you pee on it, so I squatted over the toilet and put it between my legs.

I can't even describe the dread I felt as it slowly told me it was positive. I dropped it into the toilet and left. Cried some more in the car. By the time I got back home, it was well past dawn. My dad was watching TV and my mom was needling. They didn't notice I came in, so I went to my room and laid down.

**

It was maybe two months into the pregnancy – I already had the talk with my parents, which wasn't exactly pleasant – and I knew that I needed to talk with Sam. In hindsight, I shouldn't have let him know and tried to do it on my own. It would have changed everything.

It was a few hours after Sunday service and I went into my room to call him. I held the receiver to my ear but didn't dial – to the point where the dial tone changed to a voice telling me to hang up and try again. I dialed his number, which I got from a friend. It rang and rang and rang.

"Yeah?" a tired, rough voice whispered.

"Oh, hey," I said.

"Who is this?"

"Sorry, it's Debra."

"Debra?"

"Yeah, Debra Adams."

"Debra Adams?"

"Yeah."

There was a long silence of him trying to remember who I was. He sounded either hungover or still drunk.

"Oh yeah," he said. "What's up?"

"Well, can we talk?"

"That's what we're doing. Talking. What do you want?"

"Wow. Okay, well I think I might be pregnant."

"Congratulations."

"Yeah, so..."

"Why are you telling me?"

"Are you kidding?"

"What?"

"Because you're the father."

There was a long silence but I could still hear him breathing.

"Sam?"

"Yeah."

"Are you okay?"

"How do you know I'm the father, though?"

"It's yours, Sam."

"Yeah, but how do you know?"

"Because you're the only person I've ever slept with."

I heard him put the phone down and start screaming and smashing his room in the background. Pure anger. He went on screaming for maybe ten seconds as I cried and to Sam's credit, he came back to the phone and said, "Okay."

"Okay?"

"Yeah, what do you need from me? What do you want me to do?"

**

I hated the photo from the day it was taken. I look like a big fat cow. I really wanted to wait until after Cody was born to have the wedding for that specific reason. I'm standing there, turned slightly so you can see my massive belly in that *white* dress, with Sam behind me and his arms stretched around me. And I mean, *stretched*. His arms don't make it all the way around me. It's so embarrassing. Neither of us are smiling. We look like a young couple that doesn't want anything to do with the life that was ahead of us.

29

I know my mom was ashamed of me. That's not what she was planning for her daughter. The summer after high school: a big, pregnant whale stuffed into a dress that doesn't fit. Because of that, my parents wouldn't support us. It turned into this screaming match. I thought it was so unfair of her, but she said it's what she believed.

When I asked Sam what he thought about getting married, he said that we – his words – "might as well just get it over with."

When Cody was born, Sam was late because he was at the bar. He missed him actually being born. Sam looked terrible when he finally came into my room at the hospital. I was laying there after the nurse had taken Cody away.

"Is he – what does the doctor ... where is Cody at?" Sam asked. "Did you have him yet?"

Good thing Cody was born into a family, right?

After Sam was killed, I threw out all of his stuff. His clothes and magazines and his things from high school. I didn't care. If it belonged to him, I tossed it in the garbage. Except that picture of us on our wedding day. That picture I kept for myself. One night, I went into the backyard and I sat looking at it for 10 minutes. My whole life was regret and pain and hurt and there is no way to change it. Holding the frame in both hands, I snapped it back so the sides ripped away and the glass shattered. It cut my hand, but it didn't hurt. I grabbed the picture, shook off the glass and held it up one last time. I lit the bottom right corner of the photo with a lighter and the embers slowly destroyed everything in its path. It burned away our legs, then our torsos, then our unsmiling faces.

We were gone.

Now the memory is the only proof that picture ever existed.

Chapter Three

Fred Doyle

My name is Fred Doyle.

I was next door neighbors with Sam Jenkins back in 1993, when everything happened – the murder. Terrible. I was the one to call Sheriff Cremble the night it happened. I'm turning eighty-six this year, which would put me around sixty then. We thought about moving out of the neighborhood shortly after the incident – me and my wife, Helen. She couldn't stand the memory of it. We even talked about moving out of Well Springs, believe it or not. But we decided against it.

The Jenkinses moved next to us in 1985. They were a nice little family. Cody was around two and Debra was pregnant with the twins – Cassandra and Nicole. We knew of Sam and Debra before they moved next door, seeing them around town and whatnot. Sam was a heck of a ballplayer back in his day. Debra always seemed nice. Warm face.

When they were first looking at the house, Helen watched them from the window. Telling me all about it and so forth.

"It looks like that Sam Jenkins boy," she said. "He's looking at the garage with the realtor. They're out there talking."

"Helen," I said. "I know what it looks like when people are looking at houses, you don't have to keep me so *informed*."

"Freddie, Freddie, they're shaking hands. They're all smiling and – oh my word, Freddie. I think it's them. I think they're moving in."

"Well, stay right there, Helen, I'll call it into the *Well Springs News* as a news tip."

"They seem nice," she said. "He's a handsome boy and she's a cute girl. Look at how pregnant she is. My goodness. And she already has a little one. Freddie, come look. Oh, Freddie, what a darling couple."

"I'll take your word on that one, Helen. I got a feeling I'll meet them one of these days."

When they finally moved in, he pulled in with a small trailer behind his '75 Chevy truck – red with white siding. I always loved that truck. Just gorgeous. Helen made them a casserole – Southwest cheesy chicken – and we took it over to them. Maybe it was rude to come knocking while they were busy unpacking, but Helen kept persisting we go over and introduce ourselves. She got all dolled up, too. Made her hair and everything. She said it's important to make good first impressions and be stewards of the neighborhood. I'll never forget that. *Stewards of the neighborhood*, she said.

When we went to knock, the door was already cracked a little. Helen asked if I should ring the doorbell. She would ring it herself, but she was holding the casserole and all.

"Woman, you need to just calm down already."

I'd swear she was fixing to meet LBJ or something. I knocked on the hinge-side of the door, so it wouldn't open any further. After a little while, the door creaked opened.

It was Cody.

He stood there, wobbling like a drunk sailor hanging onto the door.

"Oh my, aren't you the cutest?" Helen said. "What's your name, sweetie?"

Cody stood there and stared at us. Finally, Sam came into the room and saw us at the door. He smiled, came over, and picked up Cody. He cradled him in his left arm.

"I see you've met the man of the house," Sam joked about Cody. "Sam Jenkins."

He reached out his hand and gave me a firm but friendly handshake. He was wearing a gray t-shirt that he was sweating through from all the lifting and moving.

"Fred Doyle, nice to meet you, son. How old is the little man?"

"Just started his terrible twos," Sam said, turning and smiling at Cody.

"Oh no!" I said. We all laughed and Helen not-so-subtly cleared her throat. "Oh yes, this is my beautiful wife Helen."

"Helen, I'm Sam," he said. He really did have a charming smile. "This little monster is Cody. Can you say hello, Cody?"

Cody just stared at us and we all laughed.

"Do you have any children?" Sam asked.

"No, unfortunately not," I said.

"I'm sorry to hear that," he said.

"Thank you," Helen said. "Is the mother around? We'd love to meet her."

"She's around this mess somewhere. Debbie?" he called out.

Debra came from the hallway and she looked tired — moving while pregnant with twins, can't say I blamed her. She apologized for looking a mess because she wasn't expecting company. Helen said she wished she always looked as good as Debra looked as a mess and that seemed to cheer her up.

"Well, I don't know if y'all had plans for dinner, but I made you my Southwest cheesy chicken casserole," Helen said. "Don't feel like you have to eat it if you don't like it."

"You're going to like it," I said to Sam.

"I can already tell that we will, thank you so much, ma'am," Sam said. "What a welcome to the neighborhood."

"You two are too kind," Debra said.

"What are neighbors for?" Helen said. "If you ever need any help with anything, you let us know."

**

It was a Tuesday afternoon – that's when I always got in my hay. I ran a feed shop before retiring a few years back. I remember that vividly, though. It was a Tuesday afternoon because I was helping unload the hay and my office girl Georgina came and told me that I needed to get to the hospital in Odessa right away. Helen had been rushed there.

You talk about a stressful 30-minute drive. It's the fastest I've ever driven – got up to 100 at one point. Luckily there wasn't any policemen to slow me down. When I got to the ER main lobby, I asked the lady at the reception desk about Helen. As she was looking it the room number, I saw Sam walking toward me. The front of his shirt and pants were covered in dried crimson red.

"Lord Jesus, what happened?" I said.

"She's going to be okay, Fred."

"What happened?" I could hear my voice shake.

Sam was driving home for lunch and as he pulled in, he saw Helen face down on the concrete walkway leading from the driveway to the house. He ran over and there was blood everywhere and she wasn't responding. He was crying out her name and shaking her but no response. Luckily, she had a pulse. So he picked her up and carried her to his truck. He held her head in his lap as he drove to the hospital –

34

more than 40 miles. I can't believe how lucky we were that Sam was there.

It was one of the scariest days of my life. The doctors ran tests – talking about epilepsy or stroke and other things – but nothing came back conclusive. Through it all, they say she just fainted, maybe dehydrated, and hit her head on the concrete. It gave her one heck of a concussion and she lost quite a bit of blood. A lot of blood. She was in the hospital for five days, recovering and doing tests and so forth.

Sam visited every day. Every single day after work, he came all the way to talk and cheer her up. A lot of people told me after the fact, back when we were home, they were praying for us and glad she made it through. That's nice. I don't want to sound unappreciative of that. But Sam was the only person to actually come visit her. He'd bring flowers and balloons. He took care of things around our house, too. Mowed our lawn, watered our plants, brought us things we needed.

The day we were able to come home, the Jenkins family greeted us on our lawn with a homemade sign saying, "Welcome Home Helen!"

"My word. Freddie, look!" she said, covering her mouth with her hand.

When we got out of my truck, Cody came and gave Helen a big hug around her leg. She was crying and they all gave us a big group hug. It was a touching moment. They invited us over for a nice barbeque in the backyard. Cody was running all around, Debra was looking after the twins, and Sam was cooking. I'll never forget that moment. Helen and I were sitting there, holding hands, appreciative of the life we had. We were lucky. When it was dusk, Sam and I were off on our own talking over beers. The women and children were off talking and so forth.

"She seems like she's doing good," Sam said.

"Yeah, she's on the mend, as they say."

"That's good. Good."

"Sam, I don't know if I said this, but I wanted to thank you."

"Fred, come on. No need."

"No, it really meant a lot. Everything your family – you – have done for us. We're very lucky. I don't want you to feel it goes unappreciated."

He knew he wasn't going to win that debate. He nodded. We sat there for maybe 15 minutes in silence. We watched Cody running around. We watched Helen and Debra talking and laughing and admiring the twins. We sat there as men. It was maybe the best 15 minutes in all the years living in that neighborhood. The quiet reflection. The unspoken understanding of togetherness – that we weren't alone. It really was touching.

Things were never quite the same after that.

**

Maybe a month after the barbeque, the potluck incident happened.

After a service one Sunday, the First Church of Well Springs held their annual potluck on the lawn of the property. Helen brought her pigs-in-a-blanket and everybody was having a nice time. The girls group did this choreographed dance, the choir sang some songs, and the pastor was even the one doing the cooking – wieners and burgers. Just a nice time.

The Jenkinses showed up well late. Frankly, they could have done everyone a favor and not showed up at all. Sam was already drunk and it was hardly one o'clock. You could tell he was drunk even before you smelled it on him. He carried a six-pack of beer, tucked in his arm like you'd hold a child. Debra held Cody's hand and pushed the twins in their stroller. Sam looked bad – first time I ever saw him like *that*.

When I got the chance to speak to him in private, I asked him why he brought alcohol to a church get-together.

"It said bring refreshments," he said and chuckled to himself.

"Yeah, but Sam, beer?"

Then he said something I'd rather not repeat. Told me something vulgar then kept walking. Debra looked in rough shape, too. Her hair was messy and she had dark lines under her eyes. Looked tired. She also had a bruise on her temple and when Helen asked her about it, Debra said that a can of green beans fell off the cupboard when she was making dinner. We didn't realize it in the moment, though. We felt, *Well, those things happen.*

Sam didn't waste much time at the potluck. He was drinking that beer like a man who just got done wandering across the Chihuahuan Desert. He was flirting with some of the younger women at the barbeque — joking and laughing and whatnot. When they showed they weren't interested in him, he went off and sat by himself on the curb of the parking lot. I remember that: him sitting there by himself on the ground, finishing one beer, and then starting a new one.

I went to Pastor Wilheim and asked him if we should go talk to Sam. Maybe we should have let the drinking dog lie, so to speak. Instead, we went over to talk to him together.

"Sam, we missed you in service today," the pastor said.

"Is that right?" Sam said before taking a big, long drink and letting out a belch.

"Excuse you," Pastor Wilheim said.

"Huh?"

"Excuse you," Pastor Wilheim repeated.

"What the *so-and-so* are you talking about?" Sam said, except he didn't say *so-and-so.*

"Sam, we don't need that kind of language. I was only teasing."

"Huh?"

"Sam, is everything all right?" I asked.

"Fred, everything is just *peachy.*"

"How much have you had to drink, Sam?" Pastor Wilheim asked.

37

"Why? You worried I might break your record?"

"You're clearly drunk. How come you're over here drinking by yourself?"

"Because it beats the hell out of sitting here by myself and *not* drinking."

"Maybe it's time to switch to water or some juice," the pastor said.

"Juice," Sam said laughing. "Yeah, Pastor could you get me a cup of *juice*?"

"You'll drink it?"

"Pastor, just get me a cup of juice."

"Well, okay, stay right here."

Sam gave a sarcastic thumbs up and took another long drink from his beer before crushing the can. It was tragic, you know. And I know there's little ones with diseases, nice folks who can't catch a break, and other unfair things in life. Those are *tragic*. But I knew he was a good man deep down. Hoped it, at least. He had a beautiful wife, three beautiful children – this was before Tommy was born – and he was embarrassing all of them.

I didn't know what to say to him, so I stood there while he opened his last beer. Pastor Wilheim came back with a 10-ounce paper cup of apple juice.

"We can get you as much of this as you'd like," Pastor Wilheim said to Sam.

Pastor Wilheim bent down to offer the juice and Sam grabbed the cup and threw it back at the pastor's face. Juice and the cup. Everything. It splashed everywhere and before I knew it Sam sprung up and pushed the pastor. Pastor Wilheim stumbled backward before falling on his rear end. Sam told the pastor something vulgar, saying he's a *so-and-so* and a *this-and-that*. When the pastor put his hands on the ground behind him to get up, Sam threw a wild punch and hit the pastor right across the face. Knocked him out cold. Sam took his beer and poured some on the pastor, before tossing the can on him.

It all happened so fast. I wish I could have stopped him, but you don't exactly expect somebody to knock out the pastor for no reason. Sheriff Cremble happened to be there and he ran over and fought with Sam. It was pure chaos. People were screaming and crying. I don't believe that Sheriff Cremble cuffed him. Maybe he didn't even have cuffs with him at the time. Why would you have cuffs at a church potluck anyway?

Pastor Wilheim finally came to and, bless that man, he told Sheriff Cremble that everything was okay. Don't arrest Sam, because who knows what he's going through. Sometimes a man drinks too much because he's in pain.

I felt terrible for Debra because Lord knows what everybody was thinking of her husband and her family. She didn't cry or anything, though. She took it very matter-of-factly.

It's time to go, kids.

That's when I started to fear something was really wrong. Nobody should take something like that so calmly. It was like she was used to it. *Oh, it's happening again*, sort of deal. More annoyed than shocked.

Later that night is the first time I spoke to Helen about it.

"I feel so bad for that poor girl," Helen said, thumbing through a magazine while she sat up in bed.

"Debra?" I asked, laying with my hands clasped behind my head.

"Yes. What got into that boy? Awful. You know he embarrassed his entire family in front of everybody. And Pastor Wilheim? Why on Earth?"

"Sam had too much to drink is all."

"You're excusing it?"

"No, I'm not *excusing* it. I'm just saying he wasn't thinking straight because he had too much to drink."

"Had too much to drink? Fred, he was at a church potluck. What kind of man has too much to drink at a church potluck?"

"I don't know. A troubled man?"

"A troubled man? Yeah, I'd say he's troubled. He *is* trouble."

"Helen, come on now."

"What? What he did was inexcusable and frankly it has me worried."

"He'll be okay, sweetheart. He probably just had a rough—"

"I'm not worried about him, Fred. I'm worried about *her*. I'm worried about her and the children."

"Why are you worried about them?"

"Why am I worried? You saw what I saw. The man is becoming unhinged. If he's capable of attacking a pastor like that, then he's capable of hurting her and the children."

"You're right, you're right," I said. "I don't know, Helen. What do you — I don't like thinking about this kind of stuff."

"You talk with him more than I do, Fred. Do you think he's capable of hurting them?"

"I certainly hope not."

"Well, I hope not, too. But do you think he would?"

"It's possible, I suppose."

"What do you think we should do?" she asked.

"What *we* should do?"

"Yes. What do you think *we* should do? Should we tell Sheriff Cremble?"

"Helen, he was there. He was the one to pull him off Pastor Wilheim."

"I know that. But should we tell him to, I don't know, look into it?"

"Look into what?"

"I don't know, Fred! I just know that Sam could be abusing that poor girl and those babies and we can't just do nothing."

40

"That's a heck of a stretch, Helen. Just because he happened to have too much to drink today, now he's definitely hitting his wife and children?"

"Did you see how unhappy she was? Even before Sam made a fool of himself. She looked tired and unhappy throughout the entire potluck."

"Maybe the twins and Cody are wearing her down. Because she's tired doesn't mean Sam's abusing her."

"And sometimes if something tastes like a pear, it's a pear."

"Then you talk to her. You're a woman, Helen. Have a woman-to-woman talk and see what you can learn."

"Maybe I will."

"Good. You do that."

"And what will you do? Nothing?"

"I don't know what you want me to do. *'Listen Sam, please don't take offense, but are you beating your wife and children?'*"

"So the answer is yes."

"The answer?"

"If you're going to do nothing. The answer is yes."

"Excuse me, but when did I become the bad guy in all this?"

"Because you won't do anything about it. What kind of – oh never mind," she said.

"What? What kind of man does nothing?"

"I didn't say that."

"It's what you were going to say," I snapped.

"Well, what kind of man *does* do nothing?"

"How about this: if things keep getting worse, I'll talk to him about it or I'll talk to the Sheriff about it, okay? And if I'm right and this was a one-time deal, then we can get back to living like neighbors."

"I hope things don't keep getting worse."

"Me too, honey."

41

"I'm so worried about her and the children, Fred. I can't imagine what they're feeling right now. Those poor babies."

Our conversation after the potluck was around 1987. Sam was murdered in 1993.

**

Of course, Helen was right. It didn't get better.

Years went by and it all slowly decayed. We'd hear crying and screaming from next door. Poor Debra would look all beat up. A few times we'd be in the living room and look out the window and she would be hurrying the kids into the car and speed away. Not sure where she was going, but she had to get out of there. She always came back, though. Always. Each time she left, we secretly hoped this would be it. This would be the time she finally left and never came back. But she always came back.

I tried to talk to him about everything. I really did try. Maybe I wasn't as direct as I should have been. It's a delicate deal, you know? Every time we asked Debra about it, she denied it. Said it was a misunderstanding or she tripped or fell or some unforeseen mishap was why she had those bruises or scratches.

Looking back, though, I didn't do enough. I'm ashamed of that. I truly am. I always found a reason or excuse not to talk to Sheriff Cremble or anybody else about it.

The last time I talked to Sam was the Palm Sunday before he died. It would have been April 4, 1993, and he died in the early morning hours of April 12. We hadn't seen Sam in church in ages – the family still went, but not with him. He was there that Palm Sunday, though, in a tie and everything – but he looked worn down.

The Jenkinses settled in behind us after the service had already started. Sam sat closest to the aisle next to the rest of the family – Debra,

Cody, Cassandra, Nicole, and the youngest boy, Tommy. They were such cute children. Because of a condition Helen has, we were never able to have children. We wanted them so badly and Helen would have been a great mother. We offered to babysit the children and sometimes Sam didn't mind and other times he'd tell us to stick it where the sun don't shine. We always loved having the kids over, knowing they were playing in a safe place. We always kept popsicles in the freezer. Always. Tommy loved them. His lips would turn purple because he loved the grape ones.

Those children didn't deserve to live with all that madness next door.

But I digress. The church was decorated so beautifully for Palm Sunday, with palm branches everywhere and whatnot. A donkey – a real one, too. That was a hoot. After the choir sang a few songs, Pastor Wilheim asked everybody to rise and greet those around you.

Helen turned and greeted the children and Debra. I turned around and reached out my hand to Sam.

"Good to see you in church again, Sam," I said.

"What the *you-know-what* is that supposed to mean?" he said.

"Sam, come on, watch your language. You're in church," I said. Everyone around us was laughing and talking so nobody heard.

"What's that little crack supposed to mean, Fred? *Good to see you in church again, Sam.*"

"It ain't a crack. I'm just happy to see you here is all."

"I see, because my soul is black as coal, huh?"

"I ain't saying that. Is everything okay, Sam?"

"Everything's fine with me, Fred. How are you?" he said, and poked me hard in the chest with his index and middle fingers. Debra and the children turned to see the altercation.

"Sam, stop," she said.

"I'm not doing nothing," Sam said. "This *you-know-what* is being a little *you-know-what.*"

"Sam, you're in church!" Debra said.

"Oh, shut up you stupid *blankity blank*, I didn't wanna be here no how," he said.

People started to notice and you could hear the church getting quieter. Nobody did anything, though. They all stood there in silence – watching.

"Don't call her that, Sam," I said.

"Why not, Fred? Oh, are you trying to *you-know-what* her?"

"Sam, why don't you sit down and enjoy the rest of the service," I said.

"Fred, why don't you sit down before I cave your head in, how about that?"

I looked at Debra and the kids were hiding behind her. She had this pleading look. *Just do what he says.* I looked back at Sam, nodded, and turned around and sat back down. It's the last time I ever talked with him. I heard them get up and leave late in the service, when they were passing the collection plate. I couldn't stomach to turn around and look.

**

I was nervous about Sam showing up on Easter and all the chaos that might bring. Thankfully, he didn't show – none of them did. I kept looking over my shoulder, checking to see if they were there. Never did see them.

I didn't see Sam much during that last week. I was coming back inside after doing something and before I reached the front door, Sam was pulling into the driveway. This would have been around Thursday. I could have just walked inside, you know? But I didn't. I waited and waved. I don't know if he didn't see me or ignored me, but Sam stormed into his house. And I went inside and that, as they say, was that.

It still makes me sad it was the last time I saw Sam Jenkins.

I remember Pastor Wilheim delivered a beautiful sermon on Easter Sunday. Powerful. He talked about how Jesus conquered death and how we can all face the darkness that plagues us. How Jesus can help us through that darkness because He defeated death – and there's nothing darker than death, you know? As uncomfortable as it would have been for me, I wish Sam would have been there. Maybe it would have done him some good. Maybe he wouldn't have been so cursed that night or he would have found some shred of peace before he died.

Although, maybe it wouldn't have mattered. Maybe that beautiful sermon would have been wasted on him.

I'm sorry, that's not right of me to say.

We always had Easter dinner with the Jenkins family. Always. Ham and scalloped potatoes. Of course, that year we didn't. Helen said I should go over there and invite them anyway – even after what happened on Palm Sunday. She said I was being stubborn and whatnot. She was probably right. I told her they didn't want to come over and frankly, I didn't trust Sam not to make a scene. I peeked out the window a few times during the day. Debra and the kids were outside doing some yardwork and Sam's truck was gone. But I never did ask them. Since Helen and me had no children and both sides of our family had either passed or moved away, we had a quiet dinner and night at home. The two of us. Nothing special.

There wasn't anything particular that stood out that night. I'm sure we got ready for bed, brushed our teeth, read, and talked a little bit before heading off to sleep. I remember I had this unusual dream. I was worried about a science test I had for school – it's silly because even though you haven't been in school in ages, the fear feels so real in the dream. I was worried about the test because I hadn't studied. I went next door to the Jenkins house to see if they could help me. I walked inside and the floor was sand. Like, sand you'd find on Padre Island or

45

something. I was trying to find somebody in the house but nobody was home. I was calling out for them. *Sam! Debra! I need your help!* I don't know why, but I felt this dread – in the dream – that nobody was home. Something bad must have happened, so I started running from room to room looking for them. Yelling and screaming. Nothing. I woke up shortly thereafter and it took me a few moments to get my bearings. I always had dreams like that. Still do. Helen, she sleeps like a rock. Never dreamed or nothing.

After realizing there wasn't any test and everything was fine, I got up to go to the bathroom. It must have been hot in our room because I was also thirsty, so I walked downstairs to the sink to pour myself a glass of water. I filled it up about three-quarters of the way and took a nice big gulp. I set it down on the counter and that's when I heard it. There were about five or six *pops!* that sounded like gunshots.

"What in the world," I mumbled and went to the kitchen window. I looked across the way – the window above the sink faced the Jenkins house – and there were flashes going off inside the bedroom. My heart started to beat real fast.

I lifted the window a little bit and I could hear crying and screaming coming from their bedroom. It was Debra. I never felt something like that before. I was shaking and walked out of the kitchen toward the bedroom to wake Helen, but I turned around and went back to the kitchen window. The screaming wasn't stopping. I could see their driveway and there wasn't any other vehicles or anything.

I didn't know what to do. I grabbed the kitchen phone and I couldn't believe I forgot Sheriff Cremble's number. I went over to the fridge – we had important numbers written down on a piece of paper under a magnet. I grabbed it, went back to the phone, and dialed as fast as I could.

One ring. Two rings. A third and fourth ring. I started talking after the ringing stopped and before he even said hello.

"Sheriff Cremble, something's not right! Something's happening!" I yelled. I could tell I woke him up and he must have been as confused as he's ever been. "Sorry to call you so late, it's Fred Doyle. There's gunshots going off at the Jenkins place. I don't know, I think something's going on. You need to get down here."

The gunshots kept coming. Had to be at least thirty of them. I never heard screaming like that. I thought about going over there. I did think about it. But I was too scared, to be honest. I guess you could call me a yellow-belly. What if it was somebody who would have killed all of them? And I just *stood* there? What would I be? A coward? A man with a loving wife and who's smart enough to stay out of trouble? Maybe both. Instead of rushing over there, I stayed by the kitchen window until Sheriff Cremble finally pulled up their driveway.

Chapter Four

Sheriff George Cremble

suppose you wanna hear about the *good part*. Probably the whole reason you're doing this little story of yours.

It was 1:25 a.m. early on April 12, 1993. I remember the time exactly 'cause that's one of my favorite bible verses. James 1:25. *But whoever looks intently into the perfect law that gives freedom, and continues in it – not forgetting what they have heard, but doing it – they will be blessed in what they do.*

Yes, it was 1:25 a.m. on the dot.

I was asleep – 'cause that's what you're supposed to be doing at that hour. I'd get a call that late maybe once every few months. Them calls was never fun. How'd you like waking up in the middle of the night to go deal with some drunk man's nonsense? Some of them calls over the years had to do with Sam Jenkins, as a matter of fact. And so did this one.

The phone on my nightstand started ringing and, after I reached out and accidentally grabbed my badge, I took the receiver and put it to my ear. I couldn't keep up with the voice 'cause he was talking so daggum fast. Like a firehose. It was Fred Doyle on the line. He was saying something about Sam Jenkins' place. He said something queer was going on down there. Said he thought he heard some gunshots going off and I'd better go take a look.

"Fred, did you say gunshots?" I asked, wiping my eyes awake.

"Yes, sir," he said. "There was a whole lot of them. You need to get down here. You need to get down here now, Sheriff."

"Okay Fred, I'll be there soon. You stay right there."

"Did you say gunshots, Georgie?" Maggie said, turning over as I hung up.

"It's probably nothing Maggie, you go on back to sleep." I took the covers off and got outta bed and went to my closet.

"George, he said gunshots?" she asked again.

"It's nothing, darling. You know how Fred is."

I got myself dressed, walked over and gave her a kiss on the forehead and told her to not wait up. I told her I loved her and I'd be back in a bit. That wasn't no lie, neither. It's what I thought.

I didn't have much of a drive to think about everything – maybe three or four minutes. Thought maybe Sam was shooting cans in the backyard or something. Maybe a truck backfired. I pulled into the Jenkins's driveway and his truck and her van were parked nice and cozy there. I got to the front door and knocked a few times, letting them know I was there. No answer. When I put my ear to the door, I could hear Debbie crying inside.

No time for knocking nice. I let myself in and the sound of Debbie's cries – my word, I'll never forget that. It was the kinda cries a child makes when they think they seen a monster. I walked toward the cries, with my finger on the trigger of my raised gun for the first time in God knows how long. Looking back, I ain't even know if it was loaded. Walking toward their bedroom, I saw the girls – Cassie and Nicole – standing in the doorframe of their room and they had the scaredest look on their faces.

"You go on back in your room now," I told them. "You go back in now and lock the door."

They hurried back in their room and shut the door. The cries coming from Debbie's room weren't going away. They was constant. No ups and downs. Didn't seem like she even stopped to breathe.

"Debbie!" I yelled out as I got closer to the door. "Debbie, it's Sheriff Cremble! Debbie can you hear me?"

No answer. Just screams. The door was open a little bit and I could smell smoke coming from the room.

"Lord Jesus," I whispered. With my gun raised in my right hand, I used my forearm to slowly push the door open.

There he was.

Cody.

He was standing at the base of the bed and holding a gun down by his waist with both hands. He turned to look at me. He had this blank look on his face. Completely removed of any emotion. It was the most terrifying thing I seen in all my years. That boy's blank face with a gun in his hands, bullet cases all over the floor.

"What are you doing, Cody?" I said over Debbie's cries, my gun still raised. I was pointing my gun at a damn 10-year-old boy. "I need you to drop it. Drop the gun."

What would I have done?

That thought has never left my mind since that night. What would I have done if he ain't put the gun down? What would I have done if he turned and pointed it at me? Would I have shot him? Could I have done it? Should I have done it? They'd all talk about it – justified or not.

50

Sheriff Cremble killed that boy. Sheriff Cremble shot a young child. A baby.

Hell, I don't know if I had any bullets in my gun anyway. Maybe that woulda saved me from the decision. Maybe Cody woulda turned the gun on me and I'd pull the trigger and hear nothing but a click. Then he would have shot me dead in the chest. The town would be hurting, but I wouldn't be there to see it. Hell of a deal that would have been.

That boy killed Sheriff Cremble. Poor Maggie. A lawman killed by a boy. A baby.

Thankfully for all involved parties, Cody tossed the gun onto the bed and then looked back straight ahead. The wall from the closet jutted out and blocked my view of the bed. Sort of a tiny hallway coming into the room. I could hear – but not see – Debbie crying in the back-left corner. As I walked into the room, clearing the closet wall, I turned my head and saw him.

Considering I hadn't heard Sam during all this, I was ready to see him dead. Or see somebody dead, if it weren't Sam. I wasn't ready to see what I seen, though. It ain't even look human. It looked like a butcher shop. There was so many holes in him that I couldn't tell if it was Sam or somebody else. Face was gone. Blood everywhere. Never seen blood like that – before or since. The bed, wall, floor. Everything was covered. Sam's arm dangled over the side of the bed and blood dripped from his fingers down to the carpet. Like a leaky faucet. So much worse than after my daddy shot Charles Thompson.

I suppose every man should have a war moment. See what man could do to man. I never did go overseas, but I always felt that was my war moment. That night. Seeing that. I can't imagine a foxhole that had nothing worse than that.

Debbie was sitting on the floor against the wall in the back corner. Her knees was tucked up to her chest, arms wrapped around her shins.

She ain't even notice I was there. Her eyes were closed and she kept wailing. I looked at what was left of Sam. I looked over to Debbie crying. I looked over to Cody. I put my gun down.

"Cody, what in God's name did you do?"

**

Oh, yes. The potluck.

I remember. What a story. I don't know if it comes as a surprise, but that was the only time I ever had to deal with somebody knocking out a preacher. *Sam knocked out a preacher.* I know it ain't a funny story, per se, but I can't help but laugh. The ridiculousness of it all. Knocking out a preacher. Sam could be a real piece of work.

The First Church was holding its annual potluck and everybody was having a real nice time. Good food. Lots of socializing and so forth. As pleasant as can be. Then Sam shows up all boozed up. Hell, he was carrying around his pack of beer like he was Earl Campbell. Who comes to a church potluck like that? Every once in a while, talking with whoever I was talking with, I'd try and catch a glance of what Sam was doing. If he was making a scene. One of the church ladies came and asked me to go say something to him. She said they was scared Sam might do something. I saw he was alone by the food, so I went to talk with him. He was reaching into the bowl of potato salad and picking out individual pieces of potato with his bare hand. I remember that. There was a big spoon in the bowl and everything, but he ain't care. He was reaching in and grabbing what he wanted.

"Sam, how you doing?" I said. It seemed like I startled him some.

"Oh, how's it...how are you, Sheriff?"

"Can't complain. You doing all right?"

"Yeah, you ... why did you ask me that again? You already asked that."

"Well, you ain't answer. You only asked how I was doing."

"Fair enough," he said and then he opened his mouth real big and tossed in a potato piece and gave a real sarcastic grin. "I'm just enjoying some of this potato salad, Sheriff. Is that a crime now?"

"You been drinking, Sam?"

"Hell no, never touch the stuff."

He grabbed more potato salad and put it directly into his mouth. I grabbed a small plate and took the spoon and plopped a nice portion and offered it to him.

"Here you go, Sam. Just eat this."

"Thanks Sheriff, but I'm all done," he said and put the plate on the table. "Oh, maybe one more."

He grabbed more potato salad straight from the bowl, ate it, smiled, and then walked away. He could be a real smart ass. A real smart ass. Sometimes it was funny, I admit. He was a pretty clever fella when he wanted to be. Sometimes, though, he was just a horse's rear end. Reminded me of Charles Thompson – a headache of a man that you couldn't help but laugh with sometimes.

Both of them victims of a tragic, violent end, too. Fitting, I suppose.

It weren't too much longer after the conversation at the potato salad that everything happened with the pastor. I was talking with somebody about something or another, when I heard people around me gasping and shouting. I looked around and I saw Pastor Wilheim on his rear end trying to get up – Sam was sort of hovering over him. Then Sam rears back and just – *whack!* – a punch like Joe Frazier. I couldn't believe it. The man knocked out a preacher!

So I run over and get between Sam and Pastor Wilheim. Next thing, Sam rears back like he's fixing to knock me out. It was a good thing he had so much to drink, because he stumbled when he swung at me and I took him to the ground. I put my knee into his back and grabbed his arms. He was wiggling and shaking and cussing, like wrangling a foul-mouthed hog.

"Get the *so-and-so* off me," he yelled into the ground.

"Sam, you need to shut the hell up," I said. Now I ain't usually use that kind of language on church grounds, but he had me madder than a wet cat. "What the hell you doing, Sam? Why you hit Pastor Wilheim?"

"Get the *so-and-so* off me," he said again.

"I ain't getting off you 'til you tell me what's going on."

"He called me an asshole," Sam said.

"Come on, Sam. What's really going on? I know he ain't call you that." I didn't have my cuffs with me – didn't think I'd need 'em at a church potluck – or I would have arrested him, brought him in, and called it a day.

Everybody and their grandma had come over and circled around us. Everybody looking at us. Debra and the children. That's the part that don't make the story funny. The looks on their faces. That's what made me mad.

"Sam, you're making a damn fool of yourself," I told him.

"For what?"

"Sam, you're embarrassing yourself and your family. You need to calm the hell down."

"How can I help with what needs to be calm?" he said.

It was clear he was spouting off drunken gibberish. He probably ain't even remember hitting the pastor – or at least why he done it. He stopped resisting and laid there. Fred Doyle was helping up Pastor Wilheim and bless that man of God, because he told me that everything was okay. That he didn't want anything bad to happen to Sam. He said that we should let him go and that he ain't take the punch personally. That was a new one for me. Never did meet another man who gets knocked out cold and comes to with no hard feelings.

"Sam, I'm gonna get off you, but you're gonna get home right now, do you understand me?"

"Yes, Sheriff. Thank you. I'm sorry."

"Sorry for what?" I asked. I wanted to hear him say it, you know.

"I'm sorry for what I done."

"And what's that?" I asked.

"For doing it."

He ain't remember what he done. Knocked out a preacher and he didn't realize it. In hindsight, the apology shoulda been a warning. What do they call it? A red flag. He weren't actually sorry for getting drunk, fighting a preacher, and making a scene in front of the whole daggum town. The apology was a force of habit.

**

In the closing days of 1990, little over two years before Sam got killed, me and Maggie was going to the grocery store because we was hosting a party for the Cotton Bowl – which was an embarrassment, by the way. I'll never get over that game. Lost to a bunch of hooligans, that Miami team. One lousy field goal, Texas got. Terrible.

Well, before we knew the Longhorns would embarrass the great state of Texas in front of the country, we was at Helson's to get food for the party and we was turning a corner to the next aisle and we came across Debra. She ain't look too pretty. You could tell she was trying to cover everything up with a lot of makeup and all that nonsense, but that purple was too much to hide. Thomas, he would have been about three or four at the time, was sitting inside the cart and the twins was walking behind Debra. I don't remember seeing Cody there with them.

"Hello Debbie, how are you doing, dear?" Maggie said.

"Oh, hello," Debra said.

"Are y'all gonna be watching the Cotton Bowl? Exciting ain't it?" I said. Maggie never let that one go – I wanted to talk football with her while she looked like that.

"Maybe, I don't know. Well, it's good to see you two."

"Debbie, why don't you bring the family over for dinner one of these days?" Maggie said.

"Maybe. Yeah, that would be good."

"How about next Saturday?" Maggie said. "We can make brisket."

"Yeah, that sounds good. Maybe. I'll let you know."

"Is everything okay, Debbie?" I asked.

"Yeah, everything is fine. It was good seeing you two."

Debbie smiled as she pushed her cart away from us. That was that. Maggie and me shopped in silence. We finished shopping and put everything in the truck and didn't say one word. I got into the driver's seat, put the keys in the ignition, and then stopped.

"You know I can't do nothing about it, right?" I said.

"You should just arrest him," Maggie said.

"I can't do that."

"And why not, *Mr. Sheriff*?"

"Because until she says what he's doing, I can't do nothing."

"Oh please, Georgie, you know what's happening. You should just arrest him."

"I can't."

"Why not? He's a bad man."

"The law don't work like that, Margaret."

"To hell with the law!"

Maggie never talked like that. It sorta stunned me, to be honest. She was as hot as a kettle. There was a long silence between us. She was looking out her window and I went back and forth between looking at her and out the windshield.

"Maggie," I said.

"Yes?"

"I can't do nothing. I can't arrest him just 'cause we're assuming he's hitting her."

"Give me a break."

"You want me going around arresting people just because?"

"No, I want you to arrest him because he's beating the hell out of her, George. A blind man could see it."

"That ain't how the law works, Maggie. That's what I'm telling you. If she would tell me what was happening, then I got a little leeway to do something about it. Press charges. But she ain't."

"Because she's scared of what he would do if she told people. Especially you. How do you not understand that, you fool? He's holding her and those children prisoner and you're not doing anything about it."

"Even as sheriff, I can't do nothing."

"I'm not talking about you doing something as a sheriff, George," she said. "I'm talking about you doing something as a man. Why don't you go and talk to him? Confront him about it."

"And say what? *'You beating on Debbie, Sam?'*"

"It's better than what you're doing now."

There was more silence. This time even longer. Had to be a minute or two.

"Let's go home," she said. "We got ice cream in the back."

"Let it melt. Maggie, why don't *you* talk with *her*? Let her confide in you."

"We're not that close. She wouldn't."

"Then you ain't doing nothing about it, neither. That's what I'm saying. This is a delicate situation."

"Why is it my job to be investigating crimes in Well Springs?"

"I thought you didn't want me acting like a sheriff? You turned it into me not being a man. Why don't you talk with her? Have a girl talk, or whatever you call it. Get comfortable with her and get her to tell what he's doing and then I can arrest him."

"You're scared of him."

"I beg your pardon?"

"You're scared of him, George. You're acting like a *damn coward*!"

I started the truck and drove out the parking lot. We ain't speak much the rest of the way home. Don't think there was any dialogue at all, as a matter of fact. Both of us was stubborn as a mule about it. I wouldn't talk with him because I thought she should talk with her. She didn't talk with her because she thought I should talk with him. We dug our heels in.

I regret that. Truly. Because of our stubbornness, we let him continue to hit on her. Years of it. Shameful. I mean that. Every single day I could have said something and every day I didn't. It must have been about a year and a half after that – around summer '92 – and we was at home watching this movie. What was it called? It was ... it was in Texas, I remember. Thought it had Texas in the title. This fella lost his memory or something and was wandering around trying to find his kid and found out he had a wife that he beat up. It made Maggie cry and after it was over, we sat there watching the credits.

I don't know what got into me. I stood up, pressed stop on the VCR, and told Maggie that I'd be back. I grabbed my coat and walked over to see Sam Jenkins.

**

"Sheriff Cremble?"

Cody answered the door. Everybody else was watching TV and ain't realize I was there. I knocked pretty loud, too. I walked in and rubbed the top of Cody's head. Debra saw me and seemed a bit startled.

"Sheriff Cremble, is something wrong?"

She didn't have no makeup on. She had bags under her eyes and bruises on her arms. Sam finally realized I was in his home. He had his feet up on the coffee table and was sitting back and resting a can of beer on his stomach.

"Everything is all right, Debbie," I said. "Sam, I'd like to speak to you."

"Me?" he said, cranking his head to try and see me. I was standing behind the couch.

"Yeah, let's head out back."

"Right now?"

"Yeah, let's go." I tapped him on the shoulder. "Cassie, Nikki, how are you sweethearts?"

The girls nodded at me.

"Glad to hear it. Sam, let's go."

He had two folding chairs on a slab of concrete in the backyard. I went out and sat down first – he went to the fridge and pulled out four beers attached to a six-pack plastic holder, carrying it by the two empty rings. He was holding the beer he was already drinking.

"Want one?" Sam said as he sat down, holding up the beer.

"No sir. I'm okay, thanks."

"Okay. What's going on?"

"How's everything been going, Sam?"

"Fine, why?"

"Sam, I ain't asking as an empty pleasantry. How's everything been going, really?"

"Sheriff, I feel like I'm being questioned for something."

"No, no. I'm seeing how everything's going in your world."

"I said fine. Is that not an acceptable answer?"

"And how's the family?"

"Family's fine."

"Family's fine?"

"Yes sir."

"You like your littles ones?"

"What? What the hell is this about, Sheriff?"

"I'm only asking how your kids are doing, Sam."

"No, you're asking if I *like* them. I don't know what you're getting at."

"I'm seeing how you're liking your kids these days."

"How I'm liking them? Like they're a fridge or something."

"No, no. I'm seeing how you like fatherhood."

"Oh brother," Sam said before finishing the rest of his beer. He crushed the can and tossed it on the ground and ripped off a new one and opened it. "Sheriff, I don't know what the hell is going on. You show up unannounced, barging into my home, and then ask how I like my kids? If you got something to say, say it."

"Now Sam, I'm trying to keep this friendly."

"I don't even know what this is? What the hell's going on?"

"I'm just seeing how fatherhood's treating you."

"Love it. Okay? That it?"

We sat there in silence for a little while. Painful silence. I looked around. I knew what I needed to say, but it's a hell of a deal to say it. I pointed to the beer. Sam ripped one off and gave it to me. I opened it, took a drink, and then held the can in my lap.

"Some people are worried," I said.

"About what?"

"About you, Sam. About Debbie. About the kids. They're worried about all of you."

"They're worried about my family? Wait, who's worried?"

"It don't matter. I need to know if everything is going to be fine."

"No, Sheriff, who's worried?"

"People."

"*People* are worried? *People* are worried about my family?"

"Yes sir. And I think they're right to be worried."

"Oh, that's a load of bull. So *people* aren't worried. *You're* worried. Is that more accurate?"

"It ain't matter if I—"

"Don't be a coward about this, Sheriff. I'll talk to you, but don't be hiding behind somebody's skirt."

"Okay then. Let's talk man-to-man."

"That'd be nice."

"Why you feel like you gotta hit Debra? That ain't right."

"And who said I do that?"

"Come on, Sam. You wanna talk, let's talk. I ain't dumb."

"I never said you were."

"Everybody knows what you do. You hit the kids too?"

"Ain't this a fine Saturday night?" Sam said, shaking his head. "I went from watching my show to having the Sheriff start to accuse me of hitting my wife and kids."

"It's true, though."

"I ain't hit nobody, Sheriff. That's the God's honest truth."

"Come on, Sam," I said.

"Come on, nothing. It's true," Sam answered.

"I know you're probably mad at the world or some nonsense, but you gotta realize how good you got it, Sam."

"And how's that?"

"She's a beautiful woman and you got some great kids."

"If you say so."

"Sam, a lotta folks would love to play with the hand you were dealt. I don't know what you gotta be so *unhappy* about. And why you gotta take it out on her?"

"Why you keep saying that?"

61

"Sam, don't insult me. She's always beat to hell — bruises and whatnot."

"And it has to be from me? There's no other explanation?"

"Well, let's hear it."

"Am I on trial or something? It feels like I'm getting interrogated in my own home."

"I ain't talking to you as a lawman right now, Sam. I'm talking to you man-to-man. And what kind of man hits his woman?"

"You're something else, you know that? So you're gonna judge me, is that it? Sheriff, I'm the one around here that works for a living. I put in my time to provide for them in there. Me. I sweat it out, working a job I hate, and I come home and what do I get? Somebody ate all the turkey. Toys all over. The laundry ain't done. This and that, and this and that."

"That don't give you no right."

"I think that's pretty easy to say."

"Lots of folks got it worse off than you and don't go around bullying their own family."

"Well, to each their own, as they say."

"Listen Sam, all I'm saying is it ain't gotta be this way. It better not be this way."

"Or *else*? Is that it?"

"Yes sir. Or *else*."

"Now, is that the man talking or the sheriff talking?"

"Both."

"Well, Sheriff, I sure appreciate the time. If you don't mind, get the hell out of my house. Please."

"It's gonna catch up with you, son. I'm telling you. One way or another, it's gonna catch up with you."

"Good night, Sheriff."

**

He didn't get much better. He stayed a bully until the day he died. Or at least, I believe he did. I think there was some good stretches in there. Sobered up for a week or so. Lord knows he was given enough time to turn it all around. Just never could turn the corner.

I always thought it was interesting that my last interaction with Sam – alive, at least – was a good one. Weeks before he died, I went out to Big Rock Golf Course to meet some friends for eighteen holes. It was a Saturday morning. Warm for February. I was on the putting green, when Timmy from the clubhouse came and told me my party called and cancelled. Some good they were. Big Rock is a good 45-minute drive, and my mind was set on golfing. I went into the clubhouse to think if I should play on my own. Never did like playing by myself, but it felt silly to drive back home. As I was looking around, Sam and two of his buddies – Mark and Rhett – came walking into the clubhouse.

"Sheriff, how we doing today?" Sam said, smiling.

"Howdy fellas," I said, grabbing a small baggie of tees.

"You playing today?" Sam said.

"Not so sure anymore."

"Why? What happened?"

"Looks like my group cancelled."

"Who would want to be anywhere else on a Saturday morning?" Sam said.

"Good question. Wondering the same thing."

"Well, we only got three, you're welcome to join us."

"Thanks, Sam, but I don't wanna intrude."

"Intrude nothing. You'll join us. I won't hear another word. Timmy, we're going to have four – not three."

And just like that, I spent the day on the course with Sam and his buddies. I was a bit worried at the start – about any unpleasantness and so forth. But I gotta tell you: it was maybe the most fun I ever did have

63

playing. We was cracking jokes and talking about life and whatnot. On one of the earlier holes, I sliced it hard off the tee – it went sailing over to God-knows-where and they all started laughing.

"Sheriff," Sam said. "If you shoot like you drive, I might rob the bank and take my chances."

"You see where it went?" I asked.

"Looks like it's somewhere in New Mexico," Sam said as the boys kept howling.

Then Sam steps up, puffing out his chest – talking *watch the master talk*. He lines it up and wiggles a bit, looks down, and rears back and hits. *Smack*. He pulled it hard to the left, bounced off a tree before ending up in a sand trap – a sand trap for a *different* hole. I had to let him have it.

"Sam, I made sure to write down some notes about how to drive off the tee," I joked, as Mark and Rhett were laughing. "Nice of you to give that ball a lovely day at the beach."

By the time we was on the other side of nine, we stopped keeping score. We was having so much fun that we ain't care much about score. There was nobody playing behind us, so after holes some of 'em would smoke a cigarette or pack a chew and drink some beer. Nice and easy. We was feeling pretty good by then. Sam asked me if he had permission from the Sheriff's Office of Well Springs to take a piss behind a tree before the fifteenth hole. I told him I was off the clock. He said he woulda done it no matter what I said.

I hit the best shot I had all day on the eighteenth hole – I was on the green after two shots on a par four. As I was walking down the fairway, I felt a bit of sadness. I had a whale of a time with them boys and I knew it was coming to an end. The way it turned out, the rest of them finished up before it was my time to putt. I stood on the edge of the green and watched these knuckleheads busting chops and laughing. As Rhett missed a short gimmie putt, Sam stood off to the side, leaning on his putter.

"Rhett having trouble finding the hole, what's new?" he said. I couldn't help but laugh. It was a good one. Rhett finally putted home and after he pulled the ball out he faked like he was gonna hurl it at Sam. It was pretty funny, to be honest.

"All right George, time to close out," Sam said. "Get that birdie."

I lined up and took a breath – it was probably a fifteen-footer. It felt good off the putter but pulled slightly to the left. It wrapped around the cup – left-to-right – before falling in. I pumped my fist and the boys cheered for me.

"Oooh, wee! How about that?" Sam said. "What a way to end."

"Thanks, Sam," I shook all their hands. "Thanks for letting me play with you, fellas."

"No problem," Sam said. "It was a lotta fun. We oughta do it again sometime."

A few weeks later he was dead.

**

It was a nice Easter.

I was so happy during the day, before everything happened at the Jenkins place. Pastor Wilheim had a beautiful message – really one for the ages. Sam and his family weren't there, but apparently him and Fred got into on Palm Sunday so I wasn't surprised none that he ain't show. After church, Maggie kissed me goodbye before I went to spend the afternoon at Lake Marron. It was my old friend Darren and me, fishing on the lake all day. Easter tradition. Wonderful time. We brought plenty of drinks and plenty of time to kill. We talked about life. He ain't have no family, which I always felt bad about. He didn't want none, though. No wife, no children. Never did, neither. Always talked about how he'd rather have the freedom. No one to answer to. There was times when I thought he might be the smartest man on the planet and other times I felt sorry for him – he weren't no follower of God. He died a few years back.

"Darren, what do you think is the meaning of life?" I asked as we sat there, waiting for something to bite.

"The meaning of life?"

"Yes sir."

"That's a big one, George."

"Well, what do you think?"

"'Bout the meaning of life? Shoosh. Sometimes I wonder if it even got any meaning at all."

"There's gotta be something."

"Why?" he asked.

"Well, otherwise what's the point?"

"To enjoy moments like this, I suppose," he said.

"The point of life is fishing and drinking?"

"As good as any out there, ain't it?"

"What about being a good person? Getting to heaven and all?"

"I don't know, George. I think if it helps you be a good person, at least it's something."

"You ain't believe in heaven, Darren?"

"I don't know."

"Come on. You ain't believe in heaven? What you think happens when you kick the bucket?"

"I suppose … nothing? Darkness. Everything goes black and that's *that.*"

"Darkness?" I asked.

"You scared of dying, George?"

"No, no. I believe in heaven, Darren. Pastor Wilheim was talking about it today – about how Jesus conquered death then made his way up there."

"Yeah?" he said.

"You ain't buying it?"

"George, I think it's a very nice sentiment."

"What keeps you in line, then?" I asked.

"How do you mean?"

"If you ain't believe in heaven, why ain't you go hog wild? Stealing and killing and such."

"And why would I wanna do that?"

"Because you can. You ain't got no family to let down. You don't got no moral authority to stop you."

"Sheriff, ain't you gonna stop me if I go around shooting and killing?"

"I suppose," I said, laughing. "But you know what I mean. There's goodness in you. Where you think that goodness comes from?"

"I suppose because I get enough joy outta this. Fishing and talking and drinking. This is what makes life enjoyable. Fellowship, you might call it. Togetherness. Why would shooting some fella make me feel better? Or steal from somebody?"

"Darren, I ain't agree with you about heaven but I'll drink to your thoughts on that one."

I ended up getting home around five. I walked into the house and smelled ham and mashed potatoes. Maggie made me and the little ones the best Easter dinner you ever dreamed about. I gave her a smooch and told her I loved her. Darren can keep the freedom. That ain't for me.

We ate dinner, worked on a little jigsaw puzzle and then me and Maggie made love – although that ain't any of your business. It was a nice day. Couldn't have drawn it up better.

Maggie and me stayed up a little later than usual that night, talking about the day. I was telling her all about what Darren was saying. Eventually, the sandman came calling and we kissed each other good night. It ain't take me long to fall asleep. Next thing I know, the phone rang with a call from Fred Doyle.

Cody Jenkins had just murdered his daddy.

Chapter Five

Jackie Hill (Sexton)

I haven't been back to Texas since 1993. I returned home to Colorado pretty shortly after everything happened with Cody's dad. It's a wild story, isn't it? You could feel everybody in town either thinking about it or talking about it everywhere you went. I finished out the school year and I went back to Grand Junction.

I only taught in Well Springs for that one year. I had a pretty rough break-up back home and I felt I needed someplace new – I had a friend near Well Springs and they had a fourth-grade position. Why not?

Cody was in my class when everything went down. He was a sweet boy. He was always looking out for the kids who got bullied.

There was this one boy, Wyatt, who was getting bullied a lot. He was a real nice boy, but he was a nerdy type. Glasses. He had diabetes, so he had to take his insulin shot and he always had his little kit with him. There was this group of three boys constantly picking on him. Well Springs is a small town, so everybody basically knows everybody even coming into the school year, so they were teasing him since the first day. Called him names and taped mean signs on his back.

During recess in the first month of the school year, the boys were circling around poor Wyatt. I had recess duty and I could see it coming. Like a storm forming. Here we go. Wyatt was crying and the group was laughing and pushing him around. I started to head over to them. Before I could get there, Cody had walked up behind them. They didn't see him. Cody grabbed one of the boys by the shoulder – the ringleader, Danny, who probably grew up to be a loser no-account. Cody spun Danny around and landed this punch right in his face. The force sent Danny to the ground and his nose started bleeding and he started wailing. Cody pushed another one of them with both hands and that kid went flying to the ground and *he* started crying too. The third one went running away.

"Cody!" I yelled as my jog turned into a sprint.

Keep in mind, this is my first month in Well Springs. I was thinking I'm good as fired since all this happened with my students and I'm on recess duty. Before I got to Cody and Wyatt, the three bullies had scattered like little rats. Cody extended his hand to help Wyatt up, but Wyatt shook his head. Instead, Cody sat down on the ground and put his arm around him.

"I won't let them do that to you," Cody said.

Wyatt nodded.

"Cody why did you do that?" I said as I reached them.

"Because it was the right thing to do," he said.

"Cody, you can't just go punching people during recess."

"Why not? They deserved it."

Wyatt was sniffling but he wasn't crying anymore. Wyatt looked at me and he had the saddest, sweetest look on his face. I didn't have a good answer to Cody's question. I mean, you can't have students punching other kids, but Danny deserved to get his ass kicked if I'm being perfectly honest. It was a *little* satisfying to see it. I know that's bad to say, but it's true.

There surprisingly wasn't much fallout from what happened. Maybe it's a Texas thing. Danny and Cody got called to the principal's office right after the incident. Principal Hank Greer. He was a good man. It was me, him, and the two boys. The boys were sitting in seats in front of Principal Greer's desk and I was standing behind them.

"What's this commotion during recess I'm hearing about?" Principal Greer said.

"Danny and his friends were bullying Wyatt —" I started.

"We weren't bullying him!" Danny said.

"Danny, you'll get your turn," Principal Greer said. "Please let Miss Sexton finish."

"Danny and his friends were bullying him and I was racing over to break it up, but then Cody came in and hit Danny."

"He sucker punched me!" Danny cried out.

"Danny, please," Principal Greer said. "And what else happened?"

"Well, Cody pushed over Danny's friend and the other boy ran off before I got there," I said.

"My goodness," Principal Greer said before turning to the boys. "Boys, I will not allow my playground to be turned into a boxing ring. Do you understand me?"

Both Cody and Danny nodded.

"Now, Danny, let's hear your side of the story," Principal Greer said.

"We were just talking with Wyatt and telling jokes, and then Cody came and assaulted me!"

"He *assaulted* you? *Assaulted*?" Principal Greer said. "That's a grown-up word, Danny."

71

"Well, he punched me for no reason! We were hanging out on the playground and Cody came and punched me and it hurt."

Danny started to whimper. It was pretty pathetic. I remember thinking, *What a little liar*. They weren't just talking with Wyatt. It actually made me feel bad because I wasn't more forceful when they teased Wyatt. I'd tell them to stop and they'd stop for a minute – then get right back to terrorizing him.

"Hmm. Cody, did you punch Danny?" Principal Greer asked.

"Yes sir."

"You did, huh? How come?"

"Because they're always mean to Wyatt," Cody said. "He hasn't done anything to them, but they're mean to him anyways. They're mean to him just to be mean."

"They're mean just to be mean?"

"Yes sir. I don't like that. I won't let them bully him anymore."

"Cody, that's our job, okay? I need you to promise that you won't go around punching your classmates anymore."

"I can't do that sir."

"You can't?" Principal Greer said, raising his eyebrows in surprise.

"No sir. If they keep bullying Wyatt, I'm going to punch him again. I'll punch him every time they do."

Danny started crying and said he felt scared.

"Danny, it will be fine," Principal Greer said. "Cody will not punch you again. He won't punch you again because you and your friends are going to leave Wyatt alone. Do you understand me? Danny, do you understand me? You will leave Wyatt alone."

Danny nodded. And that was that. Danny and his friends never bothered Wyatt again. Principal Greer excused everybody but told me to set up a meeting with the two of us and Cody's parents. That's the first time I met the wonderful Sam Jenkins.

**

I met Cody's parents that night. Of course, Principal Greer told me at the last minute something came up and he couldn't make it. Apparently, it would only be me and Cody's parents. I was a little nervous because I had been in Well Springs for like a month and already there was this big incident. We were supposed to meet in my classroom, so I got there way too early. Like an hour beforehand – to clean up, get everything ready, play out in my head what I would say, and prepare for what they might say.

Honestly, my first thought of Sam was he was pretty handsome. He had a little bit of scruff, but he was a good-looking guy. Dark features. He was wearing a white t-shirt and jeans. She was pretty too. You could tell she was naturally pretty. She did look pretty worn out, though. Tired. She showed up in a t-shirt with holes in it and sweats.

"You must be Miss Sexton," Sam smiled and he softly shook my hand.

"I am. Sam and Debbie?"

"That's us," he said.

"Nice to meet you, please take a seat."

I set up two adult-sized plastic chairs in front of my desk. Debbie went and sat down right away, but Sam walked around the classroom and looked at all the decorations. He saw we had a plastic toy dump truck. He picked it up and showed Debbie, pointing at it with a smile.

"This is what I do," Sam said to me. "Construction."

"Oh, is that right?" I asked.

"Glamourous, huh?" he said with a self-deprecating look.

"Well, it's very important work," I said.

"How about that?" Sam said to Debbie. "You hear that? 'Very important work.' Miss Sexton, I have a good feeling about you."

"Oh, thank you. You can call me Jackie."

"Jackie?" Sam said.

73

"Yes. My mother loved the Kennedys."

"Is that right? Well, we won't hold it against you," Sam said. "You must not be from Texas."

"No, I'm from Colorado."

"Colorado?" Sam said. "You're a long way from home, sweetheart. No wonder why I haven't seen you around town. What part of Colorado?"

"Grand Junction, if you know where that is."

"Western part of the state, right?" Sam said. "Right on the border?"

"That's right."

"It's sure nice to have you here in Well Springs with us," Sam said. "Named after Jackie Kennedy, huh?"

"Yeah, it was sort of bad timing. I was born November 20, 1963."

"November 20?" Sam asked.

"Unfortunately."

"I don't understand," Debbie said.

"Kennedy was shot November 22," Sam said.

"That's right," I said.

"Oh," Debbie said.

"Well, it's still a very pretty name," Sam said as he came and sat down.

"Thank you," I said. "So, the reason why we're here: did Cody tell you anything?"

"That he–" Debbie started.

"Something about a playground fight," Sam said.

"Yes," I said. "I was watching the students during recess and these boys were giving this other boy, Wyatt, a hard time and Cody went over and started fighting with those boys."

"It was that Danny kid, right?" Sam asked.

"Yes."

74

"He's a little punk," Sam said. "So I'm a little confused, because you said that he was fighting with them?"

"Yes."

"Okay, Cody didn't look like he was in a fight. He seemed fine when he got home."

"Basically, he punched Danny in the face and pushed another boy to the ground."

"They didn't get any licks in?" Sam said.

"No."

"You said the boys were giving Wyatt a hard time?" Debbie asked.

"Yes," I said. "Unfortunately, they give Wyatt a hard time quite often. I try to squash it when I can, but they circled around him during recess and Wyatt was crying."

"And Cody dropped Danny in one punch?" Sam said with a slight smile.

"Pretty much," I said. "He fell to the ground and his nose was bleeding and he started crying."

"He started crying?" Sam asked.

"Yes."

"What a baby," Sam said. "Good grief. He was picking on Wyatt and then Cody lights him up and he starts *crying*?"

"Is Wyatt okay?" Debbie asked.

"Yes, I think so. He was a little shaken up, but he seems like he's okay."

"Wyatt is a nice little boy," Sam said. "So, I think I have to be the one to say it."

"Say what?" I said.

"Danny is a little pain in the neck. I know him and his daddy," Sam said. "His daddy is a pain in the neck, and the boy isn't much better."

"I haven't met Danny's parents yet," I said.

"His daddy is a pain in the neck, believe me. A real sack of crap. But it sounds like Danny was being a little jerk and he got what was coming to him."

"Well, I can't say that."

"But you believe it, right?" Sam said, smiling. "Danny was bullying this poor boy and he got a knuckle sandwich and then ran off crying. It sounds like Cody was standing up for Wyatt, is that fair?"

"I suppose, but it's still not good to have fighting on the playground."

"You said yourself there wasn't much *fighting*," Sam said. "Listen, I understand. It's wrong to go around punching people, but it sounds like if Danny stops acting like a little prick there won't be any problems."

Debbie turned toward him and gave him this look. I remember Debbie didn't say much of anything during our meeting.

"What? I'm right, aren't I?" Sam said. "Come on, let's be honest here. Danny got what was coming to him."

"You're not wrong," I said. "But please do talk with Cody. I need him to know there are other ways to solve his problems than violence."

"Yeah, I can talk with him," Sam said, standing up and looking back at the posters on the wall. "Colorado, huh?"

**

Well Springs High had its homecoming game in October. It was a big deal. Everything they say about high school football in Texas is one hundred percent true. The whole town shuts down and all the old guys wore their letterman jackets. A lot of living in the past at those things. Hearing stories about teams from way back when – they had arrested development big time. They turned into teenagers telling stories about games that I'm sure didn't actually happen.

I forget who they played during that year's homecoming game. One of the other small towns, I'm sure. I didn't care much for the sport, but I thought the games were usually fun. There was a real sense of community. Everybody was wearing red and white – the school colors. It was like a Valentine's Day card or something. Most of the time, I enjoyed going to the games. The homecoming game, though, was different.

I was walking around during the game and I came across Cody and Debbie. Debbie never liked me much, I don't think. She was never friendly to me. It's not like she was mean or anything. She was short with me and didn't exactly seem like she cared to get to know me. She had the twin girls – I forget their names – and Cody's younger brother. That's a lot of kids to look after. Sam wasn't with them.

"Hey Cody, what's going on?" I said with a smile.

"Hello Miss Sexton," Cody said. He was in a good mood because Well Springs was winning. "Did you see the touchdowns we made?"

"I did! Do you think we will win?"

"Yes!"

"I do too," I said and I smiled at Debbie but she just looked at me.

"Enjoy the game, Jackie," she said and walked past me with all the kids.

I thought it was rude, to be honest. I was trying to be nice.

I never went to the restroom during halftime. The lines were always too long. The restrooms were way off to the side and were in a small U-shaped building – men's on the left, women's on the right. If I had to go, I planned to go around four minutes into the third quarter. People are settled in for the second half and there's never anybody by the restroom. No lines. It was perfect. I literally did that every home game.

Homecoming night, though, I used the restroom and as I walked out, I ran into Sam. There was nobody else around – only me and him.

"Miss Sexton, what a pleasure," he said. He was wearing his old red letterman jacket and looked pretty rough. You could smell the booze on him. He smelled like he was sitting on a bar stool for hours. He was standing in front of me so I couldn't really get around him and back to the game.

"Hey Sam, I saw Debbie and the kids earlier," I said.

"You're looking good," Sam said and he put his hand on my shoulder and then slid it down the side of my arm.

"How much have you had to drink, Sam?"

"Ha! Because I think you look good, I must be wasted?"

"No, but I smell it on you."

"Don't tell the principal, I don't wanna get in trouble," he smiled.

"Drinking at a high school football game?"

"You know I used to be one hell of a player?"

"Is that right?"

"Oh yeah. I broke a kid's leg during one game."

"You broke his leg?"

"Yeah."

"Is that supposed to impress me?"

"You know, you are a real piece of tail."

"Oh my God, Sam."

"What? I can feel how bad you want me. We can go behind the equipment shed over there."

I tried to move around him, but his hand gripped my arm.

"Sam, that hurts. What are you doing?"

"Come on, let's do it. Miss Sexy," he had this big stupid smile on his face when he said that, like he thought he was so clever.

"I don't want to, Sam."

"Why not? Because of my wife? Please. She doesn't care."

His grip on my arm got even tighter. He wasn't smiling or trying to be charming anymore. He stared right at me and it honestly was the scariest moment of my life. There was a pair of girls – probably around sixth grade – walking toward us. The lighting was bad by the restroom, so I couldn't really tell who they were. Sam could see me looking at them, so he turned around and told them to leave. They stopped walking toward us and stood there. He yelled at them to leave again and they ran off.

"Damn it," I whispered.

"Huh?" he turned back toward me.

"Nothing."

"How come you don't wanna do it?"

"How come I don't want to have sex behind an equipment shed at a high school football game?"

"It would be like we were in high school again."

"I didn't do that in high school, Sam."

"Oh, you were a goodie girl, huh?"

"If choosing not to have sex behind a shed makes me a goodie girl."

"You're so beautiful, you know that?"

"Thank you. Let's go watch the game. Please. Let's just go watch the game, Sam."

I got lucky because there was a big roar from the crowd and Sam looked back toward the field.

"See, we're missing something," I said. "Maybe we scored."

"This coach doesn't know his ass from a hole in the ground. We should be so much better than we are."

"Do you think we scored?"

"I don't know, maybe."

"Let's go see. I want to see if we scored."

"Okay, yeah, we need to build the lead."

He let go of my arm and we both walked back toward the crowd. When we got closer to the field, his walk turned into a drunken trot and he went next to one of his buddies along the fence. I didn't stop walking. I went to my car and sat inside and cried. That was literally the last time

I saw him. I didn't go to any more games and I didn't really go out in public all that much. I was scared I'd see him. Of course, he never went to any of the elementary school events for Cody's class.

In hindsight, I probably should have told somebody. But I didn't know. It was a small town where everybody knows everybody and I didn't want to stir the pot. Maybe he has friends in high places – well, *high places* relatively speaking.

Instead, I kept it to myself.

**

Cody's odd question happened the Thursday before Easter – the Thursday before Sam was killed. It's spooky looking back, but at the time, I didn't think about it. I thought it was an innocent curiosity.

The students were doing an assignment about what plans they had for Easter. You know: *Going to church. Egg hunting. Dinner with family.* One of those assignments to keep them busy. It lets them color and practice their writing while I did some more important work. When everybody was working on the assignment, Georgina broke the silence.

"Miss Sexton, what are you doing for Easter?" she said.

"Well, I'm going to go to church and maybe I'll go to the lake or read a nice book."

"Are you going to visit your family?" she said.

"Her family lives too far away," Marcus said. "She's from Colorado. It's too far."

"How do you know that?" Georgina said. "Miss Sexton, how come your family lives so far away?"

"Well, I was born in Colorado, like Marcus said."

"Grand Junction," Cody said.

"That's right, Cody."

"How far is Grand Junction from Well Springs?" Georgina asked.

"Too far. I will have to use the telephone to call my family and let them know I love them and I miss them."

"That's sad you don't get to be with your family on Easter," she said.

"Yeah, but that's okay. I know they love me and they know that I love them."

"How come you came to Well Springs?" Marcus asked.

"So that I could teach you all. If I didn't move to Well Springs, I wouldn't have met all of you."

"Miss Sexton," Georgina said.

"Yes?"

"I'm glad that you moved to Well Springs."

"Well, aren't you a sweetheart. Thank you, Georgina."

"Miss Sexton?" Cody said.

"Yes, Cody?"

"I have a question."

"And what's your question?"

"Pastor Wilheim said that Easter is about Jesus rising from the dead," Cody said.

"That's true."

"It's because he was resurrected," Georgina said.

"That's right, Georgina," I said. "Do you know what resurrected means?"

"It means he came back to life," she said.

"That's right. Good Friday is when Jesus died for us and on Easter, Jesus came back to life."

"Jesus came back to life because he's good, right?" Cody said.

"That's right. He came back to life because he's good. He did it to save you and to forgive you of your sins."

"That's good. I'm glad that Jesus did that," Georgina said.

"Miss Sexton?" Cody said.

"Yes, Cody?"

"Are bad people resurrected?"

"Well," I replied. "I don't think so. No."

"So if bad people die, like Jesus did, they don't come back, right? Because they're bad?"

"Only Jesus could come back from being dead, Cody," I said. "It's because he's God so he could be resurrected."

"So then when bad people die, they can't come back?" Cody asked.

"I suppose not," I said.

**

On the Monday after Easter, I assumed Cody was sick. No big deal. On Tuesday, it's more like, *I hope he's not too sick*. Wednesday and Thursday go by and he's still not in school, so I start to get a little worried. His homework was piling up. I definitely didn't want to drop off the work at his house and see Sam. By Friday, I was thinking maybe the family went on a vacation. Kids rarely miss a whole week being sick.

During lunch on Friday, I went into the main office to check my mailbox. When I got in, the office secretary, Violet, was on the phone. Violet was who I wanted to talk to.

"Terrible, just terrible," she was saying. "I can't believe it. ... I know, I feel the same way. ... Have you heard from anybody? ... What'd he say? ... Oh my goodness. ... They say it was some stranger. A bad guy. ... That's what I heard. ... None of your business."

I tried not to hover and seem like I was eavesdropping, but Violet could see that I was waiting to talk to her.

"Never you mind who I heard it from. ... Listen, we'll talk later. I have to...I have to go. Mmm hmm. ... Okay, bye-bye."

She hung up the phone and asked me if I needed something.

"I don't mean to intrude, but who was that?" I asked.

"Oh, just gossip. What would you like, dear?"

"By chance have you heard from Cody Jenkins' parents. He's been out all week."

"My goodness, dear. You haven't heard?"

"Heard what?"

"Bless your heart. Oh my goodness, I can't believe nobody has told you."

"Told me what, Violet?"

"Honey, Sam Jenkins was killed."

"He was killed? What? When?"

"Sunday night."

"He was killed Sunday night?"

"Yes, sweetie. Awful news."

"How'd he die?"

"I don't want to get you all riled up, sweetheart," Violet said.

"It's fine. How'd he die?"

"Murdered," she whispered.

"He was murdered? What?"

"Terrible. Gunned down."

"He was shot? Where?"

"In his own home. While he was sleeping."

"Oh my God," I said.

"I can't believe it. In Well Springs."

"Are his wife and children okay? Is Cody okay?"

"I believe so. Only Sam was killed. Word is it was a break-in gone wrong. But nobody has been caught yet."

"Oh my God, poor Cody. Is he, have you heard or seen any members of the family?

"Not yet. There's talk that – oh never mind."

"No, what? There's talk that what?"

"I don't want to upset you, dear."

83

"There's talk that what?" I asked again.

"Well, some people think it was *her*."

"Her who?"

"Debra," she whispered.

"It was her that killed Sam?"

Violet nodded.

"Are they home?" I asked. "Can I go see them?"

"I don't believe they are, but I don't know."

"This is … you shouldn't be telling people Debra killed him. That's very irresponsible of you."

"Sweetheart, I'm not saying it was. I'm saying that's what I'm hearing."

"Well, it's not right."

"See, I didn't want to upset you."

"I can't believe it," I said. "That poor boy. And Debra. And the twins and the little one. You shouldn't be telling people it was Debra."

**

Cody never returned the rest of the school year.

For a while, I kept hoping he would show up in the morning. He never did. It was already pretty late in the school year, so eventually I knew he wouldn't come back. There was a day when one of the students asked where Cody was. When I told them that he was sick, one of the boys said he heard that Cody's mom killed his dad. I snapped at him and said to never say that again. It's very mean to spread rumors about somebody.

One day I went into the office and Violet was on the phone but turned away from me. She didn't notice I came in and I probably should have interrupted her to show her that I was there.

"I can't imagine being him. … Sheriff Cremble," she said. "Sam was a drunk. … What? It's true. He was a run-down, mean drunk. … Well, even if it wasn't her, whoever killed him did that family a favor."

84

I didn't wait to talk with Violet. I turned around and went back to my room. I knew I would never be able to get over it. I decided to move back home. There was no choice, really. I packed up and literally drove home after the last day of school. There were a few teachers I was kind of close with and I let know and said goodbye. It's not like I had any ties to that town. I wonder if I would still be living there if none of that happened. Maybe. Who knows?

Instead, I moved back to Colorado. I taught in Clifton for a few years before getting out of the profession. I've been an executive assistant for the past 15 years in Denver. It's all a little silly, to be honest – I spent a year in Well Springs. It's like, *My Year in Texas.*

Jackie, remember when you lived in Texas? Ha.

I do have some fond memories from Well Springs, though. It wasn't all bad. There are some genuinely nice people. I do wonder what happened to Cody. Do you know? I never saw him again.

And I know I said I hated Violet gossiping so much – but deep down, I wondered if Cody killed him. Obviously, it's terrible a boy would murder his dad, but Sam Jenkins was a bad man and the whole thing about Cody asking me if bad men ever come back to life days before Sam shows up dead? It's a little suspicious.

But you know what? This sounds bad, but maybe it was a good thing that Sam Jenkins was killed. I wouldn't shed any tears about him dying. He should have been in jail. I know it's bad to think that because he was murdered and all. You can't have people going around killing people – no matter how bad they are. But on the other hand, if Sam treated people better, he wouldn't be dead. You can't treat people like that. He dug his own grave. That's if it wasn't some break-in, of course. That's why I think it was Cody or his mom, even if Violet's gossiping irritated me. I heard Sam beat her. You know what I thought about the whole thing? After the initial shock of something so violent happening in that small of town – the thing I thought reflecting on Sam Jenkins being dead?

Good riddance.

Chapter Six

Debra Jenkins

I t was a nightmare getting the kids ready for Easter. I woke up a little later than I should have, so I only had thirty minutes to get Cody, Nikki, Cassie, and Tommy – and myself – dressed and fed and out the door. When I got up, they were all in the living room watching cartoons with the sound down. There's strategy to getting four kids ready. You can either start with the oldest, Cody, and get him ready because it's easiest and you work your way down the line. Or you can start with the youngest and hope that Cody can take care of himself.

I did the second option.

It was chaos getting them all dressed and ready – had to make sure they ate their breakfast too – while also getting myself presentable. Sam was still in bed – I assumed he wouldn't be going, especially after what happened on Palm Sunday with his argument with Fred Doyle. After a crazy thirty minutes, I brushed my teeth and was ready to go.

I walked back into the living room expecting chaos, but all the kids were all sitting on the couch watching cartoons. They were dressed and ready. I asked if they brushed their teeth and they all nodded. Cody was sitting with his arm around Tommy. It was a sweet moment. I told them I'd tell daddy we were leaving and I went back to our room. Sam was laying on his stomach with his face turned away from me.

"Are you awake?" I asked.

He mumbled something into the pillow.

"Okay, well we're off to church. We might stay a little bit after because I think they're having a little get together. We should be back at–"

"Where you going?" he turned over on his back, his eyes barely open and the inside of his elbow resting on his forehead.

"We're going to church. It's Easter."

"No, you're not."

"What?"

"You're not going."

"Sam, it's Easter."

"Yeah, I'm not deaf. I heard you. Y'all ain't going back to that church. You're staying home."

"The kids are all dressed and ready, Sam. We were getting ready to leave."

"Deb, you are *not* going, how simple do I need to say it?" he said, with his arm still draped across his face.

"Sam, you're being unreasona– "

"Jesus. Debra, I can't make it any more clear. You are *not* going."

He could be so petty sometimes. Ridiculous. My hands were on each side of the doorframe. I could feel Cody walking up behind me.

"Are we going mama?" he said.

"No, sweetie, it looks like we're not going to church today," I said.

"But it's Easter. We have to go to church," Cody said.

"I know. It's okay. Daddy said no."

"I want to go to church, daddy," he said to Sam.

"Cody, shut the hell up. You're not going. End of discussion."

Sam turned back on his stomach – his bare back to us. Cody looked up to me with this sad expression. I nodded at him and then motioned my head to the living room. He sunk his head and walked away. I closed the door and stood there – my face four inches from the door. I stayed there for a little while, hand on the knob, wondering if I took them anyways. He probably wouldn't even know. Chances were he would stay in bed until around noon. It would give us plenty of time to run to church, enjoy the service, and even say hello to everyone afterwards before getting back home. He wouldn't know. But people might ask him where he was during Easter service and he'd find out that I went behind his back and took them. It wasn't worth it.

I went back into the living room, sat on the couch with the kids, and we spent Easter morning watching cartoons. I suppose it's better than humiliating us in front of the whole town, like he did on Palm Sunday.

**

I was surprised he agreed to go to church on Palm Sunday, the week before he died. And also that he even remembered he said he would go. I asked him after dinner on the Thursday before Palm Sunday, assuming he'd say no – he never really went to church after the fight at the barbeque with the pastor. Part of me thinks he was embarrassed to be there. I told him it would mean a lot to me if he went with us. It was important for the children. You know, have the whole family at church and everything. He nodded. As if to say, *Not for myself or you, but for the kids*.

On Palm Sunday morning, I didn't even have to remind him that he agreed to go. He wasn't exactly chirpy and excited, but he wasn't being a bump on a log either. He got ready, ate breakfast while reading the paper, and then drove us all to church. Walking into the lobby, I could see a lot of people looking at us.

Looking at him.

Wow, Sam Jenkins is here.

I made my rounds to say hello to everybody. They were all being nice and saying it was good to see Sam. Nothing judgmental or anything. As we walked down the main aisle, we saw Fred and Helen Doyle on the left side near the front. There were seats available behind them, so I walked us over there. In hindsight, that was probably a mistake. They smiled at us but the choir started so we didn't have time to exchange pleasantries. They sang a few songs – the choir at First Church is actually really good – and then Pastor Wilheim told us to say hello to those around us.

Helen was talking with me and the kids, about how nice it was to see everybody in church and what we had planned for the rest of the day. I was in the middle of telling Cody to tell Helen about what we were going to do – he was going to do yardwork with Sam – and then I heard Sam say the f-word talking with Fred. Swearing in church.

Apparently, Fred was saying how good it was to see Sam in church again and Sam took it all personal. He was telling Fred off. Like, Fred Doyle is *such* a sweet man. Why are you using that kind of language not only directed toward Fred, but in *church*? I thought he was going to take a swing at Fred. Luckily, we all sat down – Sam with his arms crossed the rest of the service. Like a big baby. Pastor Wilheim had a sermon about how Palm Sunday was the calm before the storm. How Jesus came into Jerusalem as a king on a donkey. How it was a necessary step in the process. The whole sacrifice process. He said something along the lines of:

"Only Jesus knew what would be coming. Only he knew of the violence that would be coming upon him. Only he knew it was necessary violence. Only through that sacrifice would others – all of us – be free from the evil of sin. How many of us would be willing to make that sacrifice?"

Sam didn't grunt or make any objections to anything in the sermon. He sat there, arms folded, waiting for it to end. When they started the offering, ushers coming down the aisle with a basket, I reached into my purse to get some money. Sam grabbed my wrist.

"No," he said.

"Why not?" I whispered.

"We're not giving a dime to this place. Let's go."

"You want to leave? The service isn't over."

"I don't care. Kids, let's go. It's time to leave."

It was so embarrassing because it made us look so cheap. It made us look like we were too cheap to even give to God. People looked at us as we walked out. Sam led the way and didn't break stride. He walked right out.

He wasn't mad in the car. He just drove – didn't say anything. Nobody said a word and the radio wasn't working. It was total silence.

When we got back home, as we were eating lunch, Sam came into the kitchen and said that he was going fishing with Rhett and Mark – his buddies. Didn't say goodbye. Didn't kiss the kids. Didn't kiss me. Just, *I'm leaving*. Cody and me did yardwork. He mowed the grass – he liked doing that – and I trimmed hedges and cleaned out the gutters.

Sam was gone all day. At night, I watched TV with the kids – I think we watched a movie – before I got them all ready for bed. It was around 10 p.m. or so when I heard Sam pull into the driveway. I was already in bed. He walked into the house and I heard him open the fridge and I heard the *psst* of a beer can. For the next hour or so, he stayed in the living room and watched TV. At one point I heard him laugh really loud at something. Eventually, probably close to midnight, he came into our room.

"You awake?" he said in the dark.

"Yes."

"How was your day? I didn't catch anything, but it was still fun," he said.

"Well, that's good."

"Yeah, Rhett fell in," he said with a big laugh.

"He fell in?"

"Yeah," he said with another big laugh.

"Is he okay?"

"Yeah, yeah. We gave him a bunch of guff about it. He said it was because he didn't expect the fish to pull that hard, but I think he was too hammered and slipped and fell in."

"Sounds like you had fun."

"Yeah, I needed that. I'm gonna take a shower. You can go ahead and go to sleep."

And a week later, he was dead.

**

By the end, Sam was drinking a lot.

The Wednesday before he died, I went to pick up the kids from school and took them to get some ice cream to celebrate Cassie winning the class spelling test. We were all having a nice time and when we got back home, Sam's truck was parked half on the driveway and half on the grass, with the driver's door open. He was laying facedown on the front yard. I thought, *Oh my God, he had a heart attack*. So I sped up and parked and told the kids to stay in the car. I ran over and started to shake Sam and call his name. I was ready for him to be dead.

I turned him over and he was squinting.

"Debra, what are you doing here?" he mumbled.

He wasn't having a heart attack. He was just drunk. He was just really drunk and facedown in the front yard at four in the afternoon. In front of the kids and all the neighbors.

"Sam, what is wrong with you?" I said.

"Did I cash out?"

"What?"

"I didn't mean to leave without paying the tab."

"Sam, what the hell are you talking about?"

"Tell Dennis that I'll pay my tab next time. I'm good for it. He knows I'm always good for it."

"Your tab?"

"I hope he's not mad. I didn't mean to."

"Sam, get up and go inside and lay down."

"Inside the bar?"

"Jesus, Sam, you're home. You're lying in the front yard of your home. In front of everybody. The kids are in the car. They thought you had a heart attack. Go inside now."

"I'm home?"

He looked around and saw where he was. He laid his head back down in relief. After struggling to position his hands so that he could push himself up, he got about halfway up before stumbling backwards and falling to the ground again. I looked around to see if anybody else was watching. LeeAnn, our neighbor across the street, was snooping through the window. It was so humiliating. I walked over and grabbed Sam by the arm to help his bloated ass up.

"Get up," I said. "Sam, get inside now."

"Where are the kids?"

"Get your ass inside now. Go into the bedroom and lay down."

I got him up and he stumbled toward the house. He knocked on the front door, like he was seeing if anybody was home, before walking inside. I composed myself and then walked back to the car. Cassie asked if daddy was all right and I told her he would be fine. I said that he was sick and that he needed to lay down and rest and couldn't wait until he was inside so he laid down in the yard.

I called Dennis' bar later and asked if Sam was there and how big of a tab he ran up. It turned out Sam paid his tab and then some. Left a huge tip.

Meanwhile, Tommy was wearing shoes with holes in them.

**

There was a little stretch back in January when Sam was actually doing pretty good. About four months before Sam died, Sheriff Cremble came over randomly one night and the two of them talked in the backyard. Sam wouldn't tell me what they talked about. After the sheriff left, Sam sat in the backyard by himself for hours. I went to go tell him I was getting ready for bed, but I could see him through the window pouring his beer into the grass. Not the last sip. It was close to a full beer. I didn't go talk to him. I don't know why I didn't. I was nervous for some reason. It looked like a moment that he needed for himself. Instead, I went to bed.

I forget if it was the next day, but on a Saturday morning Sam woke up all the kids and told them to get ready. He didn't tell me anything.

"Sam, what's going on?" I said, still in my pajamas.

"Get ready, baby," he said.

"What? Where are we going?"

"It's a surprise," he said and then kissed me.

We got into my car – he's driving – and he would not tell us what was going on. I assumed we were going to get breakfast or something. The kids kept asking and asking where we were going and Sam would deflect the question and tell them some trivia or science facts or something.

"Daddy, where are we going?" Cassie asked.

94

"Cassie, my favorite spelling extraordinaire, you know the movie *ET*? The one with the alien?"

"Uh huh," she said.

"I'm putting you on the spot, baby girl. How do you spell *extraterrestrial*? That's what *ET* stands for. Extraterrestrial."

"Extraterrestrial?" Cassie said.

"That's right. Nobody help her," Sam said.

"E-x-t-r-a..."

"So far, so good."

"Extraterres...t-e-r-r..."

"Half-way there. Keep it going."

"E-s...."

"Let's go! Bring it home sister, you're almost there!"

"Extraterrestrial....t-r-i-a-l?"

"Yes!" Sam yelled out and he started honking his horn over and over and the kids were laughing and yelling. It was so much fun. He really could be fun. We were in the car for about an hour and when he exited for Mokina, the kids started to realize what was happening. He was taking them to the children's museum. There was more yelling and singing. When he finally parked, he put his arm behind my headrest and turned toward the back.

"So here's the deal team, me and mama are gonna go in for a while and y'all need to wait in the car here, unfortunately. Is that okay?"

They all screamed and yelled — they knew he was teasing — and they all got out of the car and ran toward the museum. I couldn't believe it, but I wasn't going to question anything. I didn't have to do anything. He either planned everything the night before or woke up early and did it all.

It may have been the best day of my life, to be honest. He played with the kids in the exhibits, teaching them all about dinosaurs and science and other things that I had no idea he knew about. We'd all walk around, Tommy on Sam's shoulders, looking and playing and learning. The kids loved it. When the kids were playing in a model train car, Sam kissed me off to the side.

Afterwards, we went to a restaurant and the waitress asked for our drink orders. I thought, *Okay, here it comes.* But he ordered a Dr. Pepper.

After eating, we got ice cream and walked along the little downtown area. It was a warm day for January. I remember we stayed in town to watch a night showing of the Muppets Christmas movie. It was a little weird because Christmas had been over for a little while, but I didn't mind. By the time we got home, the kids all went to bed pretty quick. They were all exhausted. Tommy fell asleep on the way home and Sam carried him to bed and tucked him in. He went around and said goodnight to Cody, Nikki, and Cassie.

We were gone all day.

When they were all asleep, we sat on the couch together. We were pretty tired but I couldn't help myself. We had probably the best sex of our entire marriage that night – starting in the living room before making our way to the kitchen and then the bedroom. It was like we were kids again. It was like we loved each other. After we were done, I went to the bathroom and I started crying. I didn't mean to, but the wave of emotions got to me. I was so happy. I was also so hopeful the change was finally happening. I was also afraid it wasn't going to stick – that everything would go back to *normal.*

It turned out I was right.

He was great – and I mean *great* – for about a week. Maybe ten days. Then something happened at work. He hurt his wrist lifting a cinderblock and had to go home early. The guys on the crew were calling him names but he really hurt it bad. I wasn't there when he came home. I had gone to the store to get a few things and when I got home, his truck was in the driveway. I thought, *He's come to surprise you at home.* So stupid. When I came in, he was sitting at the kitchen table with a six-pack of beer – two were already gone – and his wrist bandaged up.

"What happened sweetie?" I asked as I put the groceries on the counter.

"Don't worry about it," he said coldly.

"Are you okay?"

"I said don't worry about it."

"I want to know what happened to your wrist. Is there anything I can do?"

"No."

"Are you sure?"

"Debbie, you need to leave me alone right now."

And just like that, Sam was back.

**

The final few months were pretty tough.

After that brief stretch when he was an actual father to his children and a husband to me, he really fell off the rails. It's like he was trying to hold back the darkness as hard as he could for that great week, but then it took control. I really thought about leaving. This time, I meant it. I thought about packing up a bag and getting us out of there. He hit me pretty hard a couple times – once he almost broke my nose. I forget why he did that. Something stupid, probably. He started to think I was sleeping with Mark – which is laugh out loud funny because Mark is disgusting. But Sam was so paranoid and confronted me and said if he ever caught me, he'd kill me. We were in the bedroom, getting ready for bed when he brought it up.

"Sam, you're being ridiculous right now," I said.

"That's what you would say if you were sleeping around, isn't it? That *I'm* being ridiculous."

"Where the hell is this coming from? I don't even like Mark as a person. He's gross."

"I think you're lying."

"Okay, well, I'm not doing this," I said and I turned to leave the room and he grabbed me by the hair and ripped me back toward him. The momentum took me to the ground. I was surprised it didn't rip my hair out.

"Don't you walk away from me," he said. "Do you understand me?"

I covered my face and put my knees up to my chest. I told him I was sorry I made him mad, but I wasn't cheating on him. It's true, too. I could have. I *should* have. But I never did. He told me again that if he ever found out I was, he would kill me and take the kids.

It was two or three months of this. There was him yelling and screaming. There was him bullying the kids and being mean. Then there was the Palm Sunday incident with Fred, causing a scene in church. And wasting so much money on booze. There weren't any new toys for the kids. No jewelry. No fun dinners out.

I don't know what happened. It was a fast, downward spiral. One minute we're making love in the kitchen after a fun day with the family and the next you walk into the kitchen in the morning and he's sitting there with his forehead on the table.

You know the absolute worst part of it?

On Easter, the day he died, he goes off again with his fishing buddies. Two weeks in a row. He tells us we can't go to church then he has himself a nice day on the lake while his kids are at home. Cody is mowing the lawn. Tommy is pulling weeds. He's out drinking. Okay, fine. Whatever. He comes home, talking about how much fun he had again. Luckily, he didn't stay out past dinner, so we could all eat together one last time.

Sliced up hot dogs and mac and cheese. His last supper. He's telling the boys about the fish he caught – a real big one, yeah sure – that slipped out of his hands and back into the water. Tommy was mesmerized. Cody didn't even look up. He just ate his dinner.

"Not good enough for you Cody?" Sam asked, joking around.

"No, that's great Dad," Cody said.

"I never asked: how was y'all's day?"

"It was fine," I said.

"Well, that's good."

By the time he got in bed, I had turned on my side with my back to him. The lights were off. I could feel him put his head down on the pillow. After a few moments, he cleared his throat.

"Hey Debs?" he asked.

"Yeah?"

"I want to apologize," he said.

"For what?" I said, my back still facing him.

"That wasn't right for me not to let y'all go to church. Just because I don't like it there, don't mean you shouldn't be able to take the kids there. I'm sorry. That wasn't right of me."

"Okay."

"I mean it, Debbie. If you want to take them to church, you can. I mean it. I'm sorry."

There was a long silence because I didn't really know what to say. I could feel his hand on my hip.

"I love you," he said.

"I love you too, Sam," I said.

Then we went to bed. I can't believe the nerve of him. That *asshole*. I wasted my life with that drunk asshole. He ruins my life. He is the absolute *worst* husband and the *worst* father. I have a mountain full of memories of him embarrassing us, threatening us, treating us like dirt.

But the absolute nerve of him to say that. He sneaks it in at the last second. Our final interaction. It's the last thing that he ever said to me.

I love you.

**

It took me a little while to fall asleep because I was annoyed Sam apologized. I cried a little bit into the pillow. But eventually I got so tired that I fell asleep. I didn't even hear Cody come into the room. He probably didn't want to wake up Sam.

I felt some tugging at the end of our bed and it woke me up. There he was. Standing at the foot of our bed. It was dark so it was hard to see him.

"Cody? What's going on sweetheart?" I asked. He didn't answer. He just stood there, so I turned on the lamp on my nightstand. "What's the matter, Cody?"

He was holding Sam's gun and I shrieked. I didn't know what the hell was going on. My mind is racing. Was there somebody in the house and he had the gun to protect us? Was he going to kill me and Sam? Did he kill Tommy or the twins? I had no idea. It scared the hell out of me so I pushed myself up with my back against the wall and shook Sam awake.

"Sam, wake up. It's Cody."

"What?" he said, turning over.

"It's Cody. He has a gun."

"What?" Sam said, waking up real fast. He saw Cody and looked him up and down. "Cody, what's going on? Why you got my gun?"

Cody didn't say anything. He just stood there.

"Cody, why you got my gun?"

Cody lifted the gun with both hands and pointed it right at Sam. It's funny looking back — maybe funny isn't the right word — but I subconsciously moved away from Sam. I stayed in bed, but I leaned away from him.

100

"Cody, listen to me," Sam said calmly. "Put the gun down, right now. Cody, I'm serious. Put the gun down right now."

Sam put his right hand out as he spoke, palm facing Cody. Cody didn't say anything to Sam. He stood there holding the gun, his hands shaking a little bit. He looked at Sam when he finally said something.

"I love you, Mama."

Then there was a loud crack and Sam screams. Next thing I know, Sam's body pushed back toward the wall, his left shoulder dipping toward me. Blood splattered up onto my face and there was a giant dark circle in Sam's left shoulder. It started bleeding everywhere right away. Sam was screaming out in pain, putting his right hand over the wound but the blood kept pouring everywhere. Another bang and Sam yells. That one hit Sam in the right shoulder and it turned his body the other way. When his body turned, blood from his left shoulder sprayed me again. I think I was still in the bed at this point. I must have been.

"I'm gonna beat the shit outta you," Sam yelled, rocking his body back and forth.

He leaned back over with his left shoulder against the wall and his left hand holding his right shoulder. He was grimacing. His face had to be less than a foot from me. I remember Sam looked –

Excuse me.

I remember Sam looked up at me. I was looking in his eyes and he looked terrified. I had never seen him like that. He wanted me to do something – to say something to Cody to get him to stop. He looked at me like I had the power to do something. To tell Cody to stop.

And I didn't.

I was looking right at him when a third bang came and the bullet went through his right cheek. His head nearly exploded. Blood and who-knows what else splashed on me. It was so close to me that I instinctually fell out of bed and crawled into the corner. I put my back against the wall and tucked my knees into my chest and wrapped my hands around my legs.

I could still hear Sam. He wasn't dead. The gurgling sounds of the blood in his mouth. It was awful. There was so much red – covered the entire bed and wall. Sam was slowly moving, but I knew it was too late. I couldn't do anything. I was paralyzed. Screaming and crying. I didn't want to watch but I couldn't help it. This time Cody fired three shots in a row – *bang! bang! bang!* – and they hit Sam in the torso. One-two-three. He made more groaning noises. Cody kept firing and firing. The smell of smoke. At one point, I thought Cody was done. But he crouched down on the floor for a little while before standing back up, pointing the gun at Sam's body, and then started firing again.

You'll have to forgive me because I have no idea how long this lasted. You could tell me twenty seconds or twenty minutes and I'd believe you.

Cody put the gun onto the bed because Sheriff Cremble told him to. I don't really recall Sheriff Cremble coming into the room. He was just *there*. He told Cody to stay put and then he asked if I was okay and I don't think I answered him. Maybe I did. He had Cody go sit in the other corner and told him not to move. That's what Cody did. He went over there and sat. Sheriff Cremble kept walking around, going *"Oh my God, oh my God."*

He crouched down in front of me and grabbed my hands, looking back toward Cody to make sure he didn't go anywhere.

"Debra? Debra, are you okay?" Sheriff Cremble said.

I think I nodded.

"Debra, are you okay?" he repeated.

I nodded and whispered something. I don't remember what.

"Debra, what happened?"

"Cody," I said.

"Cody killed him? Why?"

"Cody."

Sheriff Cremble squeezed my hands to get me to look at him because apparently my eyes were darting all over.

"Debra, listen to me. Tell me what happened."

"Is Cody okay? Baby, are you okay?"

Cody nodded and went to stand up but Sheriff Cremble told him to sit back down. I tried to remove my hands from Sheriff Cremble's but he wouldn't let go. I looked back toward the bed and it was only bright red and legs. Blood was dripping off the side of the bed onto the floor.

"Debra, look at me. Debra, tell me what happened."

"Cody."

He was frustrated and got up and walked over to Cody and crouched in front of him. He asked Cody what happened and if he killed Sam.

"Don't," I cried.

"What?" Sheriff Cremble said.

"Don't take my baby, he didn't mean to," I said and I tried to get up but my legs were too weak so I crawled over to them. "Don't take him, Sheriff. He didn't mean to. Cody, tell him you didn't mean to."

Sheriff Cremble stood up when I got over to them and I put my arms around Cody. I was crying and screaming but I don't remember Cody saying or doing anything. He sat there. Sheriff Cremble walked around again, looking at Sam and back to us.

"This is bad," he said. "This is bad."

The gun was still on the bed, so he went and grabbed it. Cody and me both sat in that corner, while Sheriff Cremble went to the door. I remember he left. I don't know for how long. But he came back in, closed the door and then sat on the floor – his back up against the door. We all sat there for hours. Not a word.

I got so tired that I couldn't cry anymore. I sat with my back against the wall and my arm around Cody. Eventually, Sheriff Cremble got up and walked toward us.

"It's time to get up," he said.

"For what?" I said.

"The sun is about to come up. We need to leave when people are still in bed. We need to go now. Debra, I need you and Cody to stand up and come with me. We're gonna take all the kids with us."

"Where are we going?" I asked.

"We need to go to the station and talk. We need to get moving, though. Let's go."

"Talk about what? Sheriff, he didn't mean to. Don't do anything to Cody. He didn't mean to."

"I know he didn't," Sheriff Cremble said, looking back toward Sam's body before quickly turning toward us. "I know he didn't, Debra. We all need to talk, though."

"Talk about what? Is Cody in trouble?"

"We need to talk about what we're gonna say."

"What we're going to say?"

"Yes ma'am. We need to figure out the story."

Chapter Seven

Sheriff George Cremble

suppose it's fitting to tell you the bird story. I was a youngster – woulda been five or there abouts. I was walkin' around town with my cousin Eddie. He was around fifteen or so. It was summer and so we ain't have no school, you know, and we was walkin' around just 'cause. All a sudden, I come across this little birdie on the ground. It was laying on its back and wasn't moving. It was my first experience with death. This happened before I seen my granddaddy dead at the station.

Eddie kept walking but I stopped and looked at the bird. I believe it was some kinda wren. It made me sad. This beautiful creature gifted with flight – the ability to fly anywhere and do anything – and there it was, dead as a doornail on the side of the road. Eddie realized I wasn't behind him no more. He was probably a good fifty feet down the road before he turned around.

"Georgie," he called out. "What are you looking at?"

"It's a bird, Eddie."

"Yeah, so what?" he said, walking back to me.

We both stood there, looking down at it. This beautiful creature left for dead. People would keep going about their day, while it rotted away there. It made me think if the bird had any bird family – a bird wife and bird babies – waiting in the nest for him to get back. What would happen to them? Would they be sad?

"What do you think happened to him?" I asked.

"To the bird?"

"Yeah."

"I don't know, Georgie. Who cares?"

"It ain't right," I said. "Eddie, we oughta do something."

"Georgie, it's a dead bird. That's nature."

"What do you mean?"

"It's nature. Animals die all the time."

"Well, how did this bird die?"

"I don't know, Georgie. I ain't no veterinarian."

"Do you think something killed him?"

"Maybe it died of being old. It probably fell from the sky and landed here. It's fine, Georgie. Let's keep moving."

He grabbed me by the hand and we kept walking. I looked back at it one more time, hoping maybe it would get up but it ain't. It laid there, still as a dummy. I forget what we did, but when I got home later I looked around for a nice little box. The only one I could find was my old man's tobacco tin that still had some tobacco in it. If I got caught, I had hoped my daddy would understand – that I was doing something noble. Honoring it. Not letting it die alone.

That night, I waited and waited 'til everyone was asleep and I got up outta bed. Quiet as a mouse. I went to grab the tobacco tin and I slowly opened the back door and started running. I was scared I ain't have much time. Maybe the fastest I ever ran in my life, like I was Jimmy Saxton running for a touchdown. There wasn't a peep in town, of course.

Everybody was in bed. As I was running, I was worried the bird would be gone. That it got eaten or somebody else took care of it.

But there he was. Laying right where I left him. I got down on my knees and opened up the tin.

"I'm sorry this happened to you," I said to him.

I scooped my hands into the dirt under him, picked him up and dropped him in the tin. There he lay, motionless in a mixture of dirt and tobacco. I closed the lid, got up, and started running back home with the tin in my hands. When I reached my backyard, I went into my daddy's shed to get a shovel and started digging near a desert willow we had. I was digging like I was trying to get to China by sunrise. It's a tough deal digging with a grown man shovel when you're just a babe. After I got down deep enough, I grabbed the tin and opened it to look at the bird one more time. I picked him up and held him in my hands.

"I hope that you wasn't scared when you died," I said. "I'm sorry about your bird wife and bird babies. I hope they are okay. I'm sorry you died."

I placed him back into the tin and closed it. Set the tin in the hole and covered it with dirt. A proper funeral, I suppose. I remember thinking it was the right thing to do. It ain't right to let it die alone. I was doing something good.

Maybe it was the right thing to do, but I remember I got sicker than a dog afterwards. Throwing up. Fever. Mama ended up taking me to the doctor, but I ain't tell them about the bird. Kept it to myself. The doctor said I musta gotten a bad bug. I remember it lasting about a week. It worried my mama like nothing else. It's funny being a child. I thought I was doing something good, but I was scared I would get in trouble if I told her what I done. If she wanted to believe I was sick from a bug, then I wasn't gonna let her know what really happened.

**

Everything felt like it was happening so daggum fast. Sam was dead and Debbie was in the corner, crying and screaming. Nothing actually *was* happening, of course, but it felt like a whirlwind – like the middle of a twister. I tried to talk to Debbie but she wasn't saying nothing. Babbling. Saying over and over that Cody didn't mean to kill Sam. When I went to talk with Cody, she came crawling over and telling me to leave him be. Not to take him, and so forth. Chaos.

I kept looking over at what was left of Sam. It was brutal. Carnage. I can't imagine how many times that boy shot him. You ain't see that kinda violence but in a bad movie. The kinda violence like a mobster *sending a message* or some other nonsense. When I looked back at the two of them, Debbie was holding and squeezing him. It made me think of the other little ones. They was still in the house, you know. They ain't know what was happening and I was scared they'd walk in and see their daddy like that. I went looking for them.

The door to the twins' room was shut. When I went to turn the knob, it was locked. Good girls. Doing what I said. I opened the door across from the girls' bedroom but it was a bathroom. Another door led to a linen closet. Finally, I found the boys' room. When I opened the door, there was two beds on opposite sides of the room. The bed on the left was perfectly made with navy blue sheets. Cody's. The bed on the right had cartoon rocket ships and was all messy. I could hear Tommy whimpering under the bed.

I walked over and knelt beside the bed. When my knee hit the ground, I heard Tommy shriek. Felt bad I scared the little fella. I put my face down on the floor, and he was back against the wall – a small blanket covering his face.

"Tommy, son, it's Sheriff Cremble," I said. He kept whimpering into that blanket. "Tommy, I need you to listen to me, okay? It's Sheriff

Cremble. Everything is okay. You're safe. I need you to come with me, though."

He pulled the blanket down so he could see it was me. He had the saddest look on his little face. Eyes all red and glossy. I reached my hand under the bed and he grabbed it and I pulled him out. After he was out from under the bed, I picked him up and he put his arms around my neck. He kept crying into my shoulder.

"Tommy, we're gonna go in your sisters' room, okay?" He ain't say nothing, so I carried him to the twins' bedroom door and knocked on it. "Cassie, Nikki, it's Sheriff Cremble. I need y'all to unlock the door. Cassie, Nikki, I'm here to help. Unlock the door, girls."

I heard the door click. With Tommy in my right arm, I opened the door with my left hand. By the time I was in the room, I saw Nikki jumping into the closet and closing the door behind her. Both of the twins were in there – crying. I knew the violence was over. They ain't have nothing to be scared about. What was done was done. I knew if they was in the closet, they'd still be scared that a bad man would come and get them. Sometimes fear is worse.

"Girls, I need y'all to come out here. I know y'all scared, but there ain't nothing to be scared about no more. It's done. Please come out here, ladies."

It took a bit, but eventually Nikki come out the closet and Cassie was right behind her. They stood in the corner by the closet door. They each had their arms tightly crossed against their chest, like they was giving a big hug to the invisible man. I carried Tommy over to one of the beds and sat down – he was still squeezing me tight and his face was buried into my chest.

"Sweethearts, I know y'all scared, but what's done is done. There ain't no bad man here," I said.

"What happened Sheriff?" Nikki said.

"Well, something bad," I said, which got them crying again. "But it's okay. Y'all are safe."

"Where's Cody? Did they kill him?" Nikki said.

"Cody's okay. I promise. He's with your mama."

"What about daddy? What is mama screaming about?"

"Ladies, I need y'all to be brave for me. I need y'all to be brave for Tommy here. Can you do that?"

They nodded through their tears.

"I need y'all to be brave," I said again. "I'm gonna leave him with you two and I need y'all to stay in here. Don't gotta go into no closet or nothing like that. Y'all lay right here in bed – Tommy in the middle. Can y'all do that?"

"You aren't going to stay with us?" Cassie said.

"I can't, sweetheart. You are safe, I can promise that. But I'm going to your mama's room and I need you to keep put. I need y'all to stay and comfort Tommy here. I'm gonna go take care of Cody and your mama."

"What about daddy? Is he okay?"

"Girls, promise me you'll stay in here with Tommy. Can you do that?"

Nikki nodded and I laid Tommy down on the bed – he ain't wanna let go of me and it can be a little hard getting a scared youngster off you when they start clinging. I locked the door behind me and went back into the main bedroom. Cody and Debbie was still there in the corner. She ain't even realize I come back in. I ain't know what to do, so I sat down with my back against the door and started thinking.

**

I ain't proud of it, so you know.

This part.

I understand it went against my duties as a lawman. I understand that. And I ain't proud of it.

Everyone thinks they know what they'd do in a given circumstance. *Oh, I would do this* or *I would do that*. But they ain't know. It's a nice sentiment, but some things you gotta experience to know for sure. Maybe people in Dallas or Houston or some other big city – El Paso or San Antoine – they'd know what to do in my predicament. That's city life. We ain't used to this kinda violence out here.

Sam Jenkins laying there – least what's left of him. Debbie and Cody sitting together in the corner. The three babies locked in their room. Had to be around two in the morning.

Now what in the hell am I supposed to do?

Arrest a 10-year-old boy?

Or cover it up?

Those was my two options. And you know what's interesting? I never seriously considered the first option – arresting the boy. I knew it was an option, sure. But I ain't waste much energy thinking how that'd turn out. Maybe that says something about me as the lawman – I never considered upholding the law.

How could we explain what happened to Sam Jenkins? That's what was racing through my mind.

My first thought was make it seem like he up and left. Ran town. The man had a reputation for not exactly treating his family right. It weren't that much of a stretch, having the story be he went for cigarettes and never came back. Yes, the story would be the easy part. Maybe some people have questions on why he'd done it, but they'd say, *That poor woman and them children*. Then Debbie and the children can go about their life. Rebuilding and such.

The tricky part, of course, was what to do with what was laying on the bed there. I'd have to roll him in the sheets – maybe run to the station and find a body bag – and carry him outside and into the bed of his truck. Have to make sure nobody is seeing, so I'd have to act quick,

111

you know. I'd drive the truck out into the desert somewhere and bury him. Then what would I do with the truck? Have to burn it or some kinda deal. But how would I get home? Debbie would have to drive the truck because if somebody saw her driving my police car, that's game over. She'd drive the truck and I'd follow her with my police car, that way she ain't get pulled over or something. But then Debbie would be driving with her dead husband in the back? That ain't fair. But it's the way it had to be. We'd have to put the mattress in the back, too. Also cut out the carpet. We'd drive out to the desert together, do what we need to do with Sam's body and mattress, take care of the truck and then I'd drive her back into town.

If anyone saw us, of course, it'd be all she wrote. I'd spend the rest of my days in prison, most likely. Debbie, too. Accomplices. We'd have to plan it real cloak and dagger like. Do it in the dark of night. Drive far enough outta town and far enough off the road so ain't nobody see us digging.

But then we're leaving the children back in the house alone? Leaving Cody alone? They ain't coming with us, seeing us bury their daddy and all. We'd have to leave 'em with Fred and Helen.

Therein, they say, was the sticky wicket.

Fred.

He was the one that called me, you remember, so he knew he heard gunshots. Lord knows Helen heard them too, or Fred told her about it. Bless Helen, but she ain't the best confidant in the world. Big mouth. Again, sweet lady but she couldn't hold a secret if her life depended on it. Debbie would take the kids over there, ask Fred and Helen to watch them in the middle of the night. How you gonna explain that? No, Helen would start talking and it wouldn't hold up. The whole town would know there was gunshots at the Jenkins' house the night Sam supposedly left town. Maybe they'd never be able to pin it on us. Maybe. But there'd always be talk. Always. Black cloud hovering over. Probably some nonsense like me and Debbie was in cahoots. Having an affair or some baloney. Maggie would worry. Have her doubts. I'd tell her it ain't true, but I'm sure it'd always be in the back of her mind. Nothing I could do to set it straight.

Knowing Fred and Helen, I'm sure they was peeking out their windows at the very moment. Wondering. Maybe I could wait and we come back and take Sam outta here tomorrow night – leaving a dead body blown to bits laying there in the house for a full day ain't feel right, though. Besides, it ain't solve the problem. From Fred and Helen's point of view, they hear gunshots in the middle of the night, they see me showing up and staying here for hours, Sam's truck in the driveway, then I leave and tell them what? The next day Sam runs town? Too many holes. Too many questions.

I certainly do like Fred and Helen a whole lot. I ain't want it to come across like I don't. They are fine, Christian people. They do what's right.

However, I ain't gonna lie: this whole deal woulda been a lot easier if they weren't living next door. Or if they was outta town. Or if they ain't hear the gunshots. I knew it wouldn't work – the line that Sam left.

No.

Sam Jenkins needed to be murdered.

**

I was sitting there thinking what's the easiest explanation?

What would make the most sense? They got an expression for something like that – forget what it is, something 'bout how the most logical explanation or simplest deal that coulda happened is probably what did happen. It's something to do with a razor, I believe.

What made the most sense for why there was that dead body laying there?

I supposed it would be her, right?

Debbie.

It make sense, don't it? Woman getting beat on and beat on, and one day decided she ain't gonna take no more beatings. Decides to shoot him dead. It'd add up, wouldn't it? I felt like that would be the play. Wife kills the husband because he's a bad man. People would understand. I was about to push myself up and tell her the plan, when I looked over at her.

If I decided to let her go, some in town would have sympathy. Sure. Tell her she shoulda done it long ago. Then again, people would talk. Say how she shoulda tried to work it out. Hell, even take the kids and run. Ain't no reason for her to kill the man. Some would call her a murderer. Sam, as much of a dog as he was – and he was quite a dog, don't get me wrong – he still had friends. They'd have questions. They'd have 'em for me: saying why was I letting her get away with murder? What kinda lawman am I? People killing people in town and I do nothing? Maybe they'd get mean with Debbie. Harassing her, you know. Do things to get back at her. Some of his friends were a bit surly. I'm picturing her waking up on a Sunday morning and going to the car with the little ones to church and seeing God-knows-what those knuckleheads did: smash a windshield, spray paint something nasty.

Maybe she could move. Leave town with the kids to escape it all. Get away from all the noise and get themselves a fresh start. Sounds good on paper. Sounds real easy-like on paper. But she'd have to leave friends. Kids was in school and they'd leave all their friends. Then what would that do for me: not only did I let her get away with killing her husband, I let her skip town like a slippery bandit. I'm sure Sam's pals would track them down too, get drunk one night and do Lord knows.

The more I was thinking, the more I felt pinning this on her would be no good. Couldn't say I did it, neither. Seeing as the gunshots went off before Fred called me, you see. It goes back to that problem of Fred and

Helen — not to call them a problem, of course. Sweet as pie. But the story ain't line up. Wish it would. I wish I was there before the gunshots. I get called because Sam and Debbie are being loud and when I show up, Sam threatens me, waving his gun all around like a madman before pointing it at me and then I gotta shoot him. Yes, that woulda been a lot easier. People could say, *There's that Cremble Curse. It strikes again.*

But I could live with that.

Every idea I thought came up a bit flat.

Sam couldn't have left town.

Debbie could have killed him — it ain't off the table, but it would cause a lot of problems.

I couldn't have killed him, because the timeline ain't add up.

Sam couldn't have killed himself, cause Fred heard too many gunshots.

I ain't want to have Cody take the responsibility because that'd bring up a whole can of worms that I ain't trying to fish with.

I kept rolling through all the potential suspects, so to speak. Who in this town coulda had the motive to kill a man like Sam Jenkins? Not only that, who could kill him and no heads would have to roll? No life in prison? Who could we pin it on?

Then I thought: maybe a man who ain't exist.

**

A man came through Well Springs from outta town, I was thinking.

Yes.

A man wearing a mask. He was driving along and stopped at the Jenkins' house — we ain't know why. Probably never will know. Maybe he was robbing the unlucky Jenkins family. The man is in the bedroom and he pulls his gun on Sam. Tells Sam to not say a word. Says if he makes a peep, he'll blow his brains out.

What was Sam supposed to do? Ain't no time to play cowboy. He ain't in nothing but his undies and the man got a gun aimed at him. Had him dead to rights. Debbie is still sleeping. It's the middle of the night, you know?

Sam is hot as an August afternoon but the man has his index finger over his own mouth, telling Sam to not cause a racket. Maybe the man sees Debbie sleeping and he makes some vulgar comment. Says he's fixing to do something bad to her and Sam goes off. Yells at the man. Threatens him. Now this wakes Debbie up and maybe the man panics and starts shooting. Fills Sam with bullets. Debbie, well, she's confused and scared and she falls outta bed and rolls to the corner. She ain't recognize the man – he's wearing a mask. Or maybe he's not. He's a stranger, after all. After firing more than enough bullets to send Sam to the other side, he turns the gun to Debbie and pulls the trigger – but nothing but a click. All his bullets was in Sam. He looks back at Sam before running off. Gets into his car and speeds off, driving back to where he came from.

That don't pin it on nobody. Not Debbie. Not Cody. Not me. All her story had to be is, *It happened so darn fast. I ain't see much of anything.* Nobody gonna do nothing but give her sympathy.

It also accounts for Sam's body. We would have the funeral and ain't gotta worry 'bout burying him and the mattress in the desert and getting rid of the truck and so forth.

Would be a shock for the town, of course. People might start locking doors. I hoped that they wouldn't start being suspicious of each other – thinking one of their own done it. Everybody knew Sam had his demons and there was certainly people who'd say good riddance to find out he'd been killed. If it was a drifter that came through and killed Sam – well the foolishness with Koresh and all of them over in Waco had only recently happened. Had people wondering what the world was coming to. I'd rather have people shaking their heads at the state of the world than pointing fingers and whispering about Debbie or Cody being a killer.

There was but two concerns about this plan, as I saw it. One was Fred and what to do with him. I could leave it alone and he'd say he never saw the shooter leave. Never got a look at him. Or I would go over and have a talk with him. Tell him man-to-man, not getting Helen involved, that I needed him to say he saw a man running out the house. Mask on. Didn't get a good look. It's an awful weight to put on a man, asking him to lie about what he saw the night of a murder. He'd ask what really happened and I wouldn't be able to tell him.

"Fred," I'd say. "I just need you, if anybody asks what happened that night, to tell 'em that you saw a man in a mask running out the house after you heard them gunshots."

It would be, as they say, the alibi for the story.

The *story*.

Well, I suppose I need to call it what it is.

The alibi for the *cover-up*.

Fred would tell people he saw somebody running out the house after the shooting. They'd think some person decided to bring tragedy to a quiet little town.

The other concern I had was the situation getting outta control. How much effort would need to go into trying to find a man who ain't exist? Obviously there ain't no way to close the case, so what if there was people in town that demand I solve it? For their personal well-being and so forth. What if the state gets involved? Hell, maybe the FBI if they think it's a crime from a real person they're trying to find. What if they come to Well Springs – asking questions. Asking Debbie about what happened. Asking Cody about his daddy. Now you got a ten-year-old lying to the FBI. That ain't gonna last a minute before crumbling. This plan would

117

depend on people not caring enough about Sam being killed to demand the killer be found.

There ain't too many perfect hands to play when a young boy kills his daddy in the middle of the night. Gotta play the cards you're dealt, as the man says.

I forget what time it was. I was sitting and thinking for an hour or so. Maybe more. I wish I coulda had more time to think – maybe I coulda thought of something better. But for something like that, you gotta pick a plan and run with it. Debbie had stopped crying and she was sitting there holding Cody. Squeezing him tight. I can't imagine what she was thinking. Hell of a deal, going from watching your husband be killed in front of your eyes to switching over and worrying about your boy. Go to bed one night and then your life is changed forever. Ain't no time to brace for impact, neither.

I sat there and decided there wasn't no more time to dip my toe in. Gotta jump in. I walked over to Debbie and Cody. I was standing there for a little bit before Debbie even noticed.

"Let's go darling," I said, putting my hand out. "We gotta go."

"Go where?" she said. "You can't take Cody. He didn't mean to."

"Debbie, Cody ain't gonna be in no trouble. We just gotta get a story straight."

She squeezed Cody again, then reached out to my hand.

**

I went outside and looked for any souls around. We was in the bedroom long enough, even Fred went back to bed – least, I ain't seen him in the window there. We was all clear, so I went back into the house to get everybody and the six of us crammed into my squad car – Debbie in the passenger seat with Tommy on her lap and the other three little ones in the back. I told Tommy and the twins that everything was okay, but that we needed to go to the police station and told them not to ask

118

any questions. Wouldn't answer none. What I needed most outta them was to stay quiet.

I remember the silence on the ride to the station. All the emotion hanging there in the air. Everyone could feel it. Debbie was staring out the passenger door window – Tommy with his head buried in her chest. I snuck a glance at Cody through the rearview mirror and he had this blank expression. Looking out the window, too.

It was still dark.

I parked on the side of the station and told them to stay in the car. When I went inside, Hank was at his desk – he was the only one there that time of morning. I tried to mix it up so people took turns with that overnight shift 'cause that kinda boredom can drive a man insane. He was reading a book when I came in and you could tell I startled him a bit.

"Sheriff, what brings you in so early?" he said, putting the book down.

"Howdy Hank, anything come in?"

"No sir."

"That's good. You can probably head on home. I can take over."

"Sheriff?"

"It's okay. You go on home."

"I still got a few hours left, though, I can stay here. It ain't no biggie."

"That's okay. Go on home, Hank."

"Is everything all right, sir?"

"Yes, you can go home, though, Hank."

"How come you're in so early, sir?"

"Couldn't sleep. Hank, now this is an order. Do you understand? Go on home."

Now I ain't one to be so darn fussy but these was ... *unusual* circumstances. You could tell Hank was a bit confused and maybe a little

119

worried, but I had to lay the hammer down and get him outta there. He got his things and went out to his truck. When I heard him drive off, I went back to my car and told everyone to come inside. We walked to the back – we had this sorta meeting-room-type deal and I told Debbie and Cody to go in there and I'd meet 'em in a minute. Then I took Tommy and the twins over to the interrogation room – if you wanna call it that. It's a small room with a table and a few chairs. We mostly used it to do crosswords when we needed peace and quiet. I told them to go in there. I ain't want Cody and Debbie in that interrogation room – get them feeling like they was being grilled and such. Luckily, we had these coloring books for the youngins and a box of crayons that I brought in there and told them to share. Tore out sheets so each of them can color their own page. Got them some cups of water and asked if they had to go to the restroom because they'd be stuck in this room for a little while. Told them it was very important they stay in this room. They said they was okay, so I shut the door and went and grabbed two more cups of water. Went to the meeting room with Debbie and Cody.

I wondered if I shoulda had Cody be in the room with the other children. That I should only talk with Debbie about everything. But I suppose if you're old enough to kill a man, you're old enough to be in the room. Be at the adult table, so to speak.

"This is quite the predicament we find ourselves in," I said as I sat down.

Neither said nothing.

"I was thinking a lotta bout this," I said. "Cody, I ain't gonna arrest you. Do you understand that?"

He nodded.

"He didn't mean to do it, Sheriff," Debbie said. "He didn't mean to."

"Cody, is that true? Was it an accident?"

Our eyes was locked for a few seconds. He shook his head.

"You meant to kill your daddy?" I said.

He nodded once.

"Why?" I asked.

"Cody, you don't gotta answer that," Debbie said. She was frazzled. "We get a lawyer or something don't we? He's not supposed to say anything without a lawyer."

"Debbie, I need you to calm down. I know this is hectic, but I am on your side. Listen to me. I am on your side. Cody ain't going to no prison. We need to get this story straight if we're gonna move on."

"But he didn't mean to do it!"

"Debbie, be quiet! He did mean to do it! He just said so much. He *did* mean to kill him. And I wanna know *why* so I can understand as we move on. If you want me to help you make this go away, you're gonna need to be quiet and accept that he meant to kill Sam."

Now I was all heated but I ain't wanna scare Cody, so I had to put a blanket on my temper and calm down.

"Cody, how come you killed your daddy?"

"Because he was bad."

I ain't know what to say to that.

Out of the mouth of babes, they say. Sam *was* bad. Maybe that ain't fair – people is complicated and so forth. But Cody made it sound so simple that I ain't had no retort. I coulda said something about how just because a man is bad don't give you no right to shoot him dead. That the law ain't work that way. That you need to use your words. But we already tried that. Lots of people had tried words to get Sam to change. He ain't change. I couldn't say to remove yourself from the situation. You can't pick your family. He was stuck. They all was. Stuck like a pig in a fence.

Cody killed his daddy because his daddy was bad and nobody did anything about it.

"Well, okay," I said.

**

"The way I see it, we got one option that's better than the others," I told them. "I ain't gonna force it on y'all, but I think it's the best way."

I got a yellow legal pad and a pen to write and draw. Cody had drank half of his water and Debbie ain't touched hers.

"It has to be me," Debbie said. She said it like it was inevitable and she had accepted her fate. "Who would look after the children, though? Please, don't let it be Sam's parents. Fred! Fred and Helen can watch them. Sheriff, please give the children to Fred and Helen. Promise me you'll give them to Fred and Helen."

I always found that funny: I ain't thought about that. When I was planning and scheming about if Debbie killed him, I assumed she'd walk. Never occurred to me that it'd go to court and the judge would send her away. Then what would happen to the kids? You could tell the thought scared Cody. When Debbie was talking about it – about her taking the blame for what he done – it was sorta catching up to him. The consequences. His face changed and you could see the worry.

"Debra, you ain't going nowhere," I said.

"There's no other explanations, Sheriff," she said. "Cody did *not* do it. I did. I will take the blame. I was the one he beat. Me. I will take – I did it. That's the story. Cody will not be in trouble."

"Neither of you is gonna be in no trouble," I said. "Debra, please just listen to me."

Her hands was shaking but she stayed quiet enough for me to finally get to my plan.

"Here's what we're saying happened: A man came into your home in the middle of the night. Snuck in to steal whatever he could. The man seen you in bed, Debra, and made a crude comment that Sam ain't care for. Sam yelled at him and the man panicked and started shooting. He was shooting and shooting and shooting. Debra, you woke up and ain't have time to notice the man because you hurried off into the corner.

"The man shot Sam to death and got scared and ran away. Got back into his car and sped away. He never even took nothing. Never got a chance to. I'll do a manhunt, asking around if anybody knows what happened — if anybody knew who'd done it. Of course, nobody will. Eventually, everyone will accept that we'll never find out who done it. It was some out-of-towner who decided to rob a house and y'all happened to be the unfortunate ones. Somebody has to be the unfortunate ones. Then everything will ... go away."

I leaned back into my chair and that last line sorta hung there. We was all quiet and you could tell Debbie was thinking about it. Thinking if it would work.

"But what about," Debbie said, searching for what to say. "How would that work? Wouldn't somebody know what happened?"

"Only those in this room here," I said.

"When would it go away?" she said. "Wouldn't you always have to try and search for who did it?"

"Oh, it might be an open case. But I'd do my best to not let it spin outta control. Keep everything right here in Well Springs."

"And people would just forget about it?"

"I don't know about *forget* about it. But people would move on. Call it a shame, but it ain't worth the energy. Then time would take care of the rest."

"A burglar," Debbie said to herself. "A bad guy."

"I would need to take an official statement from you," I said. "There ain't much for you to say. One moment a man started shooting in your bedroom, the next I showed up. Simple as that."

"And the children?"

123

"Don't see no need. Maybe ask them if they'd seen a man. All they'd say was they was asleep and heard some bangs and that was that. Cody ran into your room after he heard the man leave."

Then we heard the front door of the station open. Somebody getting there for the day. Jerry Keel. I told Debbie and Cody to stay right put. I got up and went back into the lobby.

"Sheriff, what are you doing here so early?" Jerry said.

"Jerry, something big happened. I got the Jenkins family here. Debbie and Cody are in the meeting room. The smaller children are in the crossword room. I got it all under control, though. You ain't gotta worry about nothing."

"What happened?" he asked.

"Somebody killed Sam Jenkins."

Chapter Eight

Thomas Jenkins

I remember hiding under the bed, absolutely overcome with fear. It's not brave, but I was five. The gunshots woke me up and I could hear Mom screaming from their room. I'm talking about blood-curdling screams. I looked over and Cody wasn't there. I didn't know what was going on, so I hid under the bed and prayed to God everything would be all right. I guess God half-answered the prayers because only Dad got killed.

I'm not going to lie and say something overly dramatic like, "Not a day goes by that I don't think about that night." That's not true. Every once in a while, yeah, I'll think about it. But life is too busy to sit around and sulk. I haven't actually *talked* about it in quite some time. I was a little surprised when you called. My memories from back then aren't all that great and I'm sure I'm misremembering how things actually happened.

It's like a jigsaw puzzle and you have sixty percent of the pieces. You see enough to make out what happened, but some parts are missing.

Mom never really talked to us about everything. Maybe she did with Cody, Cass, and Nikki. But not with me.

I guess the thought was, *Well, we were all there. What's there to talk about?*

I remember hiding under the bed after the gunshots and hearing Mom screaming. And then hearing the door open. It's an odd feeling, being *five* and fearing for your life. Not like a monster kind of fear. An actual fear of, *This person is going to kill me for absolutely no reason.* The footsteps got closer and closer until I saw his boots. Of course, it turned out to be George – Sheriff Cremble, I guess I should call him.

He is a good dude.

Truly.

You'll never meet a better man than Sheriff Cremble. He scooped me out and took me into the girls' room. I was with them for a long time before Sheriff Cremble, Mom, and Cody came and got us. I *think* that's how it went. The girls might have come into my room.

I remember being at the police station, in this small room, and we had puzzles and coloring sheets or something. Basically, stuff to keep us busy. Then Cassie – who has always had a big mouth – starts saying stuff.

"Who do you think killed him?" she said.

"Killed who?" I said.

"Daddy."

"Cassie, be quiet!" Nikki said.

"What?" Cassie said.

"Did Daddy die?" I asked.

"I think so," Cassie said.

"You don't know that!" Nikki said.

"Then where is he? Why isn't he here with us?" Cassie said.

"I don't know, but you don't know that he's dead," Nikki said.

"Yes, I do. Do you think it was Mama?" Cassie said.

126

Nikki punched Cassie in the arm and they sort of got into it. Since I was young, I had this juvenile naivety that my parents were invincible. They were these larger-than-life figures. They were the Provider. They can't die.

"Nikki, is Daddy dead?" I asked.

"I don't know, Tommy" she said.

Then we sat in silence for a long time. I was coloring this sheet that was like a lizard or something. Maybe a turtle or Godzilla. It was something green. I was coloring and coloring and coloring. Nobody said a word for the longest time.

When you're that young and nobody will tell you anything, you learn by listening to what other people are saying. Figure it out that way. By the time I was older, nobody wanted to talk about it anymore so all I had were those little clues you picked up along the way. I don't know what there is to talk about. Sheriff Cremble tried his damndest. I'll give him that. He worked that case for years. *Years*. It's just hard, you know, when it's somebody who doesn't have a direct motive.

Some random criminal comes in, robs us, kills Dad, and then takes off. Nobody saw him. Nobody saw what kind of vehicle he drove. I always hoped that whoever killed Dad would do it again somewhere else and get caught. I know it's an awful thing to wish for – because somebody else needed to die. Another family crushed like ours. But then the dots would get connected and we'd finally know who did it. But I don't know if that day will ever come. To be honest, I don't expect it. There are random acts of violence all over the country and that means there has to be random victims on the wrong end of them. Those victims are actual people. Somebody has to be the victim. I guess Dad picked the wrong straw.

**

In movies, whenever there's a funeral, it's always raining.

Have you ever noticed that?

Everybody is wearing black and crying and people are holding umbrellas for the rain. That's how it always is. When Dad was buried, it was actually a really beautiful day. I remember the sky being blue. Mom even made a comment about how nice it was out when we were driving over to the cemetery. I think we actually went to the park later that day.

As an adult, I look back at that funeral and wonder how difficult it was for some of the people there. I don't mean difficult in the sense of emotional – crying and everything. More difficult in the sense of being an odd situation. I may have been young at the time, but I know my dad could be a real bastard. He had a short temper and was always drinking. There's no point in sugar-coating it: the guy could be a bastard. There were people who probably were glad he went under and they didn't have to deal with him anymore.

But he was still a young guy. He was thirty-one when he was killed. I'm thirty-one now. It's hard to think of somebody dying that young – somebody who had plenty of time to turn it around – and not feel *some* sympathy. A lot of people make good later in life, you know?

Dad never got the chance.

We had the service at First Church before moving over to the cemetery for the burial. The turnout was about what you would expect. Mom and us kids, some of his work buddies, Fred and Helen, and some people from the church. Sheriff Cremble was there with his wife. There were maybe twenty people or so. People came up to Mom and hugged her and gave their condolences. Pastor Wilheim delivered the final eulogy and it was nice. I actually got a copy of his speech. I got it with me. Figured it might be interesting for what you're working on. Pastor Wilheim gave it to Mom after the service and she kept it in a drawer over the years. When I was older and moved out, I found it when I came home one day and I kept it. Maybe it's in a more favorable light than he deserved, but it's still nice to have to remember him by.

I can read it, if you'd like.

It was the wise King Solomon who wrote in the book of Ecclesiastes: "I saw all that God has done. No one can comprehend what goes on under the sun. Despite all their efforts to search it out, no one can discover its meaning. Even if the wise claim they know, they cannot really comprehend it."

Friends, I can not claim to know why this shadow has come over our town. I can not claim to know why a man seemed fit to take the life of Sam Jenkins. I can not claim to know how this tragedy fits into the plan of God.

My heart is heavy today for Debra and her children. A wife now without her husband. Children now without their father.

Sam Jenkins was a complex man. He was a man not without his demons. However, he was a man that would give you the shirt off his back. We remember everything that he did for Helen when she had her traumatic health issues. He could be the kindest of men.

We remember how much pride he brought us in his playing days – seeing him tackling anything that came his way. He was a tremendous athlete who, as I can later personally attest, also had a mean right hook.

He became a father to four beautiful children – Cody, Cassandra, Nicole, and Thomas. Those four children are likely his greatest accomplishment, no doubt. Four children that he loved so dearly and was so very proud of.

It is unfair of me, however, to not acknowledge Sam as a cautionary tale. He was a man with certain flaws – however, that is what made him human. We all have flaws. That is the burden of humanity: our sinful nature. The first chapter of I Timothy reads: "I thank Him who has given me strength, Christ Jesus our Lord, because He judged me faithful, appointing me to His service, though formerly I was a blasphemer, persecutor, and insolent opponent. But I received mercy because I had acted ignorantly in unbelief, and the grace of our Lord overflowed for me with the faith and love that are in Christ Jesus. The saying is trustworthy and deserving of full acceptance, that Christ Jesus came into the world to save sinners, of whom I am the foremost. But I received mercy for this reason, that in me, as the foremost, Jesus Christ might display His perfect patience as an example to those who were to believe in Him for eternal life."

The day of the Lord, scripture says, will come like a thief in the night. We do not know the day and moment that we shall meet our Maker. Sam died at no fault of his own. He became the victim of a senseless crime. The victim of a sinful world. That's why we must ensure that his death, as pointless as it was, will not be in vein. We must take the lessons learned and live our own lives in a fulfilling way. We should live in kindness, enjoying the company of loved ones, striving to be better, and living a life pleasing to the Lord.

We are all sinners. It is true.

But Jesus came to save the sinners and Sam Jenkins is now with his savior. Lord, I pray that you watch over this small, humble town. Today, as we look down and watch our friend, our husband, our father lowered into the ground, I pray that we then look up. That we look up for wisdom on how to navigate the emotions of today. That we could become better people because of this tragedy. That we know that Sam's spirit is in heaven, watching over us now. I pray that we never lose sight of your love. I pray for strength for this town, Lord. In your wonderful and powerful name, we pray. Amen.

I remember the line about the right hook got a lot of laughs. With Dad punching the pastor at that church outing back in the day.

When I read it, I think about what Dad would be like now. If he wasn't killed. If that stranger decided on another house. If instead of shooting Dad, the guy decided to run away. If the guy stole a bunch of our cheap crap and then took off. Maybe Dad would have become older and wiser. Put all the drinking and anger behind him. Because he really could be a good man.

I guess there's no point in thinking about this stuff. It happened and there's no changing it. He's dead and that's all there is to it.

**

Every year, me and my wife, Erin, bond with the kids when we split off and go on separate trips. The girls – Erin and Nora, she's five now – went to Austin last year for shopping and spas and who-knows-what-else. Nora likes the great big buildings. Erin likes the shopping. For the boys, me and Sam – he's seven now – went on a camping trip up to Minnesota. Split Rock State Park.

It was a lot of fun. They have this lighthouse right on the lake. He really liked that. Sam's a pretty inquisitive kid. Always reading and learning about different things. He's a sweet boy. Big Sam would have liked him. I remember when I told Mom that I was naming him after Dad, she gave an uncomfortable look. She gave her blessing, but I felt deep down it bothered her. Maybe every time she gets the chance to see her grandson, it brings up the memory of some stranger killing her husband. I saw pictures of Dad when he was younger – like little Sam's age – and they really do look alike. He's got Dad's eyes and his nose. Dad was a handsome guy, so hopefully Sam grows up to be a good-looking dude. Life's always easier for good-looking people, right?

When we were on that trip in Minnesota, we built a little campfire and were roasting wienies and marshmallows. It was around dusk and there was this beautiful sunset. It was one of those moments you take the time to think, *This is really nice.* It was one of those deals. We had found these nice long sticks for our skewers and I was showing him how to put the marshmallow on there and hold it to the flame.

"Watch me. See how I rotate the stick real slow?" I said. "You want to slowly turn it so it cooks the marshmallow all over. You want to get it where the white turns golden brown. Now you try."

He grabbed his stick, smushed a marshmallow on the end, and stuck it directly into the fire. I grabbed his stick and lifted it up so it was more on the edge of the flames and together we rotated the stick around. Whenever Sam concentrates, he sticks his tongue out a little bit. It's the cutest thing. He was doing it then, I remember. We were spinning the marshmallow until it was perfect then he pulled the stick back and he ate it right off the skewer.

"What do you think?" I said.

"It's good! It's gooey!" he said. "Did Grandpa Sam teach you this?"

"He did," I said. "When I was about your age, we would go camping like this. We ate marshmallows just like this."

"I wish I could meet Grandpa Sam."

"Yeah? He would have liked you, little buddy."

"You think so?"

"Of course."

"It would be nice to do trips like this with him," he said.

"He would have liked this, that's for sure."

"Do you think they'll ever catch the bad guy?"

"I wouldn't worry about that," I said. "I hope they do, but I don't want you to worry about that."

That whole trip was something else. We went swimming and fishing and hiking. It was a perfect trip with him. I know there's going to come a time when he's older – teenage years – when he won't want anything to do with me. He'll want to be with his friends. He'll want to be with girls. He won't have time for me. That's what makes these trips so special. I get to take the time to enjoy being a father. When he still looks up to me like his hero and he wants to follow me everywhere and do everything that I do. He doesn't have a phone he's obsessed over. He's not playing video games or something. I get the spoils of having his undivided attention.

Sometimes I think if I appreciate it more – the time I spend with Sam – because of what happened. Do I appreciate it more than somebody whose dad didn't die when they were younger? Do I enjoy moments like the trip to Split Rock because I know how many trips with my own old man never happened because he was killed?

Maybe.

I know people don't have the most flattering things to say about Dad. That he could be really mean. A drunk. I remember times when he would get mad at stuff but I was too young to remember the details. A lot of those memories are foggy. Maybe it was best he got killed when I was so young. Maybe if he got killed five years later, when I was as old as Cody was, I would remember him less fondly.

But I guess that's another silly hypothetical because he died when I was five. All the thinking and pondering and philosophizing in the world could never change that. I've never really talked much with Cody, Cass, or Nikki about Dad. I don't know why. We just never did. I guess I didn't want to hear what stories they might have. Call me naïve, but I'm fine holding onto the precious little memories I have of Dad.

**

To this day, I don't know where we were.

It had to be somewhere near Well Springs, because I don't think our drive was that long. Once a year, Dad would do something with each one of us. He said it was important to have one-on-one time, so one of us would do something with him while the other three stayed at home. It's the reason why Erin and I do it with our kids.

I only really remember one of those trips. We packed a bunch of food and supplies and headed out of town in Dad's truck to go camping and fishing. I was so excited. I wore my hat the same way he did and I had this little cargo vest like he did. Wanted to be like Dad, you know? I remember being in the truck and excited for the adventure.

"How you doing little man?" he said.

"Are we going to catch lots of fish?"

"I sure hope so. We're gonna catch a lot of fish and go swimming and at night, we'll make a nice fire and roast some wienies and some marshmallows."

"Is it hard to catch a fish?"

"Not if you know what you're doing. I'll teach you. You want to be my new little fishing buddy?"

"Yes!"

"Well, maybe we oughta make this a tradition, huh? Every year we get away from everything and do some fishing."

When we got there, Dad put up the tent while I helped – he'd ask me to get him a part or a tool and I'd run and get it. When he was done, he rolled the sleeping bags inside and told me to get in. I thought it was the coolest thing. It felt so grown up. Like I wasn't a baby anymore.

I walked around the campground picking up rocks while dad was getting the boat ready. Maybe he was getting me to help build the fire pit or maybe he was just keeping me busy while he handled the boat. He told me to stay around the tent while he got the boat ready, probably because he knew he'd get mad and start cussing. To this day, I don't know how dad got the boat off the rack and into the water by himself. Somehow, he got the boat out there and he came and got me and we went out in the water. He packed me a lunch – peanut butter and honey sandwich, which was my favorite. We were out there on the water and he taught me how to bait the hook and how to cast. I had this little tiny pole. We were both sitting there – peace and quiet.

"This is nice, you know that, bub?" he said.

"It's very quiet," I said.

"Ain't it nice? No Mama or sisters yelling at you."

"Yeah, no girls," I said.

"That's right. Just us boys."

"Did you want another beer Daddy?"

"Yes sir, I think I might."

He always drank cheap beer – said he wasn't paying for the label, he was paying for the buzz. We sat there all afternoon, drinking beer and juice and enjoying each other's company and the silence.

"You got any cute girls at school, Tommy? You give any girls a kiss?"

"No, girls are dumb."

"Oh now, they aren't so bad. Your Mama's a girl, and you love her."

"Well, Mama's different."

"How you liking school? You learning a lot?"

"Yes sir."

"That's good. School is important. You're a smart boy, Tommy. You end up using your mind, so you ain't gotta break your back for a living like me."

"But you're smart, too."

"Oh bud, I may be smart but I'm stupid. You're too young to know what that means, but you will understand somebody."

He got a bite on his line, which nearly jerked him into the water. He got it under control and told me to come help him. He put me between himself and the rod and *we* reeled it in. I remember seeing the fish break the plane of the water. It looked like the biggest fish in the world – the kind of fish you tell fishing stories about. I don't remember what it was or how much it weighed or any of that. I only remember the feeling I had when we pulled it out of the water and into the boat. We both cheered and he lifted me up and said that I did such a good job.

Later that night, when we were around the campfire, he helped me put the marshmallows on the stick so we could make s'mores. He had had quite a bit of beer by then, and at one point he stumbled and almost fell into the fire when my marshmallow fell off the stick and into the flames. It was a little scary, but he played it off and we laughed about it.

He had this strategy when it came to drinking. He'd buy a twelve-pack and only drink eleven of them – he would save one for the following morning.

Hair of the dog, and all.

From what I remember and what I've been told, it's amazing how disciplined he was with that system. He never drank that twelfth beer. *Never*. You'd think after eleven and you're feeling good, you'd throw caution to the wind and drink the last one. Nope. He *always* stopped at eleven to make sure he had that beer in the morning to shake off the cobwebs.

During the day, he handed me the empty cans and I built this pyramid out of them. Four on the bottom, then three, then two, then one. That was the first ten. On the eleventh beer, he had me stand back and throw it at the pyramid and see how many I could knock over.

I only knocked them all over once. It felt like I had won the World Series or something. Dad was cheering and hooting. It was right before bed, so I remember I could hardly sleep because my heart was racing from the excitement. We were laying there and I could hear him breathing heavy.

"Dad?"

"Yeah, what's up little buddy?"

"I had fun today."

136

"It was pretty fun, huh?"

"Yeah."

"We oughta do it again sometime, huh?"

"Can we stay longer? Can we stay a few more days?"

"It was pretty fun, huh?" he said.

"Yeah, can we stay?"

He didn't respond after that. He fell asleep.

**

I've been living in Denton pretty much since college. I went to University of North Texas for my undergrad and then went to law school in Dallas. Got lucky out of school and landed a gig with a firm. I married Erin after I graduated from UNT and we had Sam and Nora. We found a nice little place in Denton. Things are going pretty well.

Nikki is doing good, too – has a couple of kids. She married this guy who does insurance. They live outside San Antonio.

Cass has had a rough go of it. Going from guy to guy – from bed to bed. I know she got into pills and all that. I haven't actually heard much from her in quite some time since we all had Thanksgiving back in Well Springs a few years ago. She can be tough to get ahold of. I hope she's doing okay, but you can only help people so much. Cody and I offered to pay for rehab. She ended up cashing the check and had herself a good time.

Cody still lives in Well Springs. I guess it's good to have one of us back home, to help out Mom and everything. If she needs it. Personally, I try not to go back if I can help it.

Around 2012, I went back home because Mom said she was getting rid of a bunch of things and told us to come grab anything we wanted or else it's going in the garbage. Nikki and Cass never showed, so it was me, Mom, and Cody. There were a few things I wanted to keep. Little stuff. I found photos of me and Dad and I asked her if she was planning on keeping them.

"No, honey. If you want to keep them, go ahead and take them," she told me.

"You were going to throw away pictures of me and Dad?" I asked. "Why?"

"They take up space. You can keep them, Tommy."

I went into my old room, which was now a guest bedroom. Only thing in there was a perfectly made bed and a little side table with a clock. I can't imagine the room gets used much, you know? What guests is Mom having? I sat there and thumbed through the photos. There were some good ones. A few from the fishing trip. There was one where both of us were smiling really big. I don't know who took the photo, but it was a good one. I didn't understand why she would throw these photos away.

That night I went to the bar to see some of my old Well Springs buddies and learn what was up in their world. We were drinking like fish, having a good time, and then one of Dad's old buddies, Rhett, was sitting there at the bar. He whispered something to the man to his left.

"Say Tommy," Rhett sarcastically said, turning toward me. "They ever find the guy that killed your daddy?"

"What do you mean by that?" I said.

"Well, they ever find the guy?"

There was some snickering at the bar from the other guys and the bartender shot Rhett a dirty look. Rhett tilted his beer bottle and took a nice big drink.

"Well, did they?" he said.

"You tell me, Rhett."

"Last I heard, the person still hasn't been caught," he said.

"There you go, then."

"Sure hope they find the guy."

"Rhett, you got something to say?"

He was pissing me off and obviously all the booze wasn't helping. I went to the bar and got in his face. They had to pull me back. Rhett has always been a real lowlife. Left his wife and kids one day, but stayed in Well Springs. Usually, if you're going to run off, you *run off*. You don't stay in the same town and refuse to provide for your family. My buddies tried to steer me away from talking about Rhett the rest of the night, but I was mad. The way Rhett said it sounded like everybody knew something but me.

Did they find out who did it and not tell me?

We stayed there for another hour or so before I said I wanted to go home. Mom was asleep when I got back to the house, so I went to the liquor store real quick, grabbed some real cheap bourbon, and took it back to my room. I was sitting there, looking through the pictures while taking pulls off the bottle. It wasn't even that late, either. Probably eight or nine o'clock.

I was looking at photo after photo. After I looked at all of them, I started from the beginning and looked at them again. He was such a young guy. That's what really stood out to me. Smiling big. A young man and his young son.

It wasn't like me to do this, because I am usually pretty level-headed – probably what got me interested in law – but I set the photos on the bed, took another pull from the bottle, and didn't even bother to screw the cap back on. I took it with me and walked over to Sheriff Cremble's house.

I finished the bottle about a hundred yards away from his house and I tossed it into Marylynn Conway's yard. I still feel bad about that. She's a sweet woman and this yahoo is tossing empty bourbon bottles into her yard. I hope she forgives me if she ever finds out it was me.

But I get to the Crembles' door and I knocked three times and Maggie opened it.

"Tommy Jenkins, well how are you sweetie?" she said.

"Hello, Mrs. Cremble, is the Sheriff home?" I said. I think she could smell the booze on me.

"Tommy, is everything okay?"

"Yes ma'am. Yes ma'am. Is the Sheriff home, though? I'd like to speak with him."

"Well, come on in and I'll get him."

"No thank you, ma'am. I mean no disrespect, I think it's best if I talk with him out here. Again, I don't mean no disrespect. I don't thi – I just would, if I could talk with Sheriff Cremble, if I could talk with the sheriff out here that would be great."

"Okay, Tommy. That's okay. I'll go and get him."

I took a few steps away from the door when she left. I was looking down at my feet. I really wish I would have left right then – when she was getting him. She was gone for a little while, probably telling him that I was at the door and smelled like a saloon at 2 a.m. Eventually, he came to the door and he was wearing a white t-shirt and jeans.

"Thomas Jenkins, what brings you back to little Well Springs?"

"How are you Sheriff?"

"Can't complain, what can I do you for?"

"Sheriff, I was wondering, well, do you know, have you found who killed my dad?"

"Is everything all right Thomas? How much you have to drink tonight?"

"I'm fine. I would like, I was talking with Rhett tonight and he said something about my dad and I was wondering, what – have you found the man who did it? Who killed him?"

"Unfortunately not."

"Why not?"

"Well, it's a hard case, you know? Don't let Rhett get you all worked up now."

"I'm not worked up. I just want to know why you haven't found him yet."

"Life ain't always work like that, son. It was a senseless crime."

"Twenty years and you don't, how – have you gotten any leads yet? Have you got any leads about it?"

"Tommy, I think it's best you go on home and get some rest."

"Rest isn't gonna bring my dad back."

"I ain't say it would."

"I don't understand how after twenty years, you can't find any leads about who killed my dad. Is there something you aren't saying?"

"Tommy, a case like this, unfortunately, sometimes it goes cold. Your mama tells me you're studying law, you oughta know."

"You never got one clue? Not one damn clue or a hunch or nothing?"

"Well, there was one."

"What was it?"

"About a year after your daddy died, there was a man in Lubbock. Got busted for breaking and entering and killing the family there."

"Lubbock?"

"Yes sir. I called up there and told them about your daddy. Told them how it played out like that with your daddy and if I could see if it was the same man."

"Same man that killed my dad? The man that killed the family in Lubbock?"

"Yes sir."

"And?"

"Turn out it wasn't. I wanted it to be, Tommy."

"How you know it wasn't? The man in Lubbock. He probably did it. He probably did – he probably killed Dad."

"I wish it was, son. It ain't. The man was living over in Georgia when your daddy died."

"Georgia?"

"Yes sir. His story checked out, too. It ain't him."

"What about around here?"

"What do you mean?"

"I mean, in Well Springs. Have you, did you detective around here?"

"Tommy, I searched under every rock and talked with everybody I could."

"Did anybody say anything?"

"Tommy, it ain't good to get worked up over this."

"Worked up? Sheriff, my dad got killed over nothing!"

"I know, it's a tragedy, son."

"Well, what are you doing about it? You give up? Did you, what about the file?"

"Tommy, you need to calm down."

"What about the file, Sheriff?"

"What file?"

"The file about the case. The file of my dad and the things you found out about it."

"What about it?"

"I want to see it."

"You can't see that, Tommy."

"Why not? I want to see the file."

"I can't do that, son."

"How come? It's my dad that died. I should be able to see the file. I want to know who killed him. I'm sick of people not talking about it."

"I know, Tommy. Lord knows. Hell, you ain't think I wanna find out who done it? You ain't the only one who had sleepless nights over this. You ain't the only one who tried to make sense of this."

"I want to know who killed him, Sheriff. Nobody ever wants to talk about it. I want to know who killed him."

"I know you do, son. I do, too. I spent so many nights staring up at the ceiling. Trying to make heads or tails about it. Sometimes life ain't work out the way you'd like."

"Why'd he have to kill my dad?"

"I don't know, son. If I'm gonna be honest, I don't know if we'll ever know. The best possible thing you can do for him, to honor him, is to live your life. Make something of yourself."

"I wish I had the chance to know him better. To learn what he was like."

"Tommy, I know he would be so doggone proud of you. Your schooling and everything. He wouldn't want you sitting around, wasting breath trying to figure out what happened to him. Life moves on, son, with or without you."

He put his hand on my shoulder and we stood there. I remember looking down at the ground and then collapsing into his arms. I was crying into his chest like a baby. He was right. What good is sitting around and worrying about it after all these years? If he found the guy, what would really change? Dad would still be dead.

There's no point in knowing who did it, because it was a senseless crime.

I never really looked into it much after that. I have a really great life and I wish he could have met his grandchildren. I wish I could call him and talk about life. About whatever. I wish we could have these Thanksgiving dinners where we pass around the dishes and we're laughing and enjoying each other's company.

But we can't. He's dead.

He's gone and he's not coming back, so I had to learn to deal with that. Every minute I worry about him is a minute I'm taking away from Erin and the kids. I won't dwell on it.

Instead, I framed that picture of us smiling on the fishing trip. It's sitting on my desk at work. Every once and a while, I'll catch a glimpse of it.

Me and Dad.

Chapter Nine

Sheriff George Cremble

Those first few days after Cody killed Sam was something else. Chaotic, as you might imagine. Everything feeling like it's coming at you a hundred miles an hour and you gotta hold on for dear life. Once Debbie and me got our plan and story straight, I knew the first person I had to see: Fred Doyle. He was the one to call me the night Sam died, so I gotta do my due diligence. Go over and have a talk with him. Start detectin' and so forth.

Helen answered the door and she was a mess. Running around crazy like a March hare. Fred came in and told her to calm down – asked if I wanted any sweet tea or anything. I told him that I was fine but that we needed to talk in private. He nodded and told Helen to run to the store. She put up a fight, telling me she wanted to know what happened next door. I told her I wasn't at liberty to say quite yet but that I needed to talk to Fred since he was a witness. It took some doing, getting her out the house, but finally it was me and Fred.

"Sam?" Fred asked.

"Yes sir."

"Oh, my Lord. Did he kill them all? Or just Debra?"

"I'm sorry?"

"Did he only kill Debra? Sam didn't kill the kids, too, did he? Please, God. Sam, why d—"

"Whoa, Fred. No. Sam didn't kill nobody."

"You said it was Sam, though."

"Sam was the one who was killed."

"*Sam* got killed?"

"Yes sir."

Fred had two fingers over his mouth, the tips under his nose, and he was tapping his index finger on his lips like it'd help him concentrate.

"Who did it?" he asked.

"Well Fred, that's why I'm here. You was the one who called me. I wanted to know what you saw and heard last night."

"Sheriff, I don't know what...where do I, I don't know what to say."

"Just walk me through everything leading up to calling me."

"I woke up and needed to get some water because I was feeling warm."

"What time was this?"

"I don't know. I went to bed around nine or so. Probably after midnight, but I don't know Sheriff. Forgive me, I didn't look at a clock because I didn't know."

"That's okay, Fred. That's okay. So you got up 'cause you was thirsty?"

"I was drinking the water and then I heard the gunshots next door. There were a lot of them. One after another. I could hear Debra screaming. It was terrible Sheriff."

"I'm sorry you had to go through that Fred. Did you see anything? Notice anything?"

"Well, I could see flashes going off inside the bedroom. They had the blinds down, but you could see it. Through the cracks around the sides, you know?"

"You see anybody?"

"No sir. Do you have any leads? Do you know who it is?"

"Unfortunately, I can't tell you nothing on my end, Fred."

"I understand."

"So you ain't see nobody. You see any truck or car in the driveway? Anything outta the ordinary?"

"No sir."

"Hmmm. So the shots is going off, now what?"

"Well, I was going to run up and tell Helen, but instead I called you right away. I swear, Sheriff. I called you right then and there."

"I believe you, Fred. I believe you. Now the time between you calling me and when I show up, anything I should know about?"

"I think there were some more gunshots going off and Debra was screaming. I thought about going over there."

"It's a good thing that you didn't, Fred."

"I'm not a coward."

"I ain't say you is. I'd say you got more smarts than to stick your neck into a buzz saw."

"I suppose."

"Now, how long was you looking out the window there?"

"For a little while."

"How long is that?"

"I don't know, Sheriff. I was scared when you arrived and went into their house."

"The bad guy had already taken off by the time I got there, unfortunately."

"They did?"

"Yes sir. That's why I'm surprised you ain't see nothing. He musta drove off like he was running for the border. You don't remember hearing anybody speeding off?"

"No sir."

"Fred, this is really important, so I need you to concentrate and try to remember: did you hear somebody speeding off?"

"I don't know. Everything seems kinda blurry."

"Maybe try this: close your eyes for a second."

"Yes sir."

"Now: did you hear somebody drive off?"

"I don't know. Maybe."

"You can hear it now?"

"Maybe. Now that you mention it."

"So in my report, I can write that you heard somebody drive off?"

"I suppose."

**

"You gonna be all right?" I asked.

Debra was sitting next to me in the church pew. Wearing all black. The kids was all sitting next to her. It was the seven of us – me and Maggie next to Debbie and the kids. The casket was sitting up there in the front of the sanctuary. Closed casket, of course. They picked out a nice photo of Sam smiling. Young man. I remember thinking that, seeing his photo at the funeral. He was such a young man. Had his whole life ahead of him. Maybe coulda turned it around. Although, maybe he woulda gotten worse.

Debra nodded back to me.

I remember it being a real nice day. Sunny and warm. It was a few days after he was killed. They really sped everything up. I guess Debra wanted him in the ground as fast as possible and have everybody sorta move on with their lives. The whole town was a bit in shock because they ain't believe somebody came into town and murdered one of us. Well Springs. It ain't happen like that here.

A lot of people came and gave Debra their condolences. Asking if there was anything they could do. Pastor Wilheim delivered a beautiful speech. He was talking about how we oughta live like our number could come up at any moment. Live like Jesus and all. It was a real nice speech. He had this great line about how Sam punched him at that potluck. I remember that got a lot of laughs. When he started talking about Sam, Debra reached out and held my hand. Lord, she was squeezing it like a boa constrictor.

There was a few speakers sharing stories about Sam. There was the drunken stories from Rhett. I thought they was a bit in poor taste, you know, with the kids sitting there. They was funny, no arguing there, but I thought they was stories you'd share in private over a beer. I told them I'd say a few words. Usually I'm an off-the-cuff shooter, but this one I wrote what I wanted to say and practiced it in the bathroom the day before the funeral. Went over it whenever I was alone in the car.

I brought my speech up with me at the funeral, thinking I'd need it. I never even took it out my pocket.

"I believe I ain't alone in saying my heart is heavy for Debra and the children – Cody, Cassandra, Nicole, and Thomas," I said. "I can not imagine the pain. Let me echo many who have said if there is anything that I can do to help, I hope that you ain't hesitate to ask. This here is Well Springs. When one of us hurts, all of us hurt. For those in this room, let me say: I understand the kinda fear that something like this can bring to a town. The worry. The questions. I hope we all come together instead of tear apart. Know that I will not rest until the man who done this is brought to justice. We will persevere.

"I remember a few months back, I came and talked with Sam. It's clear that Sam had his issues and I talked to him about changing his

149

ways. He told me how much he loved his children and Debra. Said they was his whole world. Anybody who knows Sam knows how loving and charming he could be. I hope that's how we remember him. I know that's how I'll remember him: as the man you'd spend a day with on the golf course and know by the end you got a friend for life.

"Now, I ain't much of a public speaker. Pastor Wilhiem, I believe you said it best: we can use this tragedy for good. I hope we can use it for good. To Debra and the children, I offer my deepest condolences and support. I sincerely hope we can all help you get through this difficult time. Thank you."

I ain't exactly get a standing ovation, but I thought it went all right — all things considering. I remember during the entire day, from the service to the actual burial, Debra ain't cry at all. She was a stone wall. This blank expression on her face. It was like she weren't even listening during the whole thing. I think that's why the kids ain't cry, neither. They seen her keeping everything together.

At the burial, it was only a few of us — Debra and the kids, Rhett, and a few others. Sam's parents ain't even come. That should tell you all you need to know about them. How you ain't go to your own son's funeral? Terrible. Pastor Wilheim asked if we had any other sentiments we'd like to say. Debra shook her head and everybody else followed suit. They lowered him into the ground and Debra and the kids left. As the rest of us scattered, I looked back and saw the men starting to put the dirt back into the grave.

Dust to dust, they say.

**

It's something else that Fred was the only one near the Jenkins house that heard anything. You'd think that many gunshots and Debra screaming would wake up the whole neighborhood. Nope. They all slept through it like a baby. Amazing.

Most of my conversations with the folks around Well Springs in the aftermath was pretty pleasant. Lot of them was pretty nervous. People trying to figure out who would do such a thing in a town like Well Springs. I'd tell them that I was working on it and if they remembered anything or had any information to lemme know. Talking with Rhett, though, ain't my idea of a good time. But when mystery surrounds somebody getting killed, a lawman's gotta talk with the victim's best friend, right? Find who had a motive to blow Sam away. The day after the funeral, I went over to Rhett's place. I did him the courtesy of coming in the afternoon, knowing he'd be in no shape to talk in the morning.

"Sheriff," he said after opening the door. "Isn't this a nice surprise?"

Rhett was a real piece of work. He had a wife and kids and one day decided to move out. Ain't move outta town, though. He ain't even leave the street. He moved a few houses down from where his family lived. What kind of man is that? I'll never understand some people. He answered the door in sweats and a dirty t-shirt and he had this beard — I ain't sure if it was a look he was going for or he was too lazy to shave. Bigger guy. Was quite the player back in high school. Then he became just some run-down, sarcastic horse's ass.

"How'ya doing Rhett?" I said.

"Never been better, how can I help you?"

"Well, I'd like to talk to you for a bit. Is now a good time?"

"Sure. Come on in."

We sat in his living room. He ain't even bother to move the marijuana pipe he had on his coffee table. He had this old couch with burn marks all over. Probably passed out with a cigarette in his mouth. It's a wonder he ain't burn his place down, to be honest. He lit a cigarette as we sat down – he jokingly offered me one – and he was smoking it with a chew in.

"Rhett, I'm here to talk about Sam Jenkins."

151

"Yeah, no kidding. I assumed you didn't come here to talk about gardening."

"How you holding up? I know you two was close."

"I'm fine."

"You sure?"

"Is that what you came over to talk about, Sheriff? My feelings? Cause I got stuff I gotta do today."

"Well, I'll be quick then: the night Sam was killed..."

"Yeah?"

"You know I gotta ask."

"Sheriff."

"I gotta ask, Rhett."

"I did not kill Sam. Jesus."

"What were you up to that night?"

"We are really doing this?"

"Yes sir. Where were you that night?"

"Here."

"And what were you doing?"

"Drinking and screwing."

"Who you got over that night?"

"Jeannie Rae. Go ahead and ask her if you don't believe me."

"Rhett, I ain't want this to be contentious. I believe you. I gotta ask, you know?"

"Yeah, okay."

"You got any ideas of people who'd want to kill Sam?"

"Come on. You know how people in this town are: judging him and everything. I'm sure there's plenty of people that woulda loved to be the one to ice him."

"Such as?"

"Maybe it was Pastor Wilheim, after Sam clocked his ass. How about that for a theory?"

"I ain't think the Pastor murdered Sam."

"You're not making him a prime suspect?"

"Let's be serious here, Rhett."

"What about Debra?"

"What about her?"

"Maybe she killed him."

"I don't think so."

"Why not? I know he would rough her up every once in a while. Maybe she got pissed one night and took him out. You talk to her?"

"I did."

"And?"

"It wasn't her."

"How you know that?"

"She said there was a man in the room shooting Sam."

"And you believe her?"

"I do."

"You know, I saw you and her holding hands at the funeral. You guys got an arrangement or something?"

"Rhett."

"Hey, I'm not judging you Sheriff. For having four kids, she's still got it. She's a piece of tail, for sure."

"Rhett, come on now."

"What? I could see it. She comes to you and says she wants to kill Sam and if you let her, she'll give yo–"

"Rhett, shut your mouth right now. I'm being serious here. I'm trying to figure out who killed Sam, okay? I'm trying to find who killed your friend, so how about a little respect?"

"Who you think it was?" Rhett asked, sitting back. He seemed genuinely interested.

"That's what I'm trying to figure out."

"Well, who you think? You got any theories?"

"I do."

"And?"

"I ain't at liberty to say, Rhett."

"Oh, come on. Who am I gonna tell? If you want me to help you, you gotta trust me a little bit, Sheriff. Isn't that how it works? What do you think? Who in town you think it was?"

"I ain't think it was somebody from Well Springs."

"Really? Sam didn't really go anywhere. I don't think he's got many enemies outside of this town."

"I don't think the man even knew Sam."

"Is that right?"

"I believe it was a stranger that come in to rob them and Sam found himself in the hornets' nest. Got killed because of it."

"An interesting theory."

"I believe that's what happened."

"Would you like to know what I think happened?" Rhett asked, leaning forward.

"Hit me."

"I think one of two things happened: First, Debra killed Sam and lied to you about some strange man coming into the room. I think she killed him and lied to you and you took the bait."

"And the second?"

"The second way it could have played out is Debra killed Sam and told you about it and you're covering for her."

**

154

It took some doing, but I finally got that conversation with Rhett outta my head. It ain't like he'd put any effort into digging. And no matter what I say – a man coulda come right out and confessed – Rhett would still look at me cross. Can't satisfy everyone all the time, I suppose. Besides, I had bigger fish to fry. Like the First Church Women's League. They was as relentless as badgers. Everyday calling and asking. They thought they got a clue and wanted me to know something or other about a blue car that they seen drive through town. I asked if they got a make and model or a license plate and they said no. They said I should be on the lookout for a blue car.

The First Church Women's League sounds like a big deal. Really, it was only four old ladies: Dottie Michaelson, Betty Tunsil, Ethel King, and Pat Thorne. Now individually, they was as sweet as sugar. But you get them together and they became the biggest storm you ever seen. They all took turns talking at you and you'd be lucky to get a word in. It was like they was a verbal machine gun or something. One after the other.

About a week after Sam was killed, they all come marching into the station. I was in the back but I heard the door open and then Dottie say that they demanded to see me. I think I sighed because Hank, he was at the front desk at the time, came and got me. I told him to go ahead and bring them on back to my office. They wasn't through the doorframe before they started up.

"Sheriff Cremble, we *demand* to talk with you," Dottie said.

"Sheriff, we want answers," Ethel said.

"Sheriff, we want answers," Betty said.

"Ladies, it's good to see you. Y'all look as pretty as a picture," I said.

"Thank you," they all said, before Dottie took over again. "Sheriff, the First Church Women's League demands to talk with you."

"We want answers," Ethel said.

"Yes, we want answers," Pat said.

155

"Ladies, you know y'all ain't gotta *demand* nothing. I'm happy to talk with y'all. Now, what can I do for you?"

"We want answers, Sheriff!" Pat said.

"And what's the question?" I asked.

"Don't you dare mock us, Sheriff!" Ethel said.

"Don't mock us!" Pat said.

"That's right, don't you dare mock us, Sheriff!" Dottie said.

"Now now, I ain't mocking," I said. "I just wanna know. Dottie, what are you wanting to know?"

"Have there been any arrests?" Pat said quickly.

"Yes, have you made any arrests yet?" Dottie said.

"At this time—" I started.

"Have you made any arrests?" Betty said.

"At this time, Betty, I have not."

"Why not?" Dottie said.

"How have you not made any arrests, Sheriff?" Pat said.

"Because I ain't found the man who done it yet."

"Sheriff, there is a madman killing people right here in Well Springs!" Dottie said.

"Terrible," Ethel said.

"Lord help us," Pat said.

"Ladies, I appreciate the concern y'all have, but I believe this was what you'd call an *isolated incident*."

"Sheriff, people in this town are being killed!" Ethel said.

"Come on now, it ain't like an epidemic or something," I said. "It was only Sam Jenkins who died."

"Sheriff, we do *not* feel safe," Ethel said, all dramatic-like.

"We don't feel safe," Dottie said.

"Right here in Well Springs!" Betty said.

"The killer is still out there!" Ethel said.

"Ladies, you ain't wanna raise that blood pressure," I said.

"Sheriff Cremble, this is serious," Betty said.

"The killer is still out there!" Ethel said again.

"We demand that you make an arrest," Pat said.

"That's right. We demand you make an arrest," Dottie said.

"How you gonna *demand* something like that?" I asked.

"You need to find the man who done this!" Pat said.

"The killer is still out there!" Ethel said.

"Ethel, I heard you the first time," I said. "Y'all gotta trust that I'm working on it."

"And what are your leads?" Pat said.

"Have you asked around?" Betty said.

"I have been asking and searching and asking again, ladies."

"And who are your prime suspects?" Pat said.

"My *prime suspects*?" I said.

"Yes sir. Sheriff, who are your prime suspects?" Pat said.

"Who coulda done something like this?" Dottie said.

"Ladies, you might be watching too much TV, coming in here talking about *prime suspects*."

"We want to know who the killer is," Ethel said.

"Not more than I do, believe me," I said. "By the way, Betty how's the grandson, Howie? He studying up in Lubbock?"

"Oh, he's doing wonderful, Sheriff," Betty said. "He's studying biology. He got himself a scholarship."

"Such a smart boy," Dottie said.

"Handsome, too," Pat said.

"Very handsome," Ethel said.

"He got himself a girl now," Betty said.

"Is that right?" Pat said.

"Pretty thing," Betty said.

"Good for him," I said.

"Sheriff, we ain't here to talk about Howie," Betty said.

"Why not?" I asked.

"Sheriff, you need to take this serious!" Betty said.

"The killer is still out there!" Pat said.

"So I heard," I said. "I can promise you ladies, that I won't rest until I find the man who done this."

"You best not," Betty said.

"What makes you think it was a man?" Ethel said.

"What's that supposed to mean?" I asked.

"Yeah, what's that supposed to mean?" Pat said.

"I'm just saying," Ethel said.

"You're just saying what?" Pat asked.

"Well, maybe – I don't want to do no gossiping," Ethel said.

"I think it's too late for that," Betty said.

"What do you mean, Ethel?" Dottie said.

"Well, maybe it wasn't a man. Maybe it was..." Ethel said.

"You don't think?" Betty said.

"Well, I don't know. It could have been her," Ethel said.

"No!" Pat said.

"Ethel!" Betty said.

"What? It's possible, ain't it?" Ethel said. "Sam wasn't good to her, no how. Maybe she got fed up."

"Ethel King, you are something else!" Betty said.

"Oh, none of you thought about it?" Ethel said.

"Well, of course," Pat said.

"It's possible," Dottie said.

"Sure, we *thought* about it," Betty said.

"Ladies, a woman had to watch her husband be murdered right in front of her eyes and you come in spouting off conspiracy theories about her killing him," I said.

"Ethel said it," Pat said.

"It was Ethel," Betty said.

"I'd politely ask you fine ladies to please leave my office so I can get back to finding out who actually killed Sam Jenkins," I said.

"Ethel!" the three of them all said at once.

"I didn't do anything," Ethel said. "I just said I thought it was possible!"

**

This part woulda been the night that I talked with Fred. Through all of the chaos and what-have-you, I never thought about what I would say to Maggie. It never crossed my mind. The night I talked with Fred, Maggie made a nice dinner – she cooked a roast and mashed potatoes. I believe it was the first time I actually ate something since Cody killed Sam. I ate like a man going to the electric chair. Musta had three servings of it.

I had been pretty quiet through the whole deal. Thinking. She understood and let me be. Didn't pry or nothing. She'd come and rub my back and neither of us would say a word. I was sitting in the living room and Maggie was on the phone in the kitchen, trying to whisper, talking about how much pressure I was under. How she can't believe what happened – right here in quiet little Well Springs.

That night, when we were in bed, she was reading this book and I laid there, hands behind my head, looking at the ceiling.

"Georgie," she said. "I need to ask because I am your wife and I love you: Are you okay?"

"Yeah, honey, I'm gonna be all right."

"I'm sorry this happened."

"It's okay. Part of the job. I'm just glad I'm alive. I'm still lying here next to you."

"Did you see him?"

"Sam?"

She nodded.

"Yeah, I saw him."

"How bad was it?"

"Bad. They shot him a lot."

"Lord Jesus. I can't believe it."

"I suppose dead is dead, though, ain't it? There's no such thing as *really* dead."

"You don't have to answer, but do you have any idea what happened?"

That was an odd feeling. That's why I wish I had thought about it before she asked the question: what would I tell Maggie? Do I tell her the truth? That Cody killed him. That I'm fixing to cover it up. Then I'm pulling her into it. I'm making her live with knowing the truth and asking her to keep it from people. That's a great burden to place on somebody. Then again, she is my partner in life. How can I be somebody that lies to her? What happens if she finds out somehow? If I tell her the song and dance about "what happened" and then she learns the truth some other way. Could our marriage survive that lie? I don't know. I didn't have much time to think about it.

I nodded.

"Oh my word. She killed him, didn't she?" Maggie said.

"Nope."

"She didn't?"

I shook my head.

"But ... was it – what happened then?"

"Apparently some man broke into the house. I'm assuming to rob them. Sam got caught up in it. Guy shot him dead right in his bed."

"Oh my word."

"Yes ma'am."

"Did she see him? The killer?"

"Not really, no. Just enough to know she didn't recognize him. The shooting is what woke her up."

"I can't even imagine."

"It's a hell of a thing."

"How come he only killed Sam?"

"What do you mean?"

"It seems odd. If he didn't mind killing Sam, why wouldn't he shoot Debra too?"

"I don't know. Maybe he didn't have time or he decided to run off."

"Yeah, but you said they shot Sam a lot. Why shoot him so much but not shoot Debra?"

"Well, I'm glad he didn't."

"Lord, I feel so bad for her and the children. How are they doing?"

"'Bout as well as they can be, considering."

"I wonder: why would he shoot Sam in bed?"

"How do you mean?"

"If you're robbing a house, it doesn't make any sense to go into the bedroom. You'd think they would rob the living room and leave."

"You trying to be a detective here?"

"No, sweetheart. Just funny, I suppose. Why go into the bedroom and risk getting caught?"

"I don't know, baby. Maybe the man was high on who-knows-what. Maybe he ain't know it was a bedroom. Or maybe Sam got up in the middle of the night and seen the man in the living room – then the man told him to go back into bed."

"Hmmm."

"I believe it was somebody from outta town. I don't know why he chose the Jenkins house, but I think he went to rob it and things went south."

"You don't think it was somebody here?"

"I don't believe so. Or else Debra would recognize him, you know?"

"That's true. I didn't think of that."

"It's a tricky one."

"How do you go about finding somebody like that? Nobody saw anything?"

"Fred said he heard a car speeding off. Didn't see it, though."

"How's he and Helen doing?"

"They're a bit shook, but it's good Fred was up to hear it. You know nobody else in that neighborhood heard it?"

"How's that?"

"Good question. If only one of the other houses saw something – saw the man running out to the vehicle or the vehicle driving off ... maybe it would give us a lead."

"Should I be worried, George? Please be honest."

"Maggie, no. I don't want you to feel unsafe around here."

"Well, why would a man kill Sam Jenkins? What is the world coming to?"

"Whoever done it is probably long gone and won't be coming back to Well Springs ever again."

"I can't believe ... in Well Springs."

"I may have my work cut out for me on this one, Maggie."

"I know, sweetheart. I am so sorry. I want you to know that I understand if you need to work longer or do whatever you need to do to find him."

"I appreciate that honey."

I gave her a kiss and I rolled over on my side, with my back to her. I turned off my lamp and stared at the wall. I can't believe I lied right to her face. I ain't feel good about it. The whole thing never sat well with me. Always ate at me over the years. But I'm glad I didn't rope her into the mess. I'm glad I ain't make her live with the burden. She would hear gossip and what-have-you, and there was times she'd ask me about it and I would tell her about the man who don't exist. How the trail ran cold and I never could crack it.

I heard her put her book down on the nightstand, turn off the light, and turn on her side.

"Why would he go into the bedroom?" she said to herself.

Chapter Ten

Rhett Vernon

A lot of people are surprised Sam and I used to hate each other. Everybody thinks we were always as thick as thieves, but when I moved to Well Springs before my freshman year, I didn't know anybody here. We were doing hell week football practices in the summer, so I met a bunch of the guys before school even started. Sam was the same year as me, so we were off with the other little punk freshmen. During the first tackling drill, he took me down and pushed off me to get himself up. I didn't like that. It's disrespectful. I wanted to mess him up. I'd cut in line so that I matched up tackling against him. Whenever I did something a little dirty – something to remember me by – the next time he'd do something dirty. It went back and forth, back and forth until we finally went at it.

I don't remember who instigated it. Who knows. He ripped off my helmet during the scuffle and reared it back and swung it at me. Didn't land. The team had to pull us apart and coach talked with us. We were couple of teenage guys in a pecker-swinging contest, that's all. It happens.

We hated each other for a good month or so. It was the second game of the year and we were kicking the hell outta Bentonville. Junior varsity, but still – we were freshmen and we had a good team. It was early third quarter and we were on defense. They ran a sweep to the left and I took the back down in a spinning, rolling way. The momentum sprung me back to my feet and one of their linemen came through and gave a real cheap shot. It took me off the ground and I landed hard on my back. Almost broke my neck. I didn't even have time to react because Sam comes over and lays out that fat piece of garbage. Might have broken his nose, too. All hell broke loose and Sam got tossed. As he walked off the field, he came and made sure I was good.

We never fought again after that.

We were good friends since that day. Learned we had more in common and there wasn't a reason to be all pissy with each other. If we weren't playing sports together, we'd be going into town, heading out to no man's land to drink some beer or he'd come over to my place. It was funny because he would *never* have people over to his house. With the way his parents were, I can't blame him. His old man was a mean bastard and his mama was always blitzed out on God-knows-what.

Henry and Loretta Jenkins.

I remember I went over there sophomore year. I had to swing by to drop off a scouting report of the team we were playing that week. I knocked on the door and Sam's old man answered.

"Yeah?" he said.

"I'm here to drop this off for Sam," I said.

"Okay, come on in."

I walked in and the place was a hellhole. Run down and dirty. Dishes piled up in the sink. Clothes all over the floor. His mom was sitting on the couch completely passed out. Head back and mouth open, an unlit cigarette dangling in her mouth. She was wearing this robe but the belt went loose so her tits were hanging out.

"You like getting a look?" Henry said.

"Oh, I didn't mean to, sir," I said and I looked away and walked toward the kitchen.

"You want her, be my guest. That whore will make your Johnson rot. Sam! Get your ass out here, you got company!"

Sam came out and you could tell he was thrown off. Didn't want to have anybody, especially me, see behind the curtain. I gave him the scouting report and Sam was pushing me toward the front door and saying we can go do something.

"Whoa, Sam, that's no way to treat company," Henry said, as he sat down in the kitchen and motioned toward the other chairs at the table. "Come on in Rhett, stay a while."

"It's fine, Dad, we're gonna head out," Sam said.

"Shut up, Sam. Rhett come on over. I wanna talk about the team."

We walked over and sat down. Even for somebody like me, it was uncomfortable. You could feel the tension in the room.

"How you think y'all gonna be this year? Off to a good start," Henry said.

We had won the first three games of the year and Sam was the starting varsity middle linebacker and one of the co-captains of the team as a sophomore. He was a helluva ball player. He took everybody down. We ended up winning eight games that year and Sam was named first team all-conference. I was a fullback. Got enough time to letter but wasn't a starter. The way Henry talked about Sam, though, it was rough.

"You see last game, when that black boy put the move on Sam and made him miss?" Henry said. "Sam tackling air and looking like a damn idiot."

"We won the game, Dad."

166

"You know how much shit I got for you missing that tackle?"

"I thought Sam was causing hell out there, sir," I said. "What'd you end up with? Seventeen tackles?"

"Shoulda been eighteen," Henry said.

"Yeah, Dad, well if I had eighteen you'd say it shoulda been nineteen."

"So much potential but you'll never be great 'cause you don't care."

"Yes, I do."

"No, you ain't. You don't put in the work to be great. Rhett, does Sam ever tell you about the player I was?"

"No sir," I said.

"Of course not. Why would he? It's not like I was all-conference *three years* in a row. All-state senior year. Averaged more than twenty-five tackles a game and this little fairy can't even get eighteen."

"And look at you now," Sam said.

Henry lunged out of his chair and grabbed Sam around the throat and lifted him up. He slammed him up against the refrigerator and it knocked all the magnets and pictures to the floor. It was wild, man. Henry was yelling at him to show some respect and I was yelling to let him go. Finally, Henry slammed Sam's head against the fridge and then let go. Sam stumbled forward and was struggling to breathe.

"Let's get outta here," Sam said to me and grabbed my arm.

"Yeah, you do that. Run away like a girl," Henry said.

I think that was the only time I ever went over to the Jenkins house. Never wanted to see that again. Sam led the way out of the house and when I turned back to shut the door behind me, I saw Loretta still sitting on the couch. Her head back, eyes closed, and mouth open. Passed out with her robe wide open. Henry was sitting back down at the kitchen table and was filling up a shot glass with rum.

**

167

I was at the party when Sam knocked up Debbie. Wild night. Sam used to joke that was the night his life started going down the toilet. How the trajectory of his life changed right then and there in that bedroom. What's funny is earlier in the night I was actually going after Debbie. She looked good and let me tell you: she was hot to trot. Really flirty. I thought I had a shot.

I forget if she had graduated by then but Sam and I had a few buddies still on the football team that were fun guys, so we were going to swing by – for a little bit, you know. But the booze was flowing and what 20-year-old you know passes on free booze? I remember a group of us were talking in the kitchen and Debbie was laying it on thick. I don't really recall what she said, but she was making herself *evident*. I went off to smoke a cigarette and by the time I came back, Sam and her were gone. I walked around trying to find them and came to a closed bedroom door and I could hear them in there. Lucky bastard, I thought. Sam was always real good at closing the deal.

I ended up going home. I thought nothing of it really. I called the next day because we were supposed to go shooting and he said he wasn't up for it – pretty hungover. Well, all right. I asked him how she was and he said she was a pretty good lay. Looked better under there than he was expecting. I called him a lucky SOB and we both laughed and that was that. Never really had a second thought about it.

We both went about our lives and then maybe a month later, he swings by my place and I never saw him like that. Shoulders sagging and head down – really dragging.

"What's going on?" I said, as he came in and sat down on my couch.

"My life is over, man," Sam said.

"Why?"

"You know Debra Adams?"

"Yeah."

"Remember when we hooked up at that party a while back?"

"Kinda, why?"

"Well, she's pregnant."

"Get the hell outta here."

"She just told me."

"Damn, man."

"Yeah."

"What are you gonna do?"

"I don't know."

"You know it's yours?"

"Yeah."

"Damn."

"What do you think I should do?" he asked.

"I don't know. You gonna ask her to flush it?"

"No, come on, man."

"What?"

"I ain't doing that."

"I was just saying."

"I guess I gotta marry her," Sam said.

"You do?"

"Yeah, it's the right thing to do."

"You think it's what's best?"

"Isn't it?"

"I don't know. Maybe you can skip town?"

"Stop."

"What? It's true. She can probably handle it herself. You get outta dodge and make a new life for yourself. Better for the kid if you don't even want it."

"Who said I don't want it?"

"Well, do you?"

169

"Man, I don't know. I don't feel good about skipping town though. I gotta step up."

"You sure?" I asked. "What do your folks say?"

"I don't care what they think. They'd only tell me how I wasted my life. I probably won't even tell them."

"You really gonna marry this girl?"

"I guess."

"Well, good for you, brother."

He sat there shaking his head and staring down at the floor. It's funny looking back. If he would have taken my advice, everybody would have been a lot better off. Sam and Debbie never really got along and he roughed her up a few times, so I'm sure she would have been a lot happier if he skipped town. Maybe she would have found some nice sucker to take on that baggage. She still looks good so I wouldn't have been surprised. She coulda gotten herself a new man. Cody maybe would have had a more normal childhood. Hell, they could tell Cody that the new guy was his actual dad.

And Sam? He wouldn't have been at that house that night so I guess he'd still be alive, wouldn't he?

**

I know some people probably thought Sam was a real awful father. Well Springs is not lacking in judgment, believe me. He could have a temper and liked to have a good time. I mean, the guy busts his ass working a job he hates to provide for a family he never wanted in the first place, you'd think people would understand he would need a little good time to stay sane. Booze never whines and complains at you.

I don't know if he ever loved Debbie. Probably not. How do you love somebody who you never would be with if you had worn a rubber that *one time*? If he doesn't knock her up, they both go on their merry way.

I think he had moments where he enjoyed her company, but I don't think he ever loved her.

But the kids? Damn, he *loved* those kids.

He would always be talking about them. How Cassie was a good speller — gonna win one of those spelling bees one day, he'd say. He wouldn't shut up about how she could spell this long word during a trip they took to some children's museum. *Extraordinary* or something. *Extracurricular*. Oh, no. You know what it was? It was *extraterrestrial*. Like an alien. He kept going on and on about it. I would give him crap about nobody cares about her spelling, but he was so damn proud of that. Nikki loved turtles and Sam would always look for little turtle knickknacks to give to her. I never understood it. Whenever he would find like a sticker or keychain or something, he'd get all fired up and buy it and talk about how much Nikki is gonna love it.

Cody always tended to be a big mama's boy. I think that bothered Sam a bit. Being the first-born boy and Cody always wanted to be with his *mommy*. Never showed much interest in things with Sam, at least I felt. But I'll give Sam credit, he loved that boy too. Cody was a smart kid. Sam used to brag about how Cody would end up at UT or Baylor on a scholarship. I know Cody's doing pretty well with his business here in town.

Tommy, though, was his pride and joy. He loved that boy. Sam and I were hunting, this was sorta near the end, and he was getting ready to go on a camping trip with Tommy. Sam had this set up where he would do things with just one of the kids. Each kid got a turn. Make it feel more special. I admired that. Maybe I shoulda done that with my kids. But when Sam and me were hunting, we were sitting there drinking and waiting because we hadn't seen much. Sam had this quirk — I don't know what you'd call it — but whenever we went on these trips, he would buy a twelve-pack and only drink eleven. I mean, he would *never* drink that

171

twelfth. It was the damndest thing. After he was done with his eleven, if he wanted another one he would try and bum one off me. I would tell him to drink his own, but he said that was for the morning. He was disciplined about that. But we were sitting there and Sam wouldn't stop talking about his upcoming camping trip.

"We're going out to Outpost Lake," he said.

"Oh yeah?"

"Yeah. I'm pretty excited. I like taking the little guy out. Teaching him stuff. It's funny when they're that young. They got so much to learn."

"What're you gonna teach him?" I asked.

"I don't know. Life stuff, I guess," he said.

"Yeah, I remember doing that with my dad."

"I never did any of that with my old man," he said. "Mean old son of a bitch. Glad he didn't take me on that kinda stuff."

"I was gonna say: Henry didn't take you out in the wild did he?"

"Hell no," Sam said with a laugh. "It's probably why I like doing it with Tommy. Teach him what Henry never taught me."

"Good for you, Sam."

"Yeah, I'm happy about it. It's nice to get out of that house and enjoy some peace and quiet. Don't get better than that."

"You're making me wish I could come along."

"I'm hoping it becomes something we do together every year," he said. "Me and him. Make it a tradition."

**

The last time I saw Sam alive we were talking about starting a business. It was the Saturday before Easter, so the day before he got killed. We had finished up a job pouring a new walkway at the elementary school the day before. Real mess of a project – a whatever-could-go-wrong sorta deal. I remember he messed up his wrist pretty bad, so he was fuming about that.

We were at the Wolfpack Bar and Sam had this brace on his wrist and we were giving him hell for it. Calling him an old man and everything. At the Wolfpack we were considered, let's call it *loyal* customers, so we paid a little less for the beers and I remember Sam was throwing them back. He was moody at the start of the night, but boy did he start feeling better by the end.

One of the bartenders at the time, Mary Lou, she was always all over Sam. Flirting and always available for a quickie in the back. She made some comment about his wrist and how if he wanted, she could help him feel better. He told her not tonight, but he appreciated the offer. Mary Lou seemed a bit annoyed at that – she was revved up and ready to go.

I had my suspicions. Maybe she got so damn offended after he turned her down that she went over to his house and killed him. A woman like that, I wouldn't put it past her. Plus not long after Sam died, she got outta town. Little suspicious, right? Maybe she thought she was gonna steal Sam away from his family – that he'd leave Debra and the kids and start a new life with her disease-ridden ass. When he turned her down, she decided if she can't have him, nobody can.

At the time, though, I was glad Sam turned down her offer of a quick kick because we were having a good time joking around. He always busted my chops about how I moved down the street from my ex and the kids and I'd tell him how I can do anything I want and go anywhere I want. I got that freedom. He'd always be a little prissy about that, but he knew I was teasing. He loved those kids and I didn't care much for mine, so we both were in a pretty decent set-up.

We ordered a plate of fries and the one downside about the Wolfpack is their food sucks. Just lousy. That's what got us thinking that night.

"You know what, we oughta start our own bar," Sam said.

"Is that right?" I asked, eating the fries.

"I'm serious. Why not?"

"Sam, what do you know about running a bar?"

"How hard could it be? Buy a ton of booze, mark up the price and hang around BSing with people."

"We already drink on the cheap here, what's the point?" I said, taking a final drink of my beer and motioning over to the bar for another.

"Think about it: you like busting your ass pouring concrete and making decks and all that?"

"Not particularly."

"Well, let's open up a bar. Make our money that way. Instead of breaking our back, we're serving up drinks."

"You're serious, aren't you?"

"Hell yeah, I'm serious. It could be a sports bar – with good food. Place to watch the Longhorns and Cowboys and eat food that's worth a damn."

"You know how to cook?"

"No, but we could find a guy. How hard could it be?"

"How much money you need to start a place like that?"

"I don't know. We could figure that out. But we start with one and it sorta becomes the place to be in Well Springs, right? Then maybe we start getting more locations – El Paso, Lubbock, Amarillo. Hell, even Dallas. You know how much money we'd be rolling in?"

"Be nice to get outta this town, huh?"

"I'm telling you: we gotta take a real look at this," Sam said. "Who doesn't like going to a place where the wings are big and the beer is cold? Get smoking hot bartenders. This is a winner."

"You been thinking a lot about this?"

"No, the inspiration just came to me."

"The eight beers?"

"You can joke all you want, but you know this is a million-dollar idea."

"You got a name for it? *Sam and Rhett's Sports Bar*?"

"No, no. Maybe – I don't know."

"You gotta have a good name. That's how things catch on."

"How about *Tommy's Sports Bar*?"

"Hmm."

"*Tommy's Sports Bar*," he said, all smiling. "You gotta admit, that's got a nice ring to it."

"Why does it get to be one of your kids?"

"Because you hate your kids," Sam said with a laugh.

"Good point. *Tommy's Sports Bar*. I gotta tell you, Sam, it ain't bad."

"Hell yeah, it's not bad."

Sam took a long satisfied-with-himself drink of his beer. We talked for another hour or so. I'm pretty sure it was before midnight when we called it. We'd been sitting on those chairs so long that when we got up, Sam stumbled backward and almost fell. Timmy gave him a little crap but Sam joked that his legs were asleep. He said goodbye to a couple other people and we left. When he went to his truck, he put a cigarette in his mouth, and turned back toward me.

"*Tommy's Sports Bar*," he said. "Think about it, Rhett. It's a good idea."

**

When Sam didn't show up to the job site on Monday, I thought he drank a lot on Sunday and couldn't answer the bell. It happens. I knew he was going fishing that Sunday. I didn't think much of it and I was actually ready to give him hell about it on Tuesday. Then Tuesday rolls around and he doesn't show up. I thought it was weird because I didn't recall him saying he was taking time off or going somewhere. Tuesday morning, I went to our foreman, Earl Landry, and asked him if he fired Sam. He said that he didn't, but if he keeps no-showing that he might.

We were putting together some new add-ons to the grandstands at the high school and were going to do the roof of one of the buildings. The only enjoyable part about roofing is joking around with the guys, so I was a little pissed at Sam because I knew the afternoon was going to be awful.

It was around lunchtime and I was still out screwing in the seats in the grandstand additions when Earl comes over to me. He said he needed to talk to me in private. I was thinking Sam quit – told Earl to go to hell or something. Earl was having a hard time saying what he wanted to say, so I knew it was bigger than that.

"Rhett, Sam died," he said, holding his hat in his hand.

"What?"

"Sam died on Sunday night."

"Very funny."

"It's not a joke, Rhett."

"Stop messing around."

"Rhett, I wanted to tell you first because I know y'all were close. He died on Sunday night. Middle of the night."

"That doesn't make any sense. How? He crash his truck?"

"He was killed."

"He was killed? What does that mean?"

"Somebody killed Sam."

"What are you talking about?"

"I don't know much. I don't know who done it and I don't know why, but somebody killed Sam. Shot him."

"What the hell?"

"I didn't want you to find out from somebody else."

"Where did he get shot? Middle of the night, he got shot?"

"Apparently at his house."

"At his house?"

"Yes sir."

"Did ... are the kids okay? Debbie? Who shot him?"

"She and the kids are fine. Only Sam got killed. Listen, if you wanna take the rest of the day or, hell, even the rest of the week off, that's fine with me."

He patted me on the arm and then walked away.

I lost it.

I took my toolbox and tossed it like a damn shot put – tools went flying everywhere. I was screaming and hitting things. I mean, what the hell? You're sitting there doing your job and then you find out your best friend got shot to hell in his own home. I didn't pick up any of my tools. I walked to my truck and sat there for a while. Smoked a couple of cigarettes. After I flipped out, it felt real numb-like. I drove home and sat on the couch. Smoked some more cigarettes. I thought about calling Debbie but she never really liked me much. You know what pissed me off, though, about everything that went down? I never heard once from her. I mean, ever. I understand not hearing from her in the day or so after, but I learned about the funeral from Pastor Wilheim. She never said one word to me after Sam died. I get I may not be the best guy around and why she'd hate me, but not one damn peep from her. Nothing to let me know what happened. Nothing about the funeral. Nothing about nothing.

I was thinking about doing something for her and the family. Sending flowers or sending something. Isn't that what people do? But what's the use? Now that Sam was dead, there was no connection between me and her. She probably liked to keep it that way. Remember what I said: there's plenty of judgment in Well Springs.

If I remember right, the funeral was on that Wednesday or thereabout. I found out he's dead Tuesday afternoon, and I got half of a day to process it and come up with something to say. Debbie and the kids were sitting on the left side of the church, first row, and I was on the first row on the right side. It had been so long since I'd been in church, I'm surprised I didn't burst into flames.

I remember the pastor said something about Sam punching him and everybody laughed. You know what's funny about that story, though? You'd think Sam would be all proud about it: some high and mighty preacher man being all pious or what-have-you and he was able to get a good lick in. But he wasn't proud of it. When he told me about it, I was laughing my ass off, but Sam was sorta bothered that he had done it. He said it wasn't right and it was probably embarrassing as hell for the kids. He wished he didn't do it. I still thought it was funny and apparently everybody at the funeral thought so, too.

I went up and said some nice things about Sam and a couple of funny stories that happened when me and him were drinking. Some people were laughing, but I saw Debbie and she had this blank, cold look on her face. Just staring straight ahead. I don't know, I thought they were funny stories and I'm the one that had to speak, so I said what I wanted to say.

Truthfully, I don't really remember much about any of the other speakers. I was sorta out of it. I was drinking pretty good that morning, practicing what I was gonna say. I didn't black out or nothing, but I was in my own world.

We ended up out near the gravesite and a few of us were still there. Debbie still didn't say a word to me. Pastor Wilheim said a few more things and then asked if we had anything else to say. Nobody said anything. Sam got lowered into the ground and that was that.

I thought about swallowing my pride and saying something to Debbie. I didn't want to, but it was probably the right thing to do. I was going to tell her to let me know if there was anything that she needed. I was going to tell her that I know she was hurting and that I was hurting too. I would have helped them, too. Really. Not for her – she was always a bitch to me – but for the kids. He loved those kids. She looked at me, too. We made eye contact and everything. I was about to say something.

Then she gathered the kids and left.

**

I remember Sheriff Cremble came to talk with me. It woulda been shortly after the funeral. Maybe the next day? Or maybe it was before? But he came to give me the *Where were you the night of...* line. I remember I was a bit of an asshole to him, admittedly. I was real pissed off at the world during that time. He came and talked to me about stuff and I started accusing him of covering up Debbie killing Sam and how they were sleeping with each other. It wasn't right. I'll tell you this: I don't like most people, but Sheriff Cremble is a good man. Kills me to say it, but it's true. He's a genuinely good man.

Sometimes I wonder: is that just how he is? Or do you work at being good?

Do I have that same goodness inside of me? If I worked at it, could I be more like Sheriff Cremble? Not saying I necessarily want to, of course. I wonder more if it's possible. Him and I butted heads a few times over the years, but he always treated me with respect and dignity. Sometimes it drove me crazy, you know? I wanna get into the muck, but he would treat me so damn nice that we ended up smoothing things over.

His wife passed not too long ago. A few years back. He loved that woman. I'm sure you've heard about my ex-wife and the nightmare that is, so it felt like such a foreign concept to me: a man loving his wife so deeply. I still don't know if I envied it or not. I like doing my own thing, but I suppose having that kinda love would be nice. Also, to have somebody love you that much.

It makes me wonder about Sam.

179

It's trippy to think about — getting into concepts of destiny or whatever. If Sam didn't get Debbie pregnant, would he still be alive? Because I don't know if Sam and Debbie ever truly loved each other. So if Sam doesn't knock her up, they don't get married, and don't have the four kids, and he doesn't move into that house. Like I said earlier, if he's not in that house, then he's not there for when whoever came into the room that night to kill him — if that's what you believe happened. Maybe he meets somebody he actually loves and he's a totally different person. Maybe they have their own family together and move to Lubbock or something. I don't get to see him anymore, but I know he's out there.

I don't know. It's pointless to think about, I suppose. He's dead.

**

Who do I think killed Sam?

You really wanna know? There was a stretch there where I really thought about it. Initially, I was sure it was Mary Lou from the Wolfpack. It made too much sense. She wanted to steal Sam away from his family and when he turned her down, she got all pissed and killed him. Then she left town. It got me all mad and I was this close to tracking her down. That's why I didn't tell Sheriff Cremble about it when he came to interrogate me at my house. I was talking about it with the boys over at the Armadillo Bar one night.

"Y'all know Mary Lou, from the Wolfpack?" I said.

"Yeah, what happened to her? I ain't seen her in a little while," Cliff said. "I heard she moved outta Well Springs."

"You wanna know what I think?" I said.

"What's that?"

"I think she's the one to kill Sam," I said.

"No, you think so?" Cliff said.

"Think about it: she was trying to be a homewrecker and push Debbie out the picture and Sam turned her down," I said.

"Can't say I blame him," Cliff said. "Could you imagine settling down with that?"

"Well, that's the thing. I think her psycho ass got all worked up. She probably killed him and then ran town."

"But what about the man?" Cliff said, popping a few pretzels in his mouth.

"The man?"

"They say Debra told Sheriff Cremble that it was a strange man that killed Sam," Cliff said.

"Well, maybe Debbie ain't telling the truth."

"But why?"

"Why what?"

"If this girl is trying to steal Sam away from Debra, and Debra sees her killing Sam, why wouldn't she just tell Sheriff Cremble that it was her? Why would she cover for somebody trying to steal her man?"

"Well, I don't know. Maybe because ... hell, Cliff. Maybe it wasn't her. Damn it, man, why you gotta ruin stuff for me?"

"I ain't ruining nothing. It ain't my problem you got no brains," Cliff said and everybody else around the bar started laughing.

That was the end of my days thinking it was Mary Lou. Over the years, it really came down to two different theories for me.

Okay, maybe it was a stranger that went to rob the house – I have no idea why that house – and then things sorta went sideways and he killed Sam. A senseless, chaotic thing. They say there's random acts of violence all over this country, but a plain house on a quiet street in a town like Well Springs? That is something even more random than random. It doesn't make sense. And if you're robbing a place, why would you go into the bedroom? Who does that? You'd steal everything in the living room or whatever and then get out. Could it have happened that way? A random stranger? Maybe.

The other option would be more obvious: Debbie killed him. It makes sense, you know? She was in this loveless marriage and Sam could beat her up from time to time. Maybe she waited until he was asleep, pulled out the gun, and shot him. Or maybe they were getting into it one night and then she shot him. It'd explain why he was killed in the bedroom. And then when Sheriff Cremble comes knocking, all she has to do is say it was some strange man who broke in. The only living witness is the killer. I don't know how hard Sheriff Cremble grilled Debbie about it, but apparently, he believes it was the stranger. So that's the official story.

There were some things about the case that really didn't add up for me. I remember talking to one of the deputies at the time about it. The young guy. There are some holes in the story.

As I said, I never talked to Debbie once since Sam died. I had no reason. Every once in a while, I'll see her and Cody around town. I heard Tommy is doing law or something in Denton. Not sure what happened with the girls. They moved away somewhere. I wonder if Debbie ever even visited Sam's grave. Wouldn't surprise me if she hadn't. I think deep down I'll always believe she killed him. Over the years, though, I learned not to let it bother me. I used to stew in it. I'd dream of going to her house and confronting her and pressuring the truth out of her. But it's been twenty-some years. Sam's rotted away and everybody has moved on with their lives. So, who do I think killed Sam?

At this point, what does it matter?

Chapter Eleven

Debra Jenkins

The first time I met Sam's parents was at our wedding, if you can believe that. I guess if you knew them, you would believe it. They were something else – both of them. My parents weren't perfect and I have my share of flaws, but those people were plain awful. Mainly him. Henry. They didn't even go to his funeral, so that should tell you all you need to know about them. Henry was a drunk and Loretta was always in her own world. When you first meet her, you think she's sort of ditzy. Sam told me she had these pills she takes, though. Always drugged up.

Deep down I always pitied Sam. And I think he sensed that and resented it. He *hated* being pitied. It drove him up a wall. But what chance did he have with those people? I still have a lot of anger and sadness toward Sam. I felt sad for him because growing up in that house must have been miserable. I can't imagine how much damage they did to him as a boy. That's the sadness. But then I thought about it more, and that sadness became anger. Sure, he didn't have the best childhood, but he feels he has the right to take it out on me and the kids? He had his hardships but that doesn't excuse how he treated us. Because his dad was abusive, he gets to be abusive? No. That's BS. That's why it's so frustrating because I would get *so* mad at him — even after he died — for behaving the way he did.

Then I couldn't help it: I'd think about his parents and start to feel bad for him. It's a cycle.

Like I said, the first time I met the charming Henry and Loretta Jenkins was our wedding day. Nobody had any money, so it was a small little wedding at the church. My parents weren't there because, well, that's a different story. I'll tell that later. But they weren't there, so they suggested Henry walk me down the aisle. To Sam's credit, he said that wasn't a good idea. But how it worked out was literally the first time I met Henry, he got corralled next to me as I'm about to walk down the aisle. I'm really pregnant at this point and he wraps his arm around mine and looks me up and down.

"Damn," he said. "Truth be told, I thought Sam woulda knocked up a fat girl. Once you get that baby out, you're gonna look mighty fine, sweetheart."

It was the *first* thing he said to me. Right as I'm about to walk down the aisle to get married. And he smelled so bad. He smelled like a bum in an alley. After we made our walk and he handed me off, he didn't know where to stand. He went to stand to the side of us and the pastor told him he could sit down.

"Right here? Sit down on the floor up here?" Henry said, confused.

"Oh my God," I whispered.

"No, no, Henry, you can go sit down in the pew," the pastor said.

There was a little step heading back to the pews and Henry tripped going down and almost fell. He composed himself and looked back like it was funny.

"I'm sorry about him," Sam whispered to me.

184

"Is he okay?" I said.

"I mean, no. He's a piece of trash. I'm sorry."

We had a little reception after the ceremony, a buffet-style dinner and some dancing. Nothing spectacular. Maybe fifty people. Henry was trying to dance around with a lot of the younger girls and Loretta was eating alone at the table. Well she wasn't so much *eating*, as trying to stay awake. She was holding a fork with her eyes closed, and her head kept dropping a little bit. It wasn't late, by the way. It was still light out.

Sam and I went around saying hello to everyone and then Henry came up to me. Sam had gone off to get a drink or something. Henry took this flask out of his pocket, opened it up, and took a long drink from it. He wiped his mouth then gestured it toward me – like he was asking if I wanted some. Keep in mind, I'm *very* pregnant at this point. I shook my head.

"Your loss," he said. "Great party, by the way. Everything looks nice. You look incredible. Very nice."

"Thank you," I said, nervously looking around.

"I don't know what you see in Sam there. Giant waste of space, that kid."

I didn't know how to respond so I just stood there.

"Probably best thing to happen to his life was not using a rubber with you," Henry laughed. "Kudos to him. Nailing it down. You got a name?"

"A name?" I said.

"Yeah, you got a name?"

"Debra?"

"No, numbnuts, for the little one," he said, gesturing toward my stomach with the hand holding the flask before taking another drink.

"Oh. Cody."

"Cody?" he asked.

"Yeah. We like Cody."

185

"Sam ever bring up naming him Henry?"

"No, I don't think so."

"That little bastard. Well, Cody is nice, too."

I looked over and Loretta's face was in her food. Barbeque baked beans and pulled pork. Eyes closed and mouth open. She looked dead to be honest.

"Henry, I think your wife might need some help," I said, pointing over to her. Henry turned around and started shaking his head.

"That drugged up whore. Lemme give you some advice, Debra: don't start popping pills. That stuff is bad for you. You'll end up like that and you'll lose that great figure that I'm sure you got."

"I'm going to make sure she's all right," I said. "It was nice talking with you Henry."

"Hey, I'm always here. Give me a ... I don't know what the word is."

"Okay, well, have fun."

I walked over to Loretta and lifted her head out of the food. There were baked beans all over the left side of her face. Her eyes started to come open.

"Hello Mrs. Jenkins, are you okay?" I asked.

"Hello Debra, dear," she said. "Oh, what a great wedding this is. Just wonderful."

"Thank you. Let me help you with that," I said, grabbing a napkin and wiping away the sauce from her face.

"Thank you, sweetheart," she said. "Just a wonderful wedding this is. You look lovely."

"Thank you, Mrs. Jenkins," I said.

"Call me Loretta," she smiled. "We're family now."

**

My parents were no better, only for a different reason. Bill and Amy Adams are your traditional Bible Belt, over-the-top Baptist. Everything is a sin. Everything is the work of the Devil. I'm not even exaggerating that much. Now imagine being a teenage girl and telling those people that you're pregnant. It was one of the worst days of my life. Mom was crying. Daddy sat there and shook his head.

"You know you have to marry him," she said.

"Our daughter," he said. "I can't believe it. Debra, we did everything right. And then you go and do something like this."

"You know you have to marry him, right?" she said.

"An abomination," he said.

"It's not an 'abomination,'" I said. "Sometimes things like this happen."

"Seventeen years old," he said. "Can you believe it?"

"What did we do wrong, Bill?" she said.

"Oh my God," I said. "Can you not talk like I'm not right here?"

"Don't you dare use the Lord's name in vain," he said. "I don't even know who you are anymore. What happened to our beautiful Debbie?"

"You know you have to marry him, right?" she said.

"I heard you the first time," I snapped.

"Unbelievable. She talks to her mother that way now," she said.

"So you're not going to help me?" I asked.

"Help you? Help you live in sin?" he said.

"I don't know what to do!" I said.

"Maybe you should have thought about that before giving it out like some two-bit, street-walking tramp," she said.

"Oh my God, Mom, really?"

"I can't do this," she said, getting up and storming out.

"You see what you did?" he said, gesturing toward her. "Shame on you."

He got up and went to console Mom. They left me there alone on the couch and I started crying. It was the loneliest feeling in the world. I ended up living with my friend after that. Lived with them until the wedding and I moved in with Sam. They lived outside of town, so I never saw my parents. We didn't talk for a long time after that. I thought about not even letting them know about the wedding. We were putting together wedding invitations – well, I was – and I thought about them. I knew they wouldn't support it. Even if they were there, I knew deep down they resented how things turned out. Resented me. I wasn't going to invite them. Really. Then I decided it wasn't right. I sent them an invitation.

Little while later, I got their RSVP in the mail. They marked Not Attending.

**

I don't do it anymore, but there was a long stretch in my life when I wondered how other families act. They have get-togethers and look after each other. My parents wanted nothing to do with us and Sam wanted nothing to do with his parents. I'm actually grateful for Sam keeping his parents away. Who knows what Henry and Loretta would do with the kids around. We only saw them once in a blue moon. Even that was too often.

But I wish we had a more normal life.

When Sam wasn't drinking so much, we had some nice family holidays. Just us and the kids. Sometimes with the Doyles next door. But I still pictured the perfect family. Thanksgiving with everybody at our house. Everybody sitting at a big table, laughing and passing dishes. That's what family is supposed to be. When I thumbed through magazines at the grocery store or hair salon, I looked at the photos of the beautiful houses and smiling families. It all looked so *perfect*.

I don't want to make it sound like I was this prisoner serving a life sentence or something. Like I said, during the times Sam had his life under control, the six of us had some great times. That's why I would feel guilty for wishing for a better life, because I knew it could have been a lot worse. At least we had *some* nice moments. I know I should be grateful for that. But then I think: why is it selfish to wish for a better life? Why is it selfish to wish for a husband that loves you and treats you with respect? Why is it selfish to wish for have parents and in-laws that are supportive? That's not asking for a lot.

Is it?

One of my friends from school, Britt, ended up with a doctor and they moved to Fort Worth. He's really good looking. Very handsome. A good man, too. Their kids went to private school and ended up going to TCU and Stanford. Are you kidding me? Stanford. One of the worst moments of my year is when I get a Christmas card from them. They are sitting there smiling. The perfect family. And the card is really glossy. Expensive, I'm sure. But they can afford it. I don't know why everything worked out for her. I don't mean that in a bad way. We were good friends. She was with me at the party when Sam got me pregnant.

Every time I get that card, I think about if Sam had sex with Britt that night, would our lives had switched places? Maybe I meet the handsome doctor and move to Fort Worth. Maybe Britt ends up staying in Well Springs, married to Sam and all the baggage that came with that. Maybe my parents still talk to me and love me if I'm married to the doctor in Fort Worth. Maybe I'm the one that sends *her* really expensive, glossy Christmas cards and she's stuck in this small town where people wonder if she killed her husband. All of that changed because of one night when I was a stupid teenager.

I don't know.

Life is so damn unfair sometimes.

**

The phone only rang twice before she picked up.

"Adams residence, how are you today?" she said.

"Mom, it's me," I said.

"Debra," she said.

"Hi Mom."

"What's wrong? Are you okay?"

"Sam died," I said. There was a long silence on the other end. "Mom?"

"Yes, honey."

"Sam died."

"Lord Jesus."

"I know we haven't talked in a while, but I thought you should know."

"How?" she said.

"How did he die?"

"Yes. Accident?"

"No. He was killed," I said.

"He was *killed*?"

"Yes. In the middle night."

"Lord help us. Debra, are you okay? Who killed him?"

"I'm okay. I just thought you should know."

"Oh, Debra. Who killed him?"

"I don't know."

"You don't know? Honey, are you okay? What happened?"

"It was somebody robbing our house. He was in our room and he shot Sam."

"Are you okay? When did this happen? Can we – are you okay?"

"I'm okay. The kids are okay. Sam was the only one that got hurt. I know that you didn't like him, but I thought–"

"Honey, this is tragic. I am so sorry. My heart is broken for you. I can't even believe that – when did this happen?"

"Two days ago. We're having the funeral either tomorrow or the next day."

190

"What is the world coming to? Bill! Bill, honey, Sam died. Sam. Yes, I'm talking to her right now."

"Is Dad there?" I asked.

"Yes, honey he's right here. Sam died. He was *killed*. Killed by some crazed maniac. Bill what is the world coming to? Debbie, honey, your father is here."

"Debbie?" he said.

"Hi Daddy."

"Honey, I am so sorry. Are you okay?" he said.

"Yeah, I am okay."

"Somebody stormed into their house and killed him, Bill!" she said.

"Debbie, are you okay? Are you still living in Well Springs?" he said.

"Yes."

"The same house?" he said.

"Yes."

"We'll come and see you. Are the kids okay?" he said.

"Yeah, they're okay."

"I can't believe it," she said.

"Who was it?" he said.

"I don't know. I didn't recognize him."

"What is the *world* coming to?" she said. "People killing people over nothing. Bill, what is the world coming to?"

"I don't know, honey," he said. "Debbie, you stay put, we'll come and see you."

They no longer lived in Well Springs. A few years before Sam was killed, they had moved a two hours away. Later that day, they pulled into the driveway and jogged to the door. Mom didn't even knock. She let herself in and yelled out for me. We stood there in the living room and hugged. Her and I were crying and Dad was silent. The kids had been living at Fred and Helen's house. I didn't want them to deal with

191

everything. After we calmed down and I explained what happened, we sat in the living room and talked for hours. Eventually, the kids came over. I don't even know if they knew who my parents were. I had to explain they were my mommy and daddy.

They stayed for quite a while and I was talking with Dad in the living room and I saw Mom in the kitchen talking with Cody. She had her hands on his shoulders. She asked him if he was okay and what happened. It made me really nervous. I was looking at them, pretending to listen to Dad talking about whatever he was talking about. Cody looked over at me.

"Are you okay sweetheart?" she said to Cody.

I nodded to him and then he nodded to her. She gave him this great big hug.

"Is that all right, Debs?" Dad said.

"I'm sorry?" I said, turning back toward him.

"The funeral. Is it okay if your mother and I go? I don't want it to be disrespectful because we didn't really support him. Do you want us to go, honey? Or do you not want us to go?"

"Okay," I said.

"You want us to go or don't want us to go?"

"You don't have to go. It's fine."

My mom consoling Cody bothered me so much. It wasn't fearing that Cody would tell her what happened. It was because she was hugging and crying about a boy whose mere existence she said was an abomination. My parents cut me out of their lives because Cody *existed*. Now she had these waterworks? It felt so – I don't know if hypocritical is the right word. How do you turn your back on family for years, and then come and pretend that you want to comfort us?

"Are you sure, Debra?" Dad said, rubbing my knee.

"Yeah, you don't have to go. You can go home, actually. Thank you for visiting."

"We can stay," he said.

"That's okay."

**

I was pretty exhausted by that point, so the night before the funeral I passed out and slept forever. I was still sleeping on the couch in the living room. I couldn't sleep in that bedroom after everything. I slept on the couch for a few months. Fred and Helen were so gracious. They let the kids sleep at their house every night. They offered to let me sleep over there too, but I still slept at our house. Sheriff Cremble always had somebody parked outside our home each night, for protection. When I told him that wasn't necessary, he said it was important for appearances. Make it align with the story, he said.

I woke up the morning of the funeral and laid there for a little while. It felt so good. Quiet. Peaceful. Eventually, I got up and made myself a nice breakfast. Waffles with creamy peanut butter and orange juice. I walked around the house, enjoying the silence. I opened our bedroom door and looked inside. They cleaned up most of it, but there was still dried blood in the carpet on Sam's side of the bed. They moved fast. They re-painted the walls and got rid of the mattress and sheets and replaced them with new ones. There was this great big new bed that nobody slept in.

Framed photos were still on the dresser and I picked one up and looked at it. The girls were babies and Sam was holding them in his arms – Tommy wasn't born yet. We were in front of the Christmas tree that Well Springs puts up near the courthouse. Cody and I were holding hands. We were all smiling. I stared at the photo and I thought: were we smiling because we were actually happy? Or were we smiling because we were supposed to? I honestly don't remember. Maybe we were happy. I put the frame back on the dresser and went to get ready.

I don't really remember much about the funeral. It was overwhelming. Everybody coming up to you, saying how sorry they were. It didn't stop.

"We're so sorry."

"Are you okay, Debra?"

"We can't believe this happened."

One after another. Constantly. Everything felt like a blur. You get drained. Then it becomes numb. I don't remember much of what people said. I know Pastor Wilheim said some nice things and Rhett – that beast – told dirty stories of Sam and him getting drunk together. I didn't have much reaction to anything.

I remember sitting there in the church, looking at the flowers. White roses. I remember that. And I remember being outside and seeing Sam's casket being lowered down. I think Pastor Wilheim said some more things, but then Sam was in his grave. That was that.

He was dead and we all sort of went our own way.

**

Everyone in town was real nice after Sam died.

People reached out and asked if there was anything they could do – the women cooked us dishes and the men helped with things around the house. I probably didn't handle it with as much grace as I should have. Sometimes I was appreciative and other times I probably came across as bitchy. It depended on my mood. Sometimes I felt like people around town looked at me as a charity case. *Oh, that poor Debra can't take care of her children by herself.* That bothered me. But I know deep-down their hearts were in the right place. We're a small town and people were trying to help.

There was a time when I wondered if they were all acting out of guilt. I wondered if they felt guilty about not doing anything to help get Sam under control and now they were overcompensating, or whatever you call it. I know word spread about Sam being killed by a robber in the middle of the night and that I saw him get killed. I wondered how many thought that I killed him. People wouldn't ask about that night. They only asked how I was doing.

About a month after Sam was killed, we were all having dinner at Fred and Helen's house. I think they enjoyed having the kids live with them because they were never able to have children. The kids even called them Uncle Fred and Auntie Helen. They were lifesavers. Truly. I will always appreciate what they did.

But the night we were having dinner, we were finishing up and cleaning the table. Tommy and the girls had run off to do whatever. It was me, Cody, Fred, and Helen.

"Debra, I hope you will forgive me," Fred said, picking up the drinking glasses. "But have you heard anything from Sheriff Cremble about catching the bad guy?"

"Fred!" Helen commanded at him.

"I'm sorry," Fred said.

"It's okay, Fred," I said. "It's okay."

"I can't believe you, Fred," Helen said. "Debra, I'm sorry. But I suppose since the topic is already brought up, *have* you heard anything about it?"

"No, nothing yet," I said. Cody was going around the table, picking up all the dirty napkins. He didn't even seem like he noticed what we were talking about.

"I should have gone over to help," Fred said.

"Fred, hush," I said.

"It's true," he said. "I am sorry Debra. I should have gone over to help. Maybe I could have stopped him from getting away."

I stopped cleaning.

"You absolutely shouldn't have come over," I said.

"I was a doggone *coward*," he said, his voice starting to shake. "I could have helped. But I didn't. I should have. Debra, I am sorry."

"Fred, I don't want to hear another word," I said.

"Fred Doyle, you fool," Helen said.

"It's true, though," he said, tears starting to well up. "I could have helped. I could have kept the man from getting away with it. He's going to get away with it because I stayed put."

"Cody, please go play with your brother and sisters," I said. He nodded and walked into the kitchen to throw the dirty napkins in the garbage and then left.

"Fred, I don't want you to feel this way," I said.

"Well, gosh darn it, I can't help it," he said. "I could have gone and helped and I didn't. I froze. I hope you can forgive me, Debra."

"Fred, you and Helen have been so gracious through all of this," I said. "I have nothing to forgive you for. You did what you should have done. He could have killed you, too. You did the right thing."

"Then how come it doesn't feel like I did?" he said.

"The Lord works in mysterious ways," I said. "I don't know why this happened, but I am so glad that you didn't come over. I can honestly say that with all my heart. I am grateful you didn't come over."

"I don't know," he said. "I suppose. Please, if there is anything that we can do to help you through all of this, let us know."

"Fred, you've already done enough."

**

Did I ever love Sam?

That's a very *complicated* question. Did I love him? Well, if he never got me pregnant at that party, would I have ended up with him? Probably not. More than likely, we each would have gone our own way. I would have had kids, but they wouldn't be Cody, Nikki, Cass, and Tommy. Sometimes I think about this concept of alternate realities or whatever they call it. Like if there are different versions of me out there in a universe or something. How many versions of me have this life? Probably only the one that I'm living.

Something I did when I was a teenager decided my path. Maybe that's unfair to say. It wasn't only that decision. I didn't have to marry him. I could have had Cody and then moved on. But then people would see me as this hussy – had a child out of wedlock and didn't even marry the father. I could have also divorced him. Some people would have understood because they knew Sam could be abusive.

There were a ton of exits I could have taken while I was on that path – but I didn't. I kept going.

Why?

I ask myself that a lot. Why didn't I do something? I don't know. I suppose I'm being unfair to myself. Sam really wasn't this big, bad wolf all the time, you know? He had his demons. But when things were right, he could be a very sweet man and a loving father. When he was sober, I would tell him how much I appreciated him and how glad I was that he wasn't drinking. Sometimes it would last a couple of weeks and other times a few days. Then something would happen and it was back to the booze. Back to the meanness. Back to the darkness.

So, your question: Did I love Sam?

I loved versions of him. Maybe. I don't think he ever loved me. I think he felt getting me pregnant ruined his life and he always deep-down resented me. I believe he loved the kids. He enjoyed spending time with them when he was sober. You could tell. It's just he couldn't keep it together. When the wheels fell off, I felt sad because I knew he would go back to being an asshole. But I also felt bad for him. I don't want to say I pitied him, but I know the kind of man he could have been.

But I don't think I ever loved him completely.

I know it's bad to say. Maybe if he had stayed sober for good, it's possible we could have found a way to love each other. It just never happened. I always knew that whenever he was good, it was a matter of time before it was bad again. Up and down. Up and down. Up and down. By the end, it got exhausting. I can't imagine doing that for years and years.

A divorce would have been perfect. He loved the kids and would get to see him. He wouldn't be around me all the time. When things were bad, he'd have probably drank his way through the weekend without even realizing he needed to come see them, but that would be fine. A divorce would have worked but, as stupid as this sounds, I just never got around to it.

There was a time, maybe six months after Sam died, I was at the store and one of the ladies in town asked me how I was doing and said that I must miss him every day. I nodded when she said it. I know it's not genuine. I don't miss him. Back then or now. I wished people stopped bringing him up. I wanted everybody to move on. I knew the longer his memory lingered, the longer people would ask questions about that night. I knew the longer that happened, the higher the chance something would come out.

I wanted Sam *gone*.

**

I pulled the kids out of school after Sam died. It was too much. I didn't want everyone asking them questions. They stayed at Fred and Helen's house and Helen tried to teach them things throughout the day. About a month after Sam died, we all went to the park. All of us – the kids and

Fred and Helen. Tommy and the girls were playing on the jungle gym and Fred and Helen were watching after them. I asked Cody to sit with me on the bench.

"How are you doing sweetie?" I said.

"I'm okay," he said, swinging his dangling legs back and forth.

"Cody, we probably need to talk about what happened."

"Okay."

"Have you told anybody about what you did?" I said.

"No."

"Cody, be honest. Don't lie. Have you told *anybody* about what you did?"

"No."

"Your sisters?"

"No."

"Did you tell Tommy?"

"No."

"This is very important. You're not bad if you told somebody, I just want to know if you did."

"I didn't, I promise."

"Okay."

We both watched the others play. It was the first time I heard them laugh since Sam died. They were having fun. It felt nice.

"Do you think I did a bad thing?" Cody said.

"Do I think you did a bad thing?" I said. He nodded. "No, sweetheart. I don't think you did a bad thing."

"I didn't like Daddy anymore," he said. "He was mean."

"I know he was mean. Cody, what you did was a very grown-up thing, though. Because of that, we need to have a very grown-up conversation."

"About Dad?"

199

"Yes. It's very important that you don't tell *anybody* about what you did. Do you understand me? Nobody. Ever."

"Okay."

"I mean it, Cody. Even as you get older, you can *never* tell anybody about this. Not Tommy. Not Cass. Not Nikki. Not Helen and Fred."

"If what I did wasn't bad, how come I shouldn't tell anybody?" he said.

"Well, because people will think that you did a bad thing – even though it wasn't. You will get into a lot of trouble."

"I know."

"If anybody ever finds out, I will have to say that I was the one to kill Daddy," I told him. "Then I would get into big trouble and probably go to prison."

"You would? But Dad was the bad one."

"I know he was. But it's against the law to kill somebody, no matter how mean they are."

"Do you think somebody will find out?"

"I hope not. Right now, the only people who know what happened are you, me, and Sheriff Cremble. He is going to help protect us. We have to make sure to not tell anybody. If anybody ever asks you about anything, you tell them you don't know what happened. You were asleep. That's all you have to say."

"I was asleep."

"You were asleep."

"A bad guy came into our house and killed Dad," he said. "But I was asleep."

"That's right," I said. "That's right."

Chapter Twelve

Sheriff George Cremble

We had this fella in our office at the time. Young kid. Early twenties. Name was Douglas Arthur. His daddy named him after the general, you know, and we always gave him a hard time about it 'cause he was an ambitious young man. We joked how he wanted to take back the Philippines. He was a good kid, though. He was good at his job, which meant he was a bit of a thorn in my side when everything was going down with Sam Jenkins. He joined us a lil before Sam died. I wanted everything to go away as fast as possible and this kid wouldn't let it go. Looked at it as something interesting happening in this quiet town. Or maybe he looked at it as something to add to his resume. Get outta Well Springs. He was from El Paso, I believe, and I think he saw Well Springs as a starter job.

About two weeks after Sam was killed, Douglas stormed into the office holding a newspaper up in the air. He was hooting and hollering about a break in the case.

"Sheriff, Sheriff!" he called out. "Look at this. Look at this!"

He slammed the folded newspaper in front of me. It was hard to tell what he was wanting me to look at. It was the regional section, so there was all these articles. He pressed his finger on a short little story. Headline read:

Man charged in slaying of Lubbock family in botched robbery

"What do you think?" he said, all eager-like.

"What do I think?" I said. "Well, I feel bad for that family."

"No, Sheriff, it could be our guy!" he said, big smile on his face.

"I don't know about that, Douglas."

"Why not?"

"Just 'cause a man killed some people don't make him our man."

"Sheriff, read it. It adds up. Guy went to rob a place, it went sideways, and then he ends up killing them."

"I can read," I said, sliding the paper back to him.

"Well, we need to check this out. Maybe it's our guy."

"Douglas, I appreciate your...*enthusiasm*. I really do. But I think that's a bit of a reach."

"How is it a reach? We gotta at least call Lubbock about it."

"You think this fella is gonna say, 'By the way, I killed another man in Well Springs if you wanna add it to the list'?"

"We can see where he was. Had he ever been to Well Springs? I don't know. We can see if this is our guy. I don't understand how you aren't excited about this. This is a real lead."

I looked around and everybody in the office was looking at me. I could tell they thought he was making sense — 'cause he was. If situations had been different, I woulda called Lubbock in a heartbeat.

"All right," I said.

"All right?"

"I'll give Lubbock a call about it."

"Now we're talking. Sheriff, this could be the big one. I think we got him. I really think this could be it."

He went all dancing around the office, high-fiving people and cheering and what-have-you. He thought he got the big break. After making a fool of himself, he came back to my desk and motioned to the phone. I picked it up and started dialing. Thing about it was, I was actually dialing Debra. I was going to have this phony conversation, so she would understand what was happening on our end. She'd be a bit confused at first, but she woulda picked up on it after a while. Have it be a one-way conversation, they call it.

Then I wondered what if eager Douglas grabbed the receiver to start yapping – thinking he's talking to Lubbock. Debra wouldn't know what to do. It'd unravel everything. Douglas would wonder why the hell I called Debra instead of Lubbock. Or, considering how Douglas was, I thought about what if after our call, he called Lubbock himself. Tell them about how he knows Sheriff Cremble called them, but he had a few questions himself. They'd tell him that no Sheriff Cremble ever called. Raise more questions.

I stopped dialing and hung up the phone.

"Hell, I thought I knew the Lubbock number, but I forgot. Can somebody get it for me?"

Douglas had his trigger finger ready. He had it written on his notepad and put it on my desk right away. I dialed and talked with Lubbock for a while. Douglas was standing right there watching me. It's a bit annoying, somebody watching you have a phone call. I wanted to shoo him away like a mosquito. After I was done, I thanked Lubbock and hung up the phone.

"Well?" he said.

"Ain't our guy," I said.

"Why?"

"The killer over there was a homeless fella. Mental problems. Crazy as they come."

"Well, maybe our guy has mental problems. Makes sense on how erratic everything was."

"Lubbock fella lived in the streets over there. Didn't have no car. Killed them with a knife, too. I appreciate your tenacity, Douglas, but we ain't gotta make something outta something that ain't worth making."

"Hold on for a second," Douglas said.

"Good grief," I said. "What?"

"You said he killed them with a knife."

"That's right."

"Our guy shot Sam to hell with a lot of bullets. Maybe he ran out of bullets and couldn't afford to buy any more. Then he switched over to a knife."

"And how you suppose he got to Lubbock? He's homeless. He ain't got means of transportation."

"Maybe he stole a car. Nothing is *registered* to him. He stole a car from wherever. Now we have to check into recently stolen vehicles."

"Douglas, you gotta know when to let go. It ain't him."

"Sheriff, why are you so keen on squashing this? Did they say where he was two weeks ago?"

"Yes sir, they did," I said.

They didn't actually bring that up. I ain't even ask about it. I knew that I had to say something to get this young gun from tracking this even further.

"And?" he said.

"Apparently he lived in this church over there. They got a handful of hobos. They had a nice Easter dinner for everybody and they stayed the

204

night. The morning after Easter they finished painting the inside of the church and he was there helping out. He wasn't in Well Springs, Douglas. I'm sorry."

I thought it was a pretty good story. Not bad for coming up with it on the spot. He looked like he was trying to figure it out. Trying to figure out how spin it like maybe that weren't true. That he was the man we were looking for.

"Damn," he said.

"I'm sorry, Douglas. It was a good lead. It really was. But it ain't our man."

"I guess it's back to the drawing board," he said.

"That's right. You go on and do that."

**

Around late June or so, things started to calm down. The cloud over the town started to clear. People was going back to their lives. It used to be that I couldn't go nowhere without people hounding me about the case. Had I found the man? Any update? Constantly. But by June, it was getting back to, *How are you, Sheriff?* Douglas quieted down about the case, too. I had told him I'd take care of it. Remind him who was the sheriff and who was the deputy. I ain't like doing that kinda stuff, but I felt I had to.

As everything was finally starting to quiet down, here comes Douglas Arthur again.

"Sheriff, you got a minute?" he asked.

"Yes sir. What's on your mind?"

"Can we sneak into the conference room?"

"Of course."

Part of me was thinking he was telling me he landed another job. Moving up, you know. We all knew his time in Well Springs was limited.

When we sat down, I noticed he had this yellow legal pad with all these notes scribbled. Had the floorplan of the Jenkins house drawn on there.

"Sheriff, I know you have got the case under control, but I figured it could always help having a fresh set of eyes," he said.

"All right," I said, trying to hide my annoyance.

"I was thinking about the Sam Jenkins case a lot lately."

"Douglas, we gotta find you a woman or a hobby. This case has got you acting like a mad man, you know that?"

"I know, Sheriff. I find this case so interesting."

"I don't know if *interesting* is the word for a man being killed in front of his family."

"Regardless, I'd been thinking a lot about this. So, Sam Jenkins was killed in his bedroom, right?"

"Douglas, we'd been through this a million times."

"I know, but humor me. He was killed in his bedroom. Killer is somebody not from Well Springs. Otherwise Debra would have recognized him, right?"

"Yes sir."

"If the killer didn't know Sam, then the primary reason why he's in the house is to rob the place. Okay, makes sense. But if he's there to rob the place, why go into the bedroom? Right? It's a bit odd. Figure he'd steal a bunch of things from the living room or somewhere else. In and out. You never want to wake the people up. Why go into the bedroom?"

"Believe that the man—"

"The man was on drugs or something. Right. Still sounds iffy, no disrespect. But okay. He was hopped up on God-knows-what. The killer goes into the bedroom. It wakes up Sam. The killer ends up shooting Sam. Shoots him *a lot*. Again, that doesn't make any sense. Why shoot him that much and risk waking up the neighborhood? And he shoots Sam so many times and doesn't shoot her?"

"Are you gonna get to anything we ain't covered already?" I asked.

"Now, from what I learned about Sam Jenkins, he could be a bit of a hot head. Especially when he was drinking."

"Unfortunately true."

"And we know that he was drinking that Sunday."

"Okay."

"We have a guy with alcohol in his system and an anger problem, and he wakes up with a stranger in his bedroom."

"It'd scare the hell out of me."

"Me too, but for somebody like Sam Jenkins, why would he not try to fight off the stranger. Even if he had a gun, the instinct would be for Sam to lunge at him. Try to subdue him."

"Maybe he did, Douglas."

"No. No, he didn't. You can tell by the way we found Sam. He was laying on the back left part of the bed. Whoever shot him, Sam was still sitting there in bed."

"Meaning?"

"Meaning, I think Sam actually *knew* whoever shot him. Otherwise, he would have tried to take him down. Rage-filled guy finds an intruder in his bedroom … and he just sits there? That doesn't add up. And if he tried to take down the shooter, he would have either gotten out of bed and been found shot dead on the floor. Maybe he'd be at the foot of the bed. But no way he would be at the back corner of the bed."

"Douglas, I got a question for you."

"Yes, Sheriff?"

"I know you got some high hopes. No doubt in my mind that you'll be going up the ladder soon enough. But I need you to answer a question for me, son: are you using the murder of a man in this small town as a way to boost your career?"

"No sir!"

"Douglas, this town has been shattered from this killing. I get the feeling you're trying to use it to get yourself a nice job somewhere else."

"No sir. No sir. I just find the case interesting is all."

"There you go with *interesting* again."

"I find that so much about this case doesn't make sense. If it's a robbery, why choose the Jenkins' below-average house? Why go into the bedroom? Why only shoot Sam? Why wouldn't Sam try to attack the killer? How did Fred not see anybody? Why did nobody else hear a car speed away? Why di–"

"Douglas, I appreciate your passion for this case. Sometimes, though, things just happen. No rhyme nor reason."

"But sir, this cas–"

"Son, sometimes things just happen. No use at looking for a sign in the mud. Sometimes mud is just mud."

"And sometimes the simplest answer is what happened."

"Meaning?"

"All of these things that don't add up – all of these questions – they hinge on one thing."

"Being?"

"Debra saying she didn't recognize the shooter."

"Well, she was the only eye-witness, Douglas. I'd say that makes her testimony pretty damn important."

"But what if she's lying?"

"Excuse me?"

"What if she's not telling the truth, Sheriff? Everything hinges on what she is saying. So, what if what she's saying isn't actually what happened?"

"I don't like what you're getting at, son."

"I think it's important to talk about, with all due respect. Sam was an abusive husband, according to several people. Wouldn't the simplest

208

explanation be that Debra shot him and made up a story about an intruder?"

"You're saying that people around here just kill each other, huh?"

"Well, it would explain why Sam was killed in the bedroom. It'd explain why he was killed while still sitting in bed. That he knew the shooter. It'd explain wh–"

"Deputy, you've officially gone off the deep end and I gotta stop you right now."

"But sir, how do you not see that there's a chance th–"

"Deputy," I said, sternly.

He gave me this look. Youthful passion being squashed. I could appreciate it. I truly could. It was a hell of a feeling for me, you know? I was getting hot under the collar over him doing his job good. He shoulda been asking these questions. But that ain't help me in no way. I shook my head, looking him in the eyes.

"Okay," he said.

"Okay?" I asked.

"Okay. I understand."

He stood up and started toward the door.

"You want your notepad?" I asked.

"No."

He walked outta the room and I stayed in there for a bit. Thinking. Thinking how to play it. I was thinking about if this truly was the end of Douglas digging around. If this young bronc would finally let it go or if he'd keep bucking. I thought about what to say to Debra. After a little while, I got up and tossed the notepad in the waste bin.

**

The mayor of Well Springs at the time – a nice man named David Ergon – came to me asking if I had an opinion about Fourth of July. I told him that I enjoyed it, not really knowing what he was getting at.

Apparently, he was all worked up about whether it was appropriate with all them fireworks – considering what had happened. I suppose it ain't make me a *conscientious* person that the thought never crossed my mind. Would people be spooked hearing all them bangs and booms going off? Probably not. Then I thought about Debra. Maybe the town would welcome a nice firework show, but how would Debra and the children like it? Would they have that shell shock?

I told the mayor I thought it best that Well Springs has itself a nice firework show. We was coming outta the fog of everything with Sam and it could be a nice boost for the people. I was on the fence about talking with Debra. I didn't know if it would come off insulting – saying they'd be scared of some regular old fireworks. But a little after the talk with the mayor, Douglas shared his little theory about Debra.

I figured I might as well go talk to her. Kill two birds with one stone, and all.

Debra was living at the house – the kids was still staying with the Doyles – so I went and knocked on her door. She answered in a t-shirt and shorts.

"Sheriff," she said. "How're you?"

"I'm just fine, Debra, do you mind if I come in?"

"Of course," she said, motioning me inside.

I took my hat off as I walked inside and we sat in the living room. She asked if I wanted some sweet tea and I told her I wouldn't be long. She had this concerned look at her face.

"Is something wrong, Sheriff?" she said.

"No, no. I was only checking in. How you holdin' up?"

"Good as I can be, I suppose."

"And the little ones?"

"They're still living next door. Fred and Helen have been so good."

"Bless them," I said. "Bless them. You got everything you need? You need any help around here?"

"I think we're all set, Sheriff. Thank you."

"You know Fourth of July is coming up."

"Is it?"

"Yes ma'am."

"I'll be honest, sometimes I lose track of what day it is."

"My goodness. Well, yes, the Fourth is coming up."

"That oughta be fun for the town."

"How you think you gonna handle that? The explosions and whatnot?"

"I haven't thought of that."

"My granddaddy, he was in the Great War. The first one. I know he come back a little shaken up. A little on edge with things."

"Is that right?"

"You been through a lot, Debra. No shame if the fireworks make you feel a certain way."

"Well, they're just fireworks, Sheriff."

"That's right. That's right. Just fireworks. I'm hoping all them booms and bangs, you know, don't make you think about that night."

"I understand."

"I ain't wanna get you all scared, Debra. Just something I was thinking about. If you wanna stay over at our house, to sorta get through it, you are more than welcome."

"Thank you, Sheriff. I think I should be fine."

"One other thing I gotta talk to you about," I said after a long pause.

"Yes?"

"Well, this one is a bit trickier."

"What's wrong?"

211

"I ain't know if you met him yet, but we got a younger fella on the force – name's Arthur."

"Arthur what?"

"Oh, Arthur is his last name, sweetheart. Douglas Arthur."

"Douglas Arthur?"

"Yes ma'am."

"The name sounds familiar."

"Well, there was a famous general from World War II. Douglas MacArthur."

"Maybe that's it."

"He's a young kid. Good kid. Anyway, he was talking to me the other day about Sam's case."

"Okay."

"He starts talking and talking and he starts saying things about you."

"About me?"

"Yes ma'am. He starts talking like I oughta talk to you more."

"Talk to me how? Is that why you're here?"

"Well, in a way. He was saying if I asked if it was you that done it."

There was this silence that swept over the room. We both sat there quiet as a couple of scared mice. She started scratching her left palm – something that I noticed she does when she gets a bit nervous.

"What did you say?" she asked.

"I told him that it was a fanciful theory. That it was a hell of a thing for him to say."

"So what now?"

"I told him to let me take care of it. I'm the boss, and so forth. Hopefully, he understands that it ain't something I'm messing around with. However, if he gets a wild hair and decides to go off and start his own investigation, I didn't want you to be blindsided by it."

"He's going to come and talk to me about it?"

"No, no, I ain't saying that. I'm saying that if he does, I wanted you to be ready. I don't want him ambushing you and then you give something away."

"You're worried about *me* giving something away?"

"I ain't saying that, neither."

"Sheriff, why is he coming around asking questions? I thought we said the story was good. How many people know?"

"Debra, I don't wanna get you all worked up. I ain't saying he said it was you. He was just bringing it up."

"How many people know about it?"

"Know about what?"

"About what Cody did."

"Just me, you, and him, to my knowledge."

"What about Maggie? She tell anybody?"

"I ain't even tell her, Debra."

"Are you telling the truth?"

"I am. I ain't tell a soul. You tell anybody?"

"Sheriff."

"You asked me, ma'am."

"No, I haven't told anybody," she said.

"Then looks like we don't got no problem."

"What should I say to him? If he talks to me?"

"You don't gotta tell him nothing. You tell him you already talked with me. You tell him you'd rather not relive it. That it was *traumatizing*. He ain't got no authority. Remember that. You tell him that I said you didn't have to talk to no one if you didn't want to."

"This is a nightmare," she said.

To this day, I ain't know if Douglas talked to her. I wouldn't put it past him. And I understand it. Young fella. If I look at it neutrally, as they say, I suppose it's an interesting case. Random killing of a fella in a small town. Lotta stuff ain't add up. Maybe if I was in his shoes, I'd have gone my own way and went to talk to Debra. Gotten at the truth. But he never told me nothing about going over there. And she never told me nothing about him sniffing around. Maybe it happened and they both ain't tell me.

But as long as either one of them lived in Well Springs, I knew the whole thing was trouble waiting to happen.

**

Around late October, I saw Henry Jenkins at the grocery store. He looked pretty rough, but he always did so it ain't concern me none at the time. He and Loretta didn't go to Sam's funeral, so it was the first time I seen Henry in quite some time. We was around the same age – went to school together and so forth. Henry's daddy was a mean old bastard. Terrible. His daddy was a drunk and ended up dying pretty young. Don't know if he even made fifty. Liver failure or some deal. Nobody cried much when he went under, though. Just a mean, sour man.

And well, you know what they say about the apple.

"How you doing Henry?" I asked when we crossed paths at the grocery store. His cart was full of those big rum bottles. Like he was hosting a Super Bowl party. Or he was fixing to drink 'til everything turned black for good.

"Hey George, I'm doing okay, how are you?" he said.

"Can't complain. How's Loretta doing?"

"She's fine."

"Good. That's good to hear."

"Yes sir."

"Well, listen I know we had a couple of leads come in," I said. "Maybe it'll crack the case and we'll find the guy."

"Who?" Henry asked.

214

"Whoever killed him," I said.

"Killed who? What in the hell are you talking about, George?"

"Sam. The man who killed Sam, Henry."

"Oh, that's right. Well, that's good. I hope you find him."

"You doing okay, Henry? I ain't see you at the funeral. You holding up?"

"Yeah, I'm okay, George."

"I'm sorry for your loss, by the way."

"Well, what are you gonna do, you know?" he said.

"I suppose. If there's anything Maggie or me can do for y'all, please let us know."

"Aren't you just a peach," he said. "I do got something I wanna run by you."

"And what's that?"

"I know they ain't start the season off right, but I got a good feeling about these Cowboys," he said, his face lighting up. "It's a hell of a team Jimmie's got."

"I suppose, Henry."

"I'm telling you, and remember that you heard it here first: they're gonna win it again this year."

"Hope you're right, Henry. I hope you're right. Well, you take care."

He smiled and then drove his cart away. I remember him pushing the cart made the glass bottles clink together. Nobody loves football and the Cowboys more than me, but that moment always struck me. It was the last thing I ever heard him say. Talking about football. I never heard him say a word about his boy.

Loretta died first few weeks into 1994. Car crash. What we think happened was she dosed off on whatever pills she was taking. She was on the highway outside of town – why, nobody knows – and she went off the road and flipped her car. Terrible. She was a sweet woman. Really

215

was. She just fell into those pills. Never got out. Apparently, Henry didn't wanna have a funeral for her. I tried calling over there a few times and never got an answer. Even drove over and knocked on the door and didn't get no answer. Man lost a son and then lost his wife.

Like a couple of dominos.

It weren't that long after Loretta died that they found Henry. He was laying face-up on his kitchen floor. Shirt opened wide with his belly plopped out. There was so many daggum rum bottles. They was all stacked perfectly in the corner, like he had a system or something. We never found no note, but who would he be writing? We wondered around the station about his dying. Was he a drunk and things got away from him one night? Or did he decide it was time to check out – drink and drink and hope his body took care of the rest?

He died before the Super Bowl – never got to see the Cowboys beat the Bills again.

It's a terrible thing. It was a rough stretch for the town. You know, they talk about the Cremble Curse, or what-have-you, but that Jenkins family ain't exactly got it great. Granted, all of those were … I don't know if *self-inflicted* is the right word. I know a lotta people around here sorta felt, *Good riddance*. I always felt bad for the family, though. There was a dark cloud over that family from the get-go. They never could shake it.

One thing I never did talk to Debra about: I always wondered if she would change her last name and the last names of the children. Call them Adams. Couldn't blame her, wanting to get away from that Jenkins name. It never made sense to me why she ain't do it. Maybe she thought it would be *suspicious* or some kinda nonsense. Make people think she killed him if she up and changed her name.

Even after all these years, though, she never did change it. Wouldn't you wanna change it? Call yourself Debra Adams. He coulda been Cody Adams. Get a fresh start.

**

By Thanksgiving 1993, things had calmed down. This was before Loretta and Henry died. People got back to regular life in Well Springs. Nobody really asked much about the case no more. Even Doug Darren – he ran the paper back then – stopped asking me about it. He used to call me every day. And I mean that. Every day.

"Sheriff, any news in the case?" he'd say.

"No sir," I'd tell him. "Doug, I will let you know when something happens. You don't gotta call me every doggone day."

"I'm just doing my job," he would say.

Every day for months I'd get those calls. Then he called every few days. By Thanksgiving, he was on to other things. Well Springs had a pretty good football team that year, so the fall months took up a lotta energy for the paper. It was nice for the town to be excited about something again. The team gave everybody something good to talk about.

We had such a wonderful Thanksgiving. Probably my favorite day of the year. I invited Debra and the children over to our house for Thanksgiving dinner. I wanted to make sure they wasn't alone. But she said they was having Thanksgiving with the Doyles, so it was all right. I ate so much I was stuffed more than the turkey. We sat around enjoying the company. My old man and I was watching the Cowboys after dinner – that was the blizzard game. Dallas against Miami. So much snow it looked like they was playing in Minnesota or something. The Cowboys was up early against the Dolphins and he turned to me.

"Anything going on with that Jenkins case?" he said.

"Nothing much," he said.

"It's a queer case," he said. "Such an odd thing."

"Yeah, I'm trying to be optimistic, but I don't know," I said.

217

I thought about if I shoulda told him – one lawman to another. He woulda understood, I think. If ever there was somebody I could tell, it woulda been my old man – Sheriff William Cremble. But I made a promise to Debra. I told her that I wouldn't tell a soul. If something got out, it weren't gonna come from me. So instead of telling him the truth, I kept to my story.

"Seems like some of the facts of the case don't add up," he said, sipping his bourbon.

"I been trying to make heads or tails outta it since the night it happened."

"You think it was a robbery gone wrong?"

"It make the most sense don't it?" I said. "Debra said she ain't recognize the man. So why would a stranger come into some house if not to rob it?"

"I suppose."

We didn't talk much for a while after that. Just watched the game. Emmitt Smith got hurt during the game for Dallas and I believe Dan Marino wasn't even playing for Miami. The Cowboys was winning 14-7 at halftime, I remember. But in the second half, the Dolphins kicked a couple of field goals. Got us a little nervous.

My old man went to fill up his glass and got himself a slice of pecan pie.

"Debra said she ain't recognize him, huh?" he said, sitting back down.

"That's right."

"You think it's straight?" he said.

"What she's saying?" I asked.

"Yes sir."

"I think so. She ain't got no reason to lie," I said.

"I don't know, son. I don't wanna tell you your job and it ain't my place, but some things don't add up."

"Is that right?"

"Why would the robber go into the bedroom? I ain't ever hear of anything like that."

"Maybe he was hopped up on something, you know? Man like that don't got the sense he was born with."

"I suppose. You'd think a man like that would leave a clue or something. There's nothing?"

"Wish there were. It'd make it a whole lot easier."

"It's a terrible thing," he said. "Just a terrible thing."

You may remember how the game played out. The Cowboys blocked the Dolphins' last-second field goal – had the game won – and then our lineman Leon Lett went and touched the ball and gave Miami another shot. We couldn't believe it. The Cowboys had it and gave it away. They was in the clear and blew it. Stoyanovich kicked another field goal for the Dolphins – made it this time – and just like that the game was over. The Cowboys lost by two points. A total embarrassment. We sat there and talked about the game for a little while before dad brought up the case again.

"I don't know about this case," he said.

"It's a tricky one," I said.

"Georgie, I'll ask you one time and then I'll leave it alone for good."

"Shoot."

"Are you doing the right thing?" he asked.

"I believe I am," I said.

"Well, all right then," he said. He finished the rest of the bourbon and got up and went into the kitchen.

**

A little more than a year after Sam died, Douglas comes into my office holding his hat and asking if we could talk. Them was words I never liked hearing from him. It meant he was up to something or wanted to talk about the case. I told him I had some things to take care of, but he said it wouldn't take but a minute. I nodded and motioned to the chair in front of my desk and he come and sat down. It was just the two of us.

"Sheriff, you know how much I appreciate everything you've done for me," he said.

"It ain't nothing," I said. "What's going on?"

"Nobody knows about this yet, but I wanted to tell you before word got around."

My heart started racing a bit. He probably went and talked with Debra or something. Maybe he went and grilled her and got the truth out – maybe not the truth, but got her confessing to the killing. He ain't said much to me about the case in a while, so it looked like he was doing it on his own time. Digging around like a hound, building up a case.

"And what's that?" I said.

"I got myself a job in Santa Fe."

"Well, hot dog!" I said, relieved like you ain't believe. "Congratulations, Douglas! Ain't that a hoot."

"Thank you, Sheriff. I don't want it to seem like I didn't like working for you. It's just Well Springs – well it's hard to meet people. Santa Fe is probably a little more suited for somebody at my stage in life."

"Douglas, you ain't gotta explain nothing. That's a wonderful opportunity. Shoot. I'm excited for you, son."

"Thank you, Sheriff."

"When you leaving?"

"End of the month."

"End of the month. How about that? Well, we oughta throw you some kinda shindig."

"That's not necessary, Sheriff."

"Oh, my bare ass it ain't necessary, Douglas. We gotta celebrate."

The day before he left, we had a fun little party at the office. There was a lotta food and even more booze. I never seen Douglas drink so much in my life. Didn't know he had it in him. But he was laughing and joking and everything was a nice time. I had a few beers but I knew it weren't my place to go off the deep end, you know. In the middle of all the festivities, Douglas comes over and talks to me as drunk as a skunk.

"Sheriff Cremble," he laughed.

"Looks like you're having a whale of a time, son," I said.

"Thank you for doing – for putting this whole thing, uh, together," he said with a great big smile.

"You deserve it. I liked having you here in Well Springs."

"Aren't you just kinder than a ... than a – I don't know what the expression is. But you're very kind, Sheriff."

"Anything in this small little town you're actually gonna miss?" I asked.

"You know what I will, what I will remember about Well Springs?"

"What's that?"

"That damn case."

"The case?"

"The Jenkins case. It's such an odd one."

"Yeah, every day I wonder if we'll ever find the man who done it."

"That's the thing, Sheriff," he said, his eyes getting big. "That's the thing. I really looked at this thing from all angles and I gotta tell you, I think it stinks."

"Of course it stinks, a man lost his life."

"I don't mean stinks like that. Like, *aw shucks*. I mean it stinks like stuff don't add up."

"Come on, Douglas. We've been throu–"

"Yeah, yeah, yeah. We've been through it. I'm telling you Sheriff. You oughta take another look. Why would he go into the bedroom? Why

221

would he, you know, why would he choose that house to rob? Why would–"

"Douglas, why don't you enjoy the party instead of worrying about all this? We'll find him."

"That's the thing! That's the thing, Sheriff!"

"What's that?"

"I don't even know if there is a *him*." He leaned in so he could whisper. "I bet you anything *she* killed him. I think she killed him and she's spoon-feeding you BS about it."

"I don't know about that."

"Talk to her again. Talk to her again, Sheriff. See what she says. See if her story is the same. I bet you anything there's gonna be holes in it. I know I'm an outsider or whatever, but I think Sam kept beating her and eventually she had enough of it and blew his ass to hell. Then made up some story about a stranger robbing them. I'm telling you, Sheriff."

"That's a hell of a story, Douglas. I think you oughta worry about Santa Fe now."

"I don't understand, Sheriff," he said, with a puzzled look.

"Don't understand what?"

"I know it's not my place, especially not now, but why can't you see it? It seems as plain as day, and it seems like you *want* to believe it was some stranger. That nobody in this town could kill somebody."

"You better watch what you're saying, son."

"I don't mean no disrespect. Honest, I don't. And I know I'm leaving so my opinion doesn't matter. But it seems so obvious that I wonder why you don't want to turn that rock over. It's like you're fine accepting that story and chasing a ghost for the rest of your life. It's like your protecting her or something."

"When a woman sees her husband shot and killed in front of her eyes, it ain't exactly good practice going around pointing your finger into her chest and accusing her of killing him."

"But you're the police, Sheriff. That's what you're supposed to do, ain't it?"

"Douglas, my job is to protect this town. And that's what I'm doing. I'm *protecting* Well Springs."

"I see," he said after a while. He sorta scratched his chin, looked me up and down, then nodded. "I understand. Well, all right then."

Chapter Thirteen

Captain Douglas Arthur

t was her, wasn't it?

Debra.

Do you know? Has it come out?

When you called me about this, I hoped you had some news.

I always thought it was her. I've been in Santa Fe for some twenty-five years now and I always wondered if it would ever come out what really happened in that case. If the official story always was a stranger came into the Jenkins house and killed Sam Jenkins. Maybe I'm being a bit dismissive, because there's a chance that's what *actually* happened. I'd feel bad for Sheriff Cremble if that was the case, because I'm sure over the years people in Well Springs had their doubts about the official story. Or maybe in a town like that, you just believe and move on.

I was only in Well Springs for about a year or so. People there were friendly. Some fine people living there, but I never made any deep connections. Nobody for me to call and see if there was news in the case over the years. Nobody to tell me it came out that Debra confessed or maybe somebody she knew killed Sam on her behalf. Whenever I looked at the newspaper, I'd see if there was any news out of Well Springs.

To Sheriff Cremble's credit, there never was. Not once.

People on my unit in Santa Fe gave me a hard time when I started because I kept bringing up the case in Well Springs.

"You wanna head back to Well Springs and figure it out?" they'd tell me. "Because we got enough to worry about here in Santa Fe, we don't really care about crimes in the middle of nowhere."

They had a point. I came to Santa Fe and I was excited to get out of Well Springs because it was too small for a young man. Not much to do. I was happier than anything when I landed the gig here, but I couldn't let go of the case. I remember I was on a date shortly after getting to Santa Fe. When I told her what I did, she asked me about it and then I went into this big long talk about the Jenkins case. She was a little put off and asked how such a thing could happen in Sante Fe, and I had to tell her it was back when I lived in a small town in Texas. I went on and on, and how I was skeptical and thought the official story wasn't what happened.

There wasn't a second date.

Over the years, I learned to shut up about Well Springs. I'd always have my questions, but I suppose they would always be that: questions. Then you wanted to talk to me. I couldn't believe it. I was waiting forever to talk about everything that happened and I was hoping you found out.

**

Well Springs is an interesting town.

I grew up in El Paso and, while that city has grown quite a bit over the years, it was still a pretty decent size – maybe 300,000 people – when I was a kid. It was a bit of a shock arriving in Well Springs, which was around 5,000 at the time. Maybe a little bigger, maybe a little smaller. I was young and looking for a job and Well Springs was the first one to send me an offer. I was engaged at the time and she said she wasn't interested in being a cop's wife – especially if it meant moving to the middle of nowhere. We broke up right then and there.

I was young and I knew what I wanted to do with my life – there'd be other women. Once I moved to Well Springs, I really never thought much about the break-up and if I made the right choice or if I should have stayed with her. There weren't any sleepless nights or any of that stupidity. I made my decision and moved on with my life.

The day I moved to Well Springs, Sheriff Cremble came by as I was carrying things from my truck into the small house I was renting.

"Welcome to Well Springs," he said.

"Sheriff, how are you doing?" I asked.

"I do believe I should be the one asking you that, son," he said. "You're here so you must not have gotten too spooked about coming to such a tiny town like Well Springs."

"I'm excited to meet everybody here, it's got that small town charm," I said.

"Is that what city folk call it?" he said with a little smirk. "Lemme tell you what, why don't you take a break and I'll take you out to lunch. The Fox Hole makes a mean patty melt."

"That's very kind but you don't have to, Sheriff."

"Now, now. Consider this my first order. I ain't wanna hear no debate on this one. All your stuff will still be here when we get back. Hop on in."

He walked to his truck and when I didn't follow him, he gestured with his head to the truck. I locked my front door and then headed over to his truck.

"You city folk," Sheriff Cremble laughed as I got in and buckled my seatbelt.

"What's that supposed to mean?" I smiled.

"Always locking your doors. Scared of your neighbors. Hopefully we'll scrub that outta you."

"I didn't mean anything by it," I said. "Force of habit, I suppose."

"I'm only giving you a hard time, son. I understand. I hope you will learn the hospitality of small-town Texas. You'll meet some of the sweetest people around."

We went to the Fox Hole and I had the patty melt. Everyone in town always rants and raves about the Fox Hole's patty melt, but to be honest, it was only okay. I never had the heart to tell people they didn't know what a good patty melt was. But it was the first time Sheriff Cremble and I ever sat down and talked about life. There was the job interview, but I was so nervous and it was pretty quick. I think he was surprised somebody wanted to come to Well Springs to fill the spot, so I got the job pretty easily.

"You got yourself a woman?" he said when we were eating.

"Had one."

"Past tense."

"Yes sir."

"She ain't think much of moving here, huh?"

"Something like that."

"You trying to have that kinda life right now?" he asked.

"I don't know."

"I imagine Well Springs is gonna be a bit hard for a young man like yourself," he said. "Me? I was born and raised here. Wife, too. There ain't a whole lotta singles your age. Is that gonna be a problem?"

"Well, I was engaged."

"I see."

"So, I think I'm okay being on my own for a little while. I wanna learn as much as I can about the job."

"That's good, but it's important to remember that work ain't everything, son. You focus so much on work and you'll miss out on life."

"Yes sir."

"I ain't wanna give you a Sunday morning sermon on your first day in Well Springs, though. I am glad you decided to come to our humble little town. I think you'll do some good and I can teach you everything I know."

"What would you say is the most important part of the job?"

"The most important part of this job?"

"Yes sir."

"Well, that's a mighty fine question, Douglas. I suppose the most important thing about this job is what my daddy taught me – he was the sheriff before me. He used to always tell me no matter what happens in this job, I gotta make sure I do what I believe is right and true. Never lose track of what is right."

"Do situations come up a lot here where you gotta remind yourself of that?"

"Meaning is there a lot of action here?"

"I suppose."

"Unfortunately for you, not much, no. I know being a young man, you probably wanna get mixed up in some action. Me? I'm perfectly fine if everything stays nice and calm."

"Then why is that the most important part of the job?"

"What do you mean?"

"Why is remembering to do the right thing the most important part of the job if things are always nice and quiet?"

"I suppose that's another good question. Just because nothing much happens don't mean there won't be a time when something does. And when something happens, I need to make sure I do the right thing."

"That's good. I guess it would be rude of me to come to Well Springs and hope something bad happens to make things interesting."

"And if I was a young man from the city, I might feel the way you feel: you want something *interesting* to happen. I can say that no matter what happens or don't happens, I want you to know it's important for me Well Springs police does the right thing. Do you understand?"

"I do, Sheriff."

"And how you like your patty melt?" he asked.

"It's really good."

**

I had been on the job for two months before everything went down with Sam Jenkins. Maybe six weeks. It wasn't long, but not much happened in that time. I was settling in to my new home, trying to meet as many folks as I could. Lots of meeting people and telling them my story. Learning names. Learning who were the "big shots" of the town – if you could call them that. There wasn't much that actually happened, though, in terms of the job.

Sheriff Cremble was showing me the ropes, telling stories of a few things that had happened and what he'd done. How there was some drunk man that started some stuff in town one day. They weren't exactly war stories, but they were better than nothing. They gave me some hope that *something* would happened.

It was either Easter Monday or maybe the next day, but I came into the office and Sheriff Cremble was sitting by the front desk and he looked really tired. Bags under his eyes. His hat was on the desk.

"Sheriff, you have a long night or something? You look tired."

"Douglas, I had a long night all right."

"What happened? Is everything okay?"

"Something bad happened at the Jenkins house."

"Sam Jenkins?"

"Yes sir."

"What happened?"

"He got killed."

"Oh my God," I said.

"Terrible thing. Terrible."

"What happened?"

"Robbery gone wrong, it looks like."

"At Sam Jenkins place? Somebody robbed them?"

"Yes sir."

"Who was it? Do we know who did it?" I asked.

"Not yet."

"Any witnesses?"

"Just Debra."

"That's his wife, right? Is she all right? Don't they have a lot of kids?"

"Four of them, yeah. She's holding up. I've had them here all night. Wanted to get them outta that house."

"Good thinking. Nobody else saw anything? Where did they find him?"

"In his bed."

"He shot Sam in the bedroom? And it was a robbery?"

"Yes sir. Debra said she's never seen the man before."

"She got a good look?"

"Not great. She went hiding in the corner once he started shooting. Says everything went fuzzy."

"Nobody else saw anything?" I asked. "You'd think gunshots would wake up the neighbors."

"Fred Doyle, who lives next door, was the one that called it in."

"And he didn't see anything?"

"No sir."

"My God. I can't believe it."

We both sat there for a while. I could tell Sheriff Cremble was exhausted. Me? My mind was racing. This was a real, honest-to-goodness crime. Breaking and entering. Murder. Somebody on the run. Manhunt. I don't like to admit it, but it was exciting. That's why I got into this line of work. I would never wish harm on a soul, but it's hard not to want some action.

I was thinking all about life in Well Springs. Over the short time I had been there, I started to not lock my doors, either. It's something you didn't do. And now Sheriff Cremble is sitting there telling me some stranger came through town and murdered somebody.

And when all of that went down, that's initially what I thought happened. Maybe it was youthful ignorance. Maybe it was the shock of something drastic happening in the small town. Maybe it was because I wanted it to happen. I wanted my first big case.

Whatever the reason, I thought a random stranger had killed Sam Jenkins.

**

Sheriff Cremble kept everything real close to the vest. He said because he was the one to find Debra in that room, he wanted to take it on himself. He would shoo-shoo you if you asked him if he wanted any help. A lot of people around town asked me about the case. Asked if there were any leads or if I knew anything. For those who didn't ask, you could tell they wanted to ask. There was this big cloud over the town. You could feel it wherever you went. I had to tell people that Sheriff Cremble was the man on the job and he was sure to find the killer.

I believe it was a Friday evening, I had to swing by Sheriff Cremble's house because I wanted to talk to him about something. I don't remember what. I headed over and as I got closer, I saw Debra Jenkins' car parked in his driveway. As I pulled up, I saw Debra at the Crembles' front door and she was being really animated. Hands waving everywhere. She was upset about something. Sheriff Cremble looked out at me and saw I was parked out there. He put his hand on Debra's shoulder and led her into the house and he closed the door behind him.

I don't know how to describe it. It just felt *off*. That's the only way to explain it. Call it unquantifiable, but it didn't seem right. Something was up. I waited out there for a while because I didn't want to interrupt whatever was going on inside. After about 15 minutes, I could see Sheriff Cremble's head come into the window really quick before disappearing.

I believe he was looking to see if I was still there.

I stayed out there for, honestly, probably about an hour. I kept waiting for Debra to leave, but she never did. I kept waiting for Sheriff Cremble to come out and see what I wanted, but he never did. After I got sick of waiting, I drove off and decided to make an impromptu pit stop.

I drove over to the Jenkins house.

I stayed parked on the curb for a while – like I did at the Crembles. I looked at the house and thought for a while. I looked at the street. No tire marks, which I thought was a little odd. If somebody comes in and kills a random person and then wants to flee as fast as he could, it'd make sense to have some skid or tire marks. I looked back at the house.

Why would somebody rob this place?

It made no sense. It wasn't a dump, but you could tell that they were on the low-income side. It wasn't even convenient to rob. Their house was in the middle of the block, so you'd have neighbors all around that could hear any chaos. It was also in the middle of Well Springs. In order to skip town after the robbery, you'd have to drive through a good part of Well Springs. If you wanted to rob a random house in town, why not hit a house closer to the highway?

Knowing Debra was still at the Crembles, I got out and went to the front door. I heard the kids had been living next door since the murder, but to be safe, I knocked a few times. I waited and waited. Nothing. They had sidelight windows next to the front door, so I cupped my hands and looked into the house. Not a soul. I thought for a moment: should I go inside? I looked around to see if any neighbors saw me. Nothing. So I reached for the handle and put my shoulder on the front door to go inside.

But it was locked.

**

Sheriff Cremble never asked me why I showed up to his house.

I was waiting for him to ask, but he never did. I didn't bring it up, either. We both went about our lives. He was working on the Jenkins case and I was patrolling about town. Whenever I brought up the case, Sheriff Cremble squashed it right then and there. Always had a reason to not talk about it — about how it wasn't the right time. Maybe it was youthful angst, but it was infuriating Sheriff Cremble had the responsibility to work the biggest case in the town's history while I was walking around town picking up litter and saying hello to old ladies. What I was doing was a total waste of time, so why wouldn't it be good to help him a little bit? Being a fresh pair of eyes would have been a whole lot more useful than what I was doing.

As the days passed, I started to get a little pissed, to be honest. I still never overreached my rank and pushed on him. I ate the crap and smiled.

One night, after my shift, I was bored so I went to one of Well Springs' bar and grills. Forget the name. I had some dinner and a few beers at a booth off on my own. This would have been maybe late May or early June. Probably six weeks or two months after Sam was killed.

Then Rhett Vernon walks over.

Rhett was known around town for being a real piece of work. I believe he left his family but didn't leave town, if I remember correctly.

Basically moved a few houses down. He was a bigger guy, but thankfully I never had any problem with him. I knew he was friends with Sam.

"How's it going?" he said.

"Hey Rhett, how are you?"

"Pretty good, you want some company?"

"Feel free," I said, motioning to the other side of the booth. He sat down and had a beer and a bourbon – one in each hand. He took a drink of the bourbon and then washed it down with the beer.

"How's the case?" he said.

"Wish I knew."

"They ain't bring you up to the big leagues yet?" he smirked.

"Not yet. Sheriff Cremble really wants this one all for himself, apparently."

"Bit odd, isn't it?"

"A little bit."

"Why wouldn't he want help? Ain't that how it works? All hands on deck?"

"You would think, wouldn't you?

"You got any theories?" he said, taking a drink from the bourbon and then the beer.

"Oh, I don't know."

"Come on, don't BS me. What do you think? You gotta have some thoughts."

"Why? You got thoughts?" I asked, drinking from my beer.

"I got thoughts, all right."

"Hit me. Maybe I'll send it along."

"Very funny."

"What do you think, though?"

"Well, are we talking? Or are we *talking*?" Rhett asked.

"Depends what you say. You know something?"

"I don't know nothing. I got some thoughts, but I don't know nothing."

"And what are those thoughts?"

"I think a lot of this smells like crap stacked six feet tall," he said.

"Such as?"

"How much you know what happened?"

"I know a stranger tried to rob the place and shot Sam."

"And you believe that?"

"Not necessarily. Why you say that?"

"Damn, son. Do I know more about the case than you?"

"What do you know?"

"Maybe I should be asking what do *you* know?" he said with a smile.

"If we're being straight: not much. I know the shooter is somebody Debra didn't recognize and how they found Sam's body."

"How's that?"

"What do you mean?"

"How'd they find Sam?" he asked, intrigued.

"Body slumped on the back corner of the bed. Right shoulder against the wall, with him on his right side. Left hand dangling off the side of the bed."

"Damn."

"Yeah, I got a look at the photos once. Lot of blood. Whoever shot him didn't want him coming back."

"That's another thing that don't add up," Rhett said, shaking his head.

"What?"

"How they found him. Like that."

"How do you mean?" I asked.

"In the back corner of the bed."

"The robber apparently came into the bedroom, and then he—"

"I'm not even gonna touch that one – why the hell would a burglar go into a bedroom? – but why would his body be back there like that?"

"I don't understand what you're getting at."

"Damn, son," he said, taking another drink of his bourbon and beer. "That's a *defensive* position."

"And? I mean, if the guy's got a gun pointed at him, it would make sense."

"I know you ain't from here, but I'll tell you: Sam was a lot of things, but he wasn't no coward. Some stranger is in his bedroom, there's no chance he's gonna just *sit there*."

"What do you think he would have done?"

"He woulda tried to take him down. Which, okay, he probably still gets his ass killed – but he ain't laying dead in the back corner of the bed."

"Meaning?"

"I got two theories," Rhett said, holding up two fingers before putting one of them down. "The first is they shot Sam when he was still sleeping. It would explain why he was back there. They shot him and he struggled to get up and they kept shooting him until he was dead."

"Plausible."

"Yeah, but why in the holy hell would you kill a man if you wanted to rob the place? Just to kill him? Then why not kill her too? A lot of things don't make sense with that."

"And what's your other theory?"

"Maybe he knew the shooter."

"But Debra said she didn't recognize the person."

"So she says. But if he knew the shooter, that would explain why he didn't lunge at them. It wouldn't be his instinct if he knew them. Maybe he thought he could sweettalk himself out of it. But for whatever reason, they shot him. That would explain a lot about the case. If he knew the shooter."

"But Debra said she didn't recognize the person."

"Maybe she's lying."

"That's quite the theory."

"Maybe she was the one to ice him."

"You think?"

"Maybe. Or she knew who killed him and she's covering for the shooter by making up some garbage about a robbery," he said, before finishing off his bourbon. "But what do I know?"

**

I thought a lot about the case during that time. About everything. It's ridiculous that a deputy tried to piece together a case as a hobby. But I wanted to build everything before bringing it to Sheriff Cremble, because he was so protective of the case I needed to add some meat to that sandwich. I had this notepad that had all my notes – unanswered questions, maps, potential people to talk to. Everything.

After the bar talk with Rhett, I started being a little *friendlier* around town. I'd talk to people about how nice everyone was since I moved and then, of course, the conversation would find its way to Sam Jenkins and the case. I don't remember their names, but I was in line at the deli talking with a couple of ladies about it.

"Terrible thing," I'd say.

"I can't believe it Deputy," one of them said.

"Please, call me Douglas."

"Douglas, do y'all have any leads yet? Do you know who did it?" she asked.

"No ma'am, unfortunately."

"Terrible, just terrible!" the other said.

"You ladies haven't heard anything, have you?" I asked.

"We heard it was a burglar from outta town that had done it, is that true?" the first woman said.

"Is that true?" the second woman said.

"That's what Sheriff Cremble believes, yes," I said.

"I don't want to gossip," the first woman said.

"Don't you dare," the second woman said to her.

"I won't!" the first woman said.

"What? What have you heard?" I asked.

"Don't you go flapping your lips with that nonsense," the second woman said. "He's a deputy!"

"Ladies, ladies. What's this *nonsense* you heard?"

"I heard it was her," the first woman whispered.

"Her?" I asked.

"Debra," she whispered, leaning toward me.

The second woman hit the first woman in the shoulder with her purse.

"You are the worst person on Earth, you know that?" the second woman said.

"It's what I heard, is all!" the first woman said.

"You heard it was her that did it?" I asked. She nodded.

"He was a real piece of work," the first woman said. "Would get drunk and act like a beast. He didn't deserve her. Am I wrong?"

"No, but you shouldn't be saying things like this," the second woman said.

"Well, maybe it's what happened. Maybe he was hitting her and she took matters into her own hands. Isn't that possible?" the first woman said.

"It's absolutely possible," I said.

"Don't listen to her nonsense, deputy!" the second woman said. "That sorta thing wouldn't happen here in Well Springs. We don't go around shooting and killing each other."

"Maybe you're right," the first woman said.

"You shouldn't be spreading rumors about Debra. Terrible," the second woman said.

"But it's possible," I said. The first woman nodded. The second woman didn't say anything or shake her head. "So it's possible."

I worked on the case without really knowing much of the important details regarding the night of the murder. It was exhilarating and after a little while, I had everything ready to come to Sheriff Cremble about it. I went in and cornered him and told him I wanted to talk. He could tell I meant business, so we went into his office. I went through all the holes in the case. I went through all the things he should be looking into. I went through everything. Then he accused me of trying to use the case to land a better job. I told him Debra Jenkins might be lying to him.

Then he ended it right then.

I could tell no matter what, he wouldn't bring me in on this one. I was furious. This was early summer 1993. I spent the rest of the year applying to different jobs. I had to get out of there. Over time, the town sort of moved on. Nobody really cared anymore. It was really bizarre. Football season started. Then it was Christmas. Then the New Year. They didn't have any memorial on the anniversary of his death. No cross. No flowers. Nothing. It was just *Tuesday*.

In late April 1994, I got word I had been hired by Santa Fe.

To his credit, Sheriff Cremble was real nice about everything. They threw me this party and I got so drunk I hardly remembered anything from it. To this day, I hope I didn't say anything embarrassing or insult the town when I was in the bag. But the day after that, I packed up my car and headed west.

239

Goodbye Well Springs.

**

I'm pretty happy with how my life turned out. Found myself a woman, Hannah, who didn't mind being a cop's wife. We got a girl, Ariel, who's heading to college next year. I've been in Santa Fe ever since leaving Well Springs. It's a nice sized town. Big enough to get some action, but small enough that we don't got the crimes that make you lose hope in humanity.

I got a good life.

Over time, I stopped bringing up the Jenkins case with the other guys. The more I was on the job, the less I thought about the case. But truthfully, it was always in the back of my mind. I always wondered. I'd look for the news and it never came.

About five years after Sam Jenkins' murder, a case popped up here in Santa Fe. A wife killed her husband and tried to pin it on a drifter. It didn't work. They quickly destroyed her story and she admitted to killing him. Everything happened in the span of a few days. Her story crumbled fast. It made me think of Well Springs and if I should give Sheriff Cremble a call. See how everything's going with the case.

I never did. I left it alone.

Few years after that, a buddy from my childhood was getting married in Dallas, so I made that trek. I thought about flying, but I decided to drive. If I'm being honest, it's because I wanted to take a peek in Well Springs. The wedding gave me an excuse, I suppose. I wanted to stop in and check things out.

It was a long drive across that desert to get to Well Springs. Felt spooky being back, driving around town. Everything looked the same. No new businesses. No new restaurants. School looked the same. It looked like I had never left – a town frozen in time.

I drove by the station and I recognized Sheriff Cremble's truck in the lot. He was still doing it.

I drove over to the Jenkins place, parked across the street and a few houses down. The whole family was outside. They were having a water balloon fight. The boys were big. The oldest one had to be in high school and was built really solid – probably played football for Well Springs. The youngest would have maybe been in junior high. The twin girls were both teenagers now. They were all yelling and screaming and laughing.

Debra was sitting on the front porch, watching the kids playing all around the yard. Eventually, the youngest boy got pelted with a water balloon so hard that he slipped and fell. Debra jumped off her chair and asked if he was all right and when the boy started laughing, she started laughing too. The boy got up, went over to the bucket of water balloons and started walking over to Debra and she's yelling at him, *Don't you dare*. He threw it at her and missed. Then she ran over to the bucket herself to grab a balloon and they all started running away from her. She was running around the house after them and they were all laughing. Just so happy.

I drove away and I've never been back.

I don't know for sure what happened, but if everybody in Well Springs was fine living life as usual, then who am I to disturb that? Everybody moved on with their lives. They got over it. Does the truth even matter at this point? I mean, really? Does it? That's how things played out because I believe that's the way people there wanted it to play out.

But I think it was her. I'm convinced of it. The only thing I don't know: did she fool Sheriff Cremble? Or was he in on it?

Chapter Fourteen

Fred Doyle

The children lived with us for about a year after their daddy died. They were such a well-behaved bunch, so we never had a problem. Besides, their mama lived next door so they knew not to act out. It was a nice deal. I always wondered why Debra didn't move, though. I was expecting it. Could you blame her? I'd want to get away from that mess if it was me.

No. She stayed in that house ever since.

Part of me was sad they didn't move because I knew it would have been a nice fresh start for them. But I always enjoyed having them live next door. Debra and the children were nothing but sunshine to me and Helen. I remember talking with Debra after everything happened, and we insisted the children live with us. At least until everything blows over. She agreed.

The first night they stayed over, though, I heard this loud crying in the middle of the night. Tommy. I wasn't sleeping all that great myself, so I was awake when he started howling and I jumped outta bed and hustled over to his room. When I got there, Cody was already there –

holding him tight. Tommy was still crying, but he wasn't shrieking anymore. That's one heck of a big brother, right there. I went over and sat down on the bed and started rubbing Tommy's back.

"I know, Tommy," I said. "I feel the same way."

"I'm scared," he cried.

"It's okay. Nobody is gonna hurt you, Tommy," I said.

"Is daddy gone?" he asked, his head still buried in Cody's chest.

"Yeah, Tommy," Cody said before I could answer. "He's gone."

"Forever?"

"Yeah. He's gone forever," Cody said.

Tommy kept whimpering. Cody acted like such a grown up. I remember that. It was real strange. It was like a father consoling a son. I didn't quite know what to say, so I didn't say anything. You don't always gotta *say something*. The three of us sat there for a good while before Helen came into the room and asked if everything was all right.

"Yes ma'am," Cody said. "Tommy was a bit scared, but I don't think he's scared anymore. Are you scared, Tommy?"

Tommy shook his head.

"Do you want to try and go back to sleep?" Cody asked.

Tommy nodded and so I got off the bed and Cody helped put him back down. We both took his blanket and covered him up. Cody kissed Tommy on the forehead and the three of us – Helen, Cody, and myself – left the room. When we were in the hallway, Helen went back to the bedroom and I got down on a knee.

"Cody, that was very grown up of you," I said.

"Well, Tommy was scared. I didn't want him to be scared."

"The way you handled that was very mature, Cody. Your mama would be very proud."

"Everything that happened was pretty scary for him. I hope he learns he doesn't have to be scared anymore."

"Cody, are you okay? Was it scary for you too?"

"Not really," he said.

"Wow, that's very brave of you. It was scary for me," I said.

"It was scary for you?"

"Yes, it was. I heard the gunshots going off. I was the one who called Sheriff Cremble. It was very scary. I didn't know if I should go over to your house and see if I could help."

He didn't respond. He shifted his eyes around, looking down the hallway and back to me.

"Are you okay, son?" I asked.

"I should probably check on the girls," Cody said.

**

When you're living in a town like Well Springs and something happens like Sam Jenkins' murder, it can be hard to put everything into perspective. When it happened, I kept waiting for the media to come. I was expecting news vans and all the national papers to infest our little town and make Well Springs known for this gruesome act. It felt like that Kansas family back in the day – the ones that got robbed and killed and it turned into this best seller. Nobody else felt that way – that a storm of attention was coming. A senseless murder in a quiet little town? I know the news loves that kinda stuff. They are never talking about the good in humanity. Always the evil. And our little town made for the perfect story.

But you know what happened?

Nothing. No news vans. No big city journalists coming to interview me about what happened that night. It was like it never happened. Only the Well Springs paper talked to me, but they asked less about what happened that night and more about how I was feeling about life in town after the murder.

I thank God that Well Springs didn't become this media circus. We were able to go about our lives. Although, I do wonder if the story got more attention, would we have found who did it? Would we have found the killer?

I don't know.

There was this dark cloud that hung over Well Springs in the aftermath of Sam's death. I couldn't believe it, but Helen and me actually locked our doors. We didn't like doing it, but it shook us up a bit. I listened to Sam being killed. Terrible. If some bad guy would target that house, what's to say he wouldn't target my house next? What's to say he wouldn't barge in at night and kill me or – even worse – hurt Helen? Call it silly all you want, but when it's your loved one's life, you'd probably lock your doors too.

When I first brought up locking the doors to Helen, I was expecting this big, long argument. How we can't turn our backs on our neighbors. How we can't let the fear of this senseless crime dictate our lives. How we'd be letting the actions of a stranger impact how we feel about those in town. How there is nothing Well Springs needed more than a sense of togetherness – to circle the wagons and show we wouldn't let tragedy change who we are.

But when I asked her how she felt about locking the doors, she just nodded.

We lived like that for weeks and weeks. Locking the door and looking over our shoulders. Then people started to move on. Life got back to normal. We had a good team that year – think they won 10 games – and that helped lift the burden from the town. Suddenly, people had something to talk about again. Conversations went from talking with people at the grocery store about the murder to talking about Well Springs High's game the coming week. I don't want to say the team saved the town, because that's a bit too much – but then again, maybe it's not. It helped us get back to normal.

And once we got back to normal, people were friendly again. Everyone unlocked their doors again. Well Springs got back to being Well Springs.

I suppose every wound needs time to heal, as they say. Sam's death was a wound for Well Springs. It hurt but time healed it up. Using that wound analogy, did it leave a scar? Does the town still have a scar from Sam Jenkins' murder?

I believe some people completely moved on from it. They'd never think about it again unless it's brought up. Sometimes I wonder how much of that is because Sam was the one who got killed. Is that what helped the town move on? I know Sam rubbed people the wrong way sometimes. I know people felt like he didn't treat Debra all that great. He had his demons – punching Pastor Wilheim and what-have-you. Is that why the town decided to forget about it? To forget about him?

Or maybe that's unfair of me – to assume everybody decided to forget about Sam. You can't know what people are thinking. Maybe they are sad about his death, but know it isn't worth letting it run their lives. There wasn't much for the town to do but grieve and move on and help the living.

But I always wondered if he was out there.

The killer.

After a while, I decided not to bother Helen about it. I would bring it up, talking about if we'll ever find out who did it. Or I'd read a story about a similar crime and tell her about it and you could tell it bothered her. She didn't want to hear about people killing people. Can't say I blamed her. Instead, I wondered to myself. I remember years after Sam's death, it would have been around Thanksgiving time, I saw Sheriff Cremble in the grocery store. We talked about our families and so forth before I decided to ask.

"Sheriff Cremble," I said. "I know it's not my place to ask, but you think we'll ever find who killed Sam Jenkins?"

"Oh, Fred," he said.

"I don't mean to pry at all. It's just, I don't know. You ever get any leads anymore?"

"Unfortunately, not much of a bite lately," he said.

"Terrible. You ever think about it?"

"I do, Fred. I think about it a lot."

"I still can't believe it."

"Yeah, but you know, I think Debra and the kids are doing good."

"Mighty good," I said. "I can't imagine what it must have been like for her. And the children, too."

"You know, that's why I think it's important to not drag them back into it," he said. "They're moving on with their lives and I think that's what we all should do."

"Don't you have to always try and catch the man who did it, though?"

"Fred, I'll spend the rest of my life thinking about this case," he said, putting his hand on my shoulder. "I got it covered, though. I think the best thing for you to do is go about your life. There ain't no point in worrying about a dead man when you could be loving the living."

**

There was some suspicion following Sam's death that somebody from Well Springs killed him. Rumors. The sorta thing that could tear a town apart. Word finally got out it was somebody Debra didn't recognize. That it wasn't anybody from Well Springs. I was mighty grateful for that, because I couldn't think what life would be like knowing somebody here had it in him to murder a man.

There was also gossip, which I didn't appreciate at all, that you know – Debra.

Helen was at the beauty salon and they'd all get to talking about what happened and how one of them heard Debra was the one to kill him. How they wouldn't have blamed her if she did because he didn't treat her right. How she deserved better. How they wouldn't waste the energy to shed any tears if she had done it. They'd do the same thing.

I remember when Helen came back home and told me.

"Who said that?" I asked.

"Some of the ladies," Helen said.

"Who?"

"I don't know, it's not important Fred," she said.

"Come on now, who said that?"

"I don't know. Dolly might have said that."

"Dolly Henderson?"

"What are you going to do, Fred?"

Now I was hot under the collar and I stormed out of the house and Helen was yelling at me to stop. Asking where I was going and what I was doing. The Hendersons lived down at the end of the block, so I walked over and nearly had doggone steam coming out of my ears. I knocked on the door like I was a repo man.

"Fred Doyle, what in the world is all this ruckus about?" Dolly said. She had this big poofy hairdo and enough eye shadow to last three showers.

"Dolly, I'm going to ask you a question and I want an honest answer," I said.

"Fred, what's the matter? Is everything okay?"

"Are you going around telling people that Debra Jenkins killed Sam?"

"Fred, I don't know what's gotten into you."

"Dolly, are you telling people that?"

"I don't know."

"You don't know?"

"I can't believe Helen," she said.

"Are you going around telling people that?"

"What a big mouth she's got. And I am *not* saying that Debra killed Sam, no."

"You're telling me my wife is lying to me? She said that you said you heard Debra is the killer."

"Right."

"Right, what?"

"I'm not going around telling people Debra killed him. It's something I heard, is all."

"I think that's an awfully sick thing to say about somebody who lives in Well Springs. What kinda character do you got?"

"Fred, I am not going to be lectured about how I am a bad person when I haven't done anything. The ladies gossip while we get our hair done, Fred. That's all it is. It's just talk."

"Well, sometimes it's more than just talk, Dolly. You keep spreading falsehoods and eventually it'll spread like wildfire and people are going to start to believe it's true."

"And you're sure it's not true?" she asked.

"What's that supposed to mean?"

"Is it so crazy that she, you know?"

"Dolly, you didn't hear her screaming and crying the night Sam was killed."

"Fred," she said.

"No, 'Fred' nothing," I said. "You didn't hear her screaming and crying when the gunshots were going off. I did. You didn't hear the children, in the days after, crying and screaming in the middle of the night. Wondering if their daddy was ever coming back."

"Maybe you're right," she said, softly.

"No, there ain't any *maybe* about it," I said. "The way I heard Debra screaming and crying that night – I am telling you she did not kill Sam. And it sure would be nice if you didn't go around telling others that she did."

Dolly stood there like a five-year-old who got caught with their hand in the cookie jar. She knew she didn't have a leg to stand on. Instead, she just nodded. I told her I didn't mean to be so hot, I apologized for getting rabid on her, but then we said goodbye and I left. Helen was standing outside the front door when I walked back.

"What in the world did you do?" she asked, arms folded.

"I settled things."

**

It was December 1999 when Helen was in the hospital. She had another episode and was plugged up to all these machines. Terrible. I remember it was getting close to the new millennium and there was all this talk about the computers going haywire and it made me nervous because she was hooked up to these things. I worried things would stop working when the new year started and God forbid, Helen would pass. It was a stressful few weeks in there.

One of the worst parts about it was the solitude. It was only me and her in that hospital room. Nobody ever came to visit. It had been years since Sam had died, but there were times when I sat in that hospital room and thought about him. I thought about how he helped her during that episode way back when – rushed her to the hospital himself. He'd come to visit her. I truly believe if Sam was still alive in '99, he would have visited her then, too. Even though she was barely there mentally during that time, he would have still come. He would have made the time.

We didn't come home until the middle of January and there wasn't hoopla this time. No banners. Nobody was waiting for us. Instead, I pulled into the garage and helped Helen into the house. The next time we saw Debra and the kids, they were really sweet about it. Asking how she was and saying how happy they were that she was feeling better and out of the hospital.

It was a dark time for me – that stretch she was in the hospital. It made me wonder: is it selfish to want people to visit you in the hospital? Is it immature to be disappointed in people when they don't? It wasn't like I was asking them to come every day or stay overnight. But nobody came to visit once. It made me a little steamed toward them, but then it made me feel bad for feeling that way – made me feel selfish. Then I got steamed at them for making me feel bad for being mad for them not coming. It was a terrible thing.

I suppose me bringing it up is evidence it still bothers me. That Helen had done so much to help those children over the years, especially during that tumultuous time, and nobody cared to make the time and drive to the hospital. I suppose it made me miss Sam.

**

Debra never married again. That surprised me. She was young enough and she was pretty enough. She could have found a man. Maybe she felt like she would have had to leave Well Springs to find somebody. I don't think she wanted to do that. Maybe she felt it wouldn't be fair to Sam if she married again. Like she wanted to honor his memory or something. I don't know. I know he could be abusive, but they were together for years and had the four children. That's gotta count for something, right? Maybe she felt like she never wanted to be married again because she'd always be comparing the new man to Sam. Helen even tried to set her up a few times and Debra said she wasn't interested.

I always wondered, but didn't feel it was right to ask, whose situation she would rather have: hers or ours. For her, she had four beautiful children but had her partner taken from her at a young age – I believe he was thirty or so at the time. For us, we had each other for our lifetime but we never were able to have children. Obviously, neither Debra or our lives could ever be perfect. There'd always be something missing. I'd guess if she was given the choice, she would have chosen her life. She'd want the children even if it meant sacrificing Sam.

**

I still think about the night Sam was killed.

It was awful.

Hearing the gunshots.

Hearing the screams.

To know somebody was getting killed twenty yards from you and you're just standing there. It's one of those moments you don't know what you would do until it happens. Unfortunately, I froze. I called Sheriff Cremble and I stood in the kitchen while everything happened. While the bad guy killed Sam and then ran out the house and drove away.

I stood there. Helpless.

I could have gone outside, at least. I could have looked at the driveway to find the car or truck he was driving. Get the license plate. I could have tried to hide and see what the man looked like as he was leaving the house. That way I could get a description to Sheriff Cremble. I could say what he looked like, gotten a license plate, make and model and color of his vehicle. Instead, I stayed in my house. The only helpful thing I provided was a phone call to Sheriff Cremble.

Whenever I talked to Helen about this, she'd always say the same thing.

"Sweetheart, you did the absolute best thing you could have done," Helen told me one night when we were in bed talking about it.

"You gotta say that," I said.

"Fred, what did you want to happen? You go over there like John Wayne and get yourself killed? And where would that leave me?"

"Honey, I didn't mean that."

"It's bad enough that one soul died in this whole senseless event, now you're wanting to have me lose my husband because your pride," she said.

"It ain't my pride, honey. You don't understand."

"Why can't you see you did the right thing by not going over there?"

"If I did the right thing, then how come I feel so ashamed about it?" I said, starting to get all choked up.

"Fred, I don't mean to—"

"Honey, I'm struggling with this is all. I could have helped more and instead, I was a coward and stayed here. I'm glad I didn't get killed and I don't wanna think about putting you through what Debra went through. But I feel like I failed Sam. My neighbor needed me and I didn't answer the bell."

"Sam would be dead even if you went over there."

"Helen, that's a terrible thing to say."

"I don't mean to be cruel, but it's true. By the time you got over there — if you went over there — the bad guy had killed him already. I understand you think you could have helped, but the only thing that would have happened was he would have killed you too."

She was right, you know. If I look at it logically, I understand it was the right thing to do — on paper, as they say. And even though I know that's the case, I still have that little spot in the back of my mind that wonders what would have happened if I went over. Maybe I wouldn't have been able to save Sam's life, but maybe seeing the man or seeing

253

his vehicle could have helped the case. Maybe it would have helped Sheriff Cremble catch the guy and at least bring Sam a little justice. It would have at least closed the book on everything.

And you know the biggest thing it would have helped? It would have ended all those vicious rumors about Debra once and for all. All the whispers and what-have-you that she was the one who killed him. Like what Dolly was saying. I told anybody who would listen that I heard her screaming and crying the night Sam was shot. Most of the time, people took it to heart and changed their mind. But like weeds popping up over the yard, it was hard to keep the rumors from swirling again. Some people told Helen that Debra was only crying and screaming after the fact. That she was crying because she realized what she had done shooting and killing Sam.

Terrible.

That's what would have changed if I went over there. If people said maybe it was Debra that shot Sam, I could tell them, "Listen, I was there. I saw the man who did it. Don't you ever say that Debra was the one to kill him."

I don't know how big of a deal that would even be nowadays. I don't think many people talk about Debra or Sam or what happened much anymore. People moved on with their lives and found better things to do with their time. But I still think about it. I think about what happened and it upsets me that there are people in Well Springs, when reminded of what happened, probably still think Debra killed him.

**

Every Easter morning, before church, I go visit Sam's grave.

I did it the first year after he died. I didn't want to make a big show of it. The only person I told was Helen. Then it became this tradition. Every year I bring a package of beef jerky and set it on his grave. I know it's silly. The first time that I went, when I was at the grave, I felt compelled to lay something down. The only thing I had in my coat pocket was a small package of beef jerky. I didn't want to lay flowers down because Sam wasn't exactly a flower fella, you know? Wasn't exactly manly. I thought about laying down a beer can, but I didn't think that was appropriate – due to his drinking, and all. I figured beef jerky was a nice compromise.

The second anniversary of his death, I asked Debra if she wanted to come. I told her what I had done the previous year and I thought about making it an annual thing. To go pay my respects. She thanked me but told me she wasn't interested in doing that. I told her I understood. It was probably too difficult for her – to relive what happened. I can't blame her. I went by myself that year too. And every year after. She never did join me. I wondered if enough time passed, maybe she would go – I suppose the pain was always too much.

When Cody got older, high school age and all, I asked him. I didn't want him to feel pressured to do it, but I thought it was a nice gesture for a first-born to visit his daddy's grave. But he said no too. I never pressed him either. I told him if he ever did want to join me, he was more than welcome.

Never did.

Instead, I went to the cemetery by myself – still do.

My folks are buried there and I got some friends there too. So I make my rounds every Easter morning. Saying hello to those no longer with us. I always end with Sam. I feel it's fitting. It's a nice way to update Sam on his family. I always feared Debra would find another man and wondered if I would tell Sam or not. But she never did. Instead, I let him know what his children were up to.

I told him when Tommy moved away to go to school and become a lawyer. I joked that Tommy could have represented Sam if he ever found himself in trouble. He would have been so proud of Tommy. He turned into a fine young man. Smart.

I told him about Nikki getting married and moving to the San Antonio area. I believe she has two children herself, if I remember. Occasionally she'll call Debra. I don't see her much anymore now that she moved away. She rarely comes to Well Springs for holidays or anything. I think Debra visits Nikki's family over there. I miss seeing her, but I know she's got a good little life in the city. Sam would have been proud and probably tickled to see his grandchildren.

It's always hard to tell him about Cassie, how she sowed her wild oats and never came back. I would be surprised if you get ahold of her for this deal you're working on. She wants to get clean. I know that. But when you start fooling around with those pills, it can be hard. I see her every once in a blue moon, although it's been a little while now. She'll come to a Thanksgiving or she'll stop by and ask for some money to get her life together. She was such a sweet little girl. It's hard. I know Sam had his own problems and I wonder if Cassie got dealt a bad hand by Sam. If he passed on that addiction to her. Or I wonder if Sam getting killed is what sent Cassie down the wrong path. I can't imagine what it's like for a little girl to lose her daddy like that.

I'll tell Sam about Cody – the only Jenkins child to stay here in town. He started this landscaping company and I think he's doing quite well. I keep waiting for him to find a woman and start a family. Helen always gives him a hard time. Tells him he oughta find a nice girl. One of these days he'll find one, I'm sure. I know he's busy with his business and checking up with Debra. He'll stop by our place and see if we need help with anything. Heck, he helped me with this maple we had that was getting out of control. Sam would be so doggone proud of how Cody turned out. I wish Sam had the chance to see him. I wish he had to chance to see all of his children.

Last Easter, when I went on his visit, I don't know why but I felt a little more sentimental than usual.

"Sam, how you doing bud?" I said. "Me and Helen are getting up there in age now. We'll probably be seeing you soon. I hope you're doing well. Debra and the children are doing well. You'd be so proud, Sam. So proud. You raised your kids right. Fine people they've become.

"I know you'd probably tease me about it, but I can't help but think about that night every once in a while. Especially this time of year. Last week, I was at the sink washing a plate and I looked out the window at your house. Made me think of it. Made me hear the gunshots again. I play it out in my head – still to this day. I hear the shots going off and I march over to your house. I wait by the front door and as the man comes charging out to his car, I tackle him to the ground. Sheriff Cremble comes over and arrests him. He goes to prison and gets what he deserves for killing you. It's the way things should have turned out. It's what I should have done.

"I can't help but feel like I failed you, Sam. Call me a loon, but I can't help but feel it. That I failed you.

"I'm sorry, Sam. I hope you can forgive me. I should have done more to help."

Chapter Fifteen

Debra Jenkins

By the end – before he died – Sam was a lot to put up with. It was miserable. Then, suddenly he was gone. It was like wearing a heavy backpack for years. It wore me down and hurt and there was nothing in the world I wanted more than to take off the backpack. Then it finally comes off. Maybe it feels good, but you still feel the pain in your back. It's like a reminder of the weight you carried all those years. That's the best way I could describe the aftermath of everything. Part of me felt good that I didn't have to live in fear of what Sam would do, but I still felt the weight.

In the weeks and months after Sam died, people reaching out and asking if they could help went from reassuring to a little bit annoying. All these people who never cared about our family when Sam was alive were now lining up around the block to give me baked dishes or offer to help around the house. Nobody ever tried to help when Sam made life a nightmare. After a little while, I got upset about people asking how I was.

Truthfully, I was exhausted.

About a year after everything, I noticed people stopped asking how I was. They stopped offering things. They stopped going out of their way to talk to me at the grocery store. At first, I thought it was because I was rude.

I was at the grocery store and people saw me coming and turned away. It was like I was a leper. I was in the produce section when Susanne Patterson – she was one of the office ladies at the school district – came to talk to me.

"Debbie, how are you doing sweetheart?" she said.

"How are you, Susanne?" I said, looking at the limes.

"How's the family?" she asked. It startled me the way she asked it. Most of the time its asked either emptily – people just exchanging pleasantries – or overly concerned because of everything that happened. Susanne sounded different. She had this almost skeptical tone to her voice.

"The children are fine, Susanne. Thank you," I said.

"That's good. Debra, there's something I need to ask you," she said.

"Okay?"

"I just want you to know, that no matter what, I am on your side," she whispered. "You would be one thousand percent justified, you know. I understand it."

"What are you talking about?"

"Well, some of the others were talking. It's not our place and I don't even want to ask it, but I will only ask you once."

"What's wrong, Susanne?"

"Debra, was it you?"

"Was what me?" I said.

"You know," she said, looking around. "Sam."

"I'm confused."

259

"Honey, I don't mean to pry or gossip or nothing. We just wanted to hear it from you. At least once."

"Are you asking if I killed Sam?" I asked in a slightly louder than normal voice. That startled her and she looked around again.

"I hope you aren't mad about us asking," she said.

"Us?"

"Well, me. But I know there's a lot of people that want to know. Word spreads fast in Well Springs."

"I'm aware of that. Who is asking?"

"It's not important. Forget I ever asked. I'm so very sorry, Debra. I shouldn't have asked."

"The answer is no."

"No?"

"No."

"Oh darling, I'm so sorry that we even doubted you. It's just, we couldn't believe such a terrible thing could happen in Well Springs. An intruder?"

"I pray it never happens again," I said.

"That makes two of us. That makes two of us. Debra, I am so sorry."

"It's okay. Make sure you tell all your little friends that it wasn't me."

"Of course. Of course, I will. Is there anything we can do?"

"No, Susanne. Not at the moment."

That interaction was so painful, but I'm glad we had it. I noticed after I talked with Susanne, people got back to their old friendly ways. They'd smile and ask if there was anything they could do. It was back to those empty pleasantries. People smiled and asked how my day was going. They waved to me when they passed by. More and more, people stopped asking about Sam and the children and how everyone was handling it.

Eventually, people moved on.

**

I started thinking about what I would do for the anniversary of Sam's death – I don't know if anniversary is the right word for it. Is it? The anniversary was the late Monday turning into Tuesday – the week after Easter. I was scared to death that Pastor Wilheim would say something in his sermon. He never came during the week and asked if it was okay if he did, which made me think he wouldn't talk about it – but I wasn't sure.

I really didn't want to do anything, in terms of Sam. What was the point? But after my talk with Susanne in the grocery store, about how some people thought I killed Sam, a few days before the anniversary I decided I should do something – for appearances.

On the morning of April 12, 1994, I went to visit Sam's grave. It sounds awful, but the reason I went was that I hoped people saw me. I know. Terrible. But that's what I did. I figured if people saw me – the grieving widow – they would accept the story about an intruder. I left the children at the Doyles' house. I wanted to go alone. I didn't want to use the kids like that

I hadn't been to his grave since the day he was buried. It was overcast and a bit colder than usual. I remember there was a 12-pack of cheap beer sitting on his grave, but with a hole ripped in the case. One beer was gone. I'm sure that was Rhett. There was also a bag of beef jerky Fred left on Easter the previous week. I didn't bring anything. His parents were laying there next to him. That was new.

Henry Jenkins. Loretta Jenkins. Sam Jenkins.

They were all lined up in a row. One, two, three. What a family. How did I get so lucky to get pulled into that?

"Hello Sam," I said, my hands in my coat pockets. "I don't know where you are right now, but today is the anniversary of when everything happened. With Cody."

261

I looked around the cemetery and didn't see anybody.

"I know it's been a while since then. Things were pretty hard for a bit. I'm not sad about it – you being dead. I meant things were hard for the town. They think a burglar killed you. Maybe some think I killed you. I know. It probably would have been easier if it was me.

"I still can't believe Cody did it. I had no idea he was going to do it. I didn't tell him to do it, so you know. You probably think I did. You probably think I was too scared to kill you myself, so I had Cody do it. I would never. I don't know why he – you know what, why couldn't *you* be better?

"Why are we the bad ones? Everybody crying over you dying. Why are we bad? You should have been a better man. A better husband. A better father. If you weren't such an asshole maybe you'd still be alive.

"I see your folks ended up right next to you. You didn't have to be like him, you know that? I know they say that stuff gets passed down. Father to son. But you didn't have to be that way. You made a choice. You had a family, Sam. You could have enjoyed it. Things were not all that bad. I know we had to get married, but we could have made it work. Life could have been all right if you actually worked at it. If you tried to be a better man. But you didn't.

"I don't feel bad for you. I don't. You brought this on yourself. You would rather go get drunk with Rhett – I see he left you a nice present. Drinking with your friends was more important to you than I was. Than the kids were. You had so many chances. So many.

"Why couldn't you work at it? Why? Why couldn't you at least try? We could have made something. We could have been happy. You wouldn't be laying here with your folks. Your mom died in a car crash. Word was she dosed off on those pills. She probably wasn't even conscious when it happened. It makes me wonder how many times you could have killed yourself driving around. It would have been so much easier that way. God forgive me, but it would have been so much easier if you crashed your truck or something.

"Cody wouldn't have to live his life knowing he killed his father. We would have been heartbroken, probably. Hearing you crashed your truck into a pole. Terrible. But it would save us from the guilt. You would be dead because of something *you* did. But you never did. You always ended up at home. Why? How? So many times you drove home drunk and all we needed was *one time*.

"Your dad – what a winner he was. Drank himself to death. You didn't need to be like him. I pray Cody and Tommy don't end up like you. But you know what? If Cody didn't do what he did, who knows what would have happened? You probably would have gotten even worse. You'd end up like Henry. And how is that fair for us? We would have to live with it. You drinking and losing control.

"You could have been a great man, Sam. You didn't need to be like Henry. Things were good when you actually tried. Why is that so much for me to ask for? For you to try? The kids miss you. They don't know. I never told them. I didn't want them to know what happened. Maybe when they are older and can understand better. Maybe. They still miss you. I know Tommy does. He worships you. He doesn't know.

"Would you want them to know? Would you? Would you want them to know it was Cody? It would destroy us. I probably won't tell them.

"I can't believe he did it. Truly. I can't. I wish he didn't. I should have just left. You didn't need to die. I should have left. I don't know why I didn't. There are times when I feel like everything is my fault. I should have left when things got bad. You would have moved on. I know you never really had feelings for me. I could have left and we could have handled the children through it.

"Why didn't I leave?

263

"I don't know. I didn't. What's the point of thinking about all this? You're gone. And you know what? We'll be okay. I know it. We will be okay and you'll still be dead."

I looked around the cemetery and didn't see anybody. I didn't want to stay there all day waiting for somebody to see me. I looked at Sam's grave:

Sam Jenkins
1962-1993

I remember thinking that's all he deserved to have on his tombstone. I looked at Henry and Loretta's graves. I took a deep breath and then walked away. It was the last time I ever went to see Sam.

**

There's been times over the years when I felt the guilt creep in. The kids — especially Tommy — talked about how much they missed Sam. That they wish he wasn't gone. Tommy used to cry about it a lot. I held him and let him cry. I felt guilty about it and I'd feel terrible for Cody. What a weight to bear for a child — seeing your little brother crying over the man you killed. Cody was ten! It was such an adult thing to have to carry, but there were times when Sam's behavior forced Cody to be the grown up. He watched over Tommy, Cass, and Nikki when Sam was drunk and angry or when he drank himself into a stupor. I resented Sam for that. Cody couldn't just be a boy.

But I couldn't escape that guilt.

That feeling of, "Yeah, Sam was not a great man, but did he really deserve to die?" You know what helped me? Here, look at this. It happened about two years after Sam died. I cut it out of *The American* and brought it with me because I knew I'd tell this story:

Amarillo man charged with murder of wife

An Amarillo man was charged with first-degree murder on Thursday after authorities were called about a domestic disturbance. George Hill, 31, was arrested after police say they found the body of his wife, Darlene, 30, beaten to death after an altercation. Hill had been previously arrested twice for domestic battery and had three DUIs.

I remember reading it and thinking two things: First, the death of that woman at the hands of her husband was so insignificant that the paper only ran it as this short little story. It was three damn sentences. She had an entire life and was her own person, and her death was only good enough for *three sentences*. The other thing I thought was how easily that could have been me. There but the grace of God go I. Sam could have gotten a little too out of control one night and killed me. Would I get more than three sentences? If Cody wouldn't have killed him, maybe Sam would have killed me. And then what? He gets arrested, I'm hoping, but then what happens with the kids? They would have gone with either my parents or, God forbid, Sam's parents.

That's why I'm at peace with what Cody did.

I remember after reading the story about Darlene Hill, I looked around for a bigger story. Our library didn't get *the Amarillo Globe-Times* or *the Daily News* so I literally drove to Amarillo. I didn't know what I was doing. I had no plan. I wanted to go there and learn more about what happened. The kids stayed at Fred and Helen's house and I went by myself. I finally got to the public library, or at least one of them, and went through the newspapers. It took a little while but I finally found a bigger article about what happened and I remember crying while I read it.

They had been together since high school and had four children together. He had a drinking problem and had been on-again, off-again. They had split up briefly but he said he would change and they got back together. Apparently, one of her friends said he was a jealous type and he was convinced she was having an affair. That's probably what drove him to kill her. He didn't even use a weapon or anything. The police said he literally beat her to death with his bare hands – he laid on top of her and beat her and beat her. I can't even imagine.

The sense of helplessness.

In the article, they said their children were left with her parents. Tom and Kathy Loren. I can't believe I did this, but I went to the Yellow Pages and found where in Amarillo they lived and I drove over there. I parked out on the street and looked at the house. I hoped somebody would be out in the yard, so I wouldn't have to go knock on the door. After sitting there for a while, I got up and went to the door. Right when I knocked, I felt this sense of fear come over me. I hoped nobody answered. When nobody opened the door, I turned back toward my car.

"Yes?" a soft voice said behind me.

"Oh, hello," I said, turning back to the house.

"How can I help you dear?" Kathy said.

"Well, this is really random and I probably shouldn't even be here, but my name is Debra Jenkins and I'm from Well Springs."

"My goodness, what brings you to Amarillo?"

"I read what happened to your daughter and it really moved me," I said, my voice starting to shake.

"Oh my word. Come inside, sweetheart," she said.

Tom was at the store with the children, she told me as we sat in the living room. She offered me some tea but I told her it was okay.

"Did you know Darlene?" she asked.

"No. No, I just read about her. I am so sorry if I'm bringing up something that hurts to talk about. I shouldn't even be here."

"It's okay, sweetheart. It's okay. If you came here all the way from Well Springs, it must mean a lot to you."

"It does. I am so sorry that happened to Darlene. I can't imagine how – did you know how bad of a man George was?"

"Of course. He was a sweet boy when he was younger. Handsome and gentle. Sometimes sweet boys turn into bad men, though. Are you married?"

"No."

"Well, when you do, make sure you find the right man."

"I didn't mean no, as in I wasn't married. I was married."

"To a bad man?"

"Yes."

"That's why you're here," she said.

"Partly."

"I'm glad that you're here. That means the bad man didn't do to you what George did to my Darlene."

"Why do you think nobody did anything? About George?"

"That's a question that will always haunt me, to be honest. We could have done something. All of us. And we didn't."

"That's how I felt about my husband."

"Did he hurt you?" she asked. I nodded. "Terrible. I don't understand men. They can be so unhappy even with a nice life. They can be ungrateful animals."

"Do you ever think about if George was the one who died?"

"How nice that would have been," she said with a half-hearted smile.

"That's what happened with my husband," I said.

"Did you...?" she asked.

"No."

267

"Oh, I see."

My hands were shaking and I kept telling myself to say it, but the words wouldn't come. We sat there in silence. *Say it,* I thought. I could feel the tears forming in my eyes and then I finally said it.

"My boy did," I said.

"Your boy?" she asked, confused.

"My boy, Cody. He's ten. He did."

She tried to contain a gasp. She couldn't believe it.

"Was it an accident?" she asked.

"No," I said, unable to stop myself from crying. "He killed him."

Kathy got up and sat next to me and rubbed my back as I collapsed into her arms. We sat there crying. For minutes I wept as she comforted me. She was so kind. When I was done, she held my hands.

"What happened? If you don't mind me asking," she asked.

"He shot him. In the middle of the night. He came into our room and shot him."

"Honey, I am so sorry."

"But it's okay, though. That's the thing. It's *okay*. That's why I came here. To find you. To find out what happened to Darlene. Because if Cody wouldn't have shot him," I said.

"Maybe the same thing would have happened to you," she said.

"That's right," I said.

"And what happened to your boy?"

"He's doing okay," I said.

"Did they arrest him?"

"No," I said, shaking my head.

"Is that right?"

"Yeah. The sheriff in our town, he's very understanding."

"So what happened? Did you say it was you?"

"The official story is it was a burglar."

"He covered it up?" she asked. I nodded and we sat there in silence once again.

"Well, good," she said.

"You think?" I asked.

"Absolutely. The only victim is a victimizer, in my opinion. If Cody didn't do what he did, maybe you would have ended up like my Darlene. I think you all did the right thing."

"Thank you," I whispered. "Thank you."

I didn't stay much longer after that. She was so incredibly gracious. To this day, she's the only person I told what really happened. She said if I ever needed to talk to her, I shouldn't hesitate to reach out – but I never did.

I found out George Hill got sentenced to 20 years in prison for killing Darlene. Twenty years. He was charged and sentenced in 1994 so that means even if he served the maximum time, he was released in 2014.

For the past four years, George Hill has been a free man.

**

I never *decided* that I wouldn't marry again. Maybe one day I will. I'm fifty-two. Maybe I'll meet somebody one of these days. I'm not opposed to it. I've been on a couple of dates over the years. I remember the first one was about two years after Sam died. It was painfully awkward at first. I literally had never been on a date. I didn't have a boyfriend in high school and Sam getting me pregnant forced how that played out.

The date was with a nice man living in Well Springs. I don't want to say who – he still lives here. He really is a sweet man, but I don't want to betray any confidences. We had talked at the grocery store one day and then he asked if I would have dinner with him. I didn't realize it in the moment – I thought he was being nice because of everything that happened.

"No," he told me. "Maybe you don't understand: did you want to grab *dinner*?"

"Like a date?" I asked.

"If you want to call it that," he said.

We met for dinner out of town, which was my idea, so nobody in Well Springs would see us. I had known him for years, so it felt odd looking at it as a romantic dinner. We had a nice time and he paid, but at the end of the date I told him that I wasn't ready. He understood. Looking back, I probably could have been happy with him. He would have made a sweet step-father to the kids. But I remember at the time almost being scared about how nice he was.

"Sam could be nice too," I'd think. "And look how that turned out."

I was afraid he would be nice for a little bit and then he'd start drinking and get abusive. I was scared he would change. I told him the timing wasn't right and it wouldn't be smart for us to be romantic. He understood. I still see him around town. He got married and has some children and you know what happened? He has stayed the same sweet man. He didn't get fat and didn't lose interest in his family. Lucky woman, I suppose.

I thought about moving out of Well Springs too. You're probably thinking, *Why wouldn't she move and get a fresh start?* I had an old high school friend who lived in Wichita Falls and she mentioned this house for sale that was perfect for me and the children. I thought about it. The house was cute and it was in a nice quiet neighborhood. There was a little more to do in Wichita Falls. I wouldn't be the *Jenkins widow* in Wichita Falls.

I even drove to see it in person. There were sidewalks and trees lining the street. It was close to the elementary school. I figured I could find a new job. Maybe I could work for the university. I told the real estate agent I needed some time to think and I would let her know in a few days. Driving home after seeing the house, I decided I would put in an offer.

It never made it that far. The real estate agent called me when I was driving home and left a message saying the family had a change of heart and was taking the house off the market.

Of course.

That was pretty disheartening, to be honest. After that, I stopped looking because I assumed we wouldn't get the house or something else would go wrong. Besides, the kids had friends at school. I didn't want to move and upend their lives. I thought maybe after the kids were done with school. Once Tommy was done with high school, I'd look to move.

But truthfully, I like Well Springs. We're comfortable here. And over the years, things have changed. People moved on. I'm no longer the Jenkins widow. I am Debra Jenkins.

**

We had a nice party at our house on Cody's eighteenth birthday. A lot of people came and Fred grilled up food. It was an interesting day. Part of turning eighteen is people coming around and talking about how now you're a man. That's a big day – although really all it means is you can buy lottery tickets and cigarettes or join the military. People kept coming up to him, telling him he's officially a man. But Cody was an adult the day he killed Sam. He never was a regular teenage boy – getting into trouble and breaking the law. He watched over Tommy and the girls. He became their unofficial daddy.

One of the guys at the party asked Cody what kinda beer he wanted. Cody is a man now, so he should have a beer on his birthday, the guy said. I wouldn't have cared, but before I could say anything, Cody thanked him but said he didn't want one.

"No?" the man said.

"No, I'm all set. Thank you though," Cody said.

I remember feeling this sense of pride. He really did turn into a good young man. I always feared Cody would fall victim to his own genetics. Henry was a drunk, Sam was a drunk, and I always worried Cody would become a drunk. He never did. I don't believe he's ever even touched the stuff. He saw what it turned men into.

Later in the party, Fred and Helen were sitting with Cody and myself. We were talking about how things have changed over the years. They asked Cody if he was going away for school or not. Cody had talked about potentially going to Tech. He wasn't sure what he would study, but he said he worried about me and the kids. That he was scared to go away.

"You know what, Cody?" Fred said.

"Yes sir?"

"You've turned into quite the young man."

"Amen," Helen said.

"You're too kind, Fred," Cody said.

"Your father would be so doggone proud," Fred said, his voice starting to crack.

"Fred," I said.

"I'm not going to cry, come on now," Fred said. "It just needed to be said. Cody, you are a good young man and Sam would be proud."

"Thank you sir," he said.

It was a bit uncomfortable, so I asked them if they would like any more food or their drinks freshened to change the subject. It worked – everybody moved on from the subject.

That moment always stayed with me – Fred saying Sam would be proud of Cody. I wondered if it's true. Cody is so unlike Sam. Cody has always been so damn selfless. Looking out for others. Sam had this stubborn machismo about him, so he would have thought Cody was soft. He'd say Cody was clearly raised by his mama. He probably would have wanted to toughen Cody up. Cody never even played football. The violence of it never really appealed to him. Sam loved to talk about life lessons football taught him and it's important for Cody to learn those. But you know what, how did those life lessons work out for Sam? He had this whole toughness mentality, but where did it get him?

The funny part is Sam would probably say the thing he respected most about Cody was how he stood up to him and killed him.

Cody never did go away for school. I tried to tell him. I nearly forced him but Cody dug his heels in and said he would rather stay in Well Springs and help out around the house.

"Cody, I don't need help around the house," I told him.

"What do I need to go to school for?" he said. "I don't even know what I want to do. Why waste the money?"

"Because that's what kids your age are supposed to do – go away and enjoy college."

"We can't afford it," he said. "It's fine. I'd rather stay here."

"Cody, you need to experience life outside this town."

"Why?"

"Because there's more to the world than Well Springs."

"But I like it here. Why go somewhere if you like where you're at? Besides, I can help around the house and take Tommy, Cass, and Nikki places if they need to go somewhere."

"Cody," I told him.

"Listen, this isn't something I feel like I'm being forced to do. I want to stay here."

"Why? It's a big world, Cody. Go experience it. Have fun. Meet new people."

"Mama, I want to stay."

I suppose there was a little bit of his daddy's stubbornness in him. I kept waiting for him to finally say he wanted to go away for school.

Maybe not that first year, but he'd eventually come to his senses. He never did. He got a job at Dickerson's Landscaping Company in town. He really took to it right away. Over time, he got more and more responsibility – he wasn't even twenty-one before they gave him a management position. He earned himself quite the reputation around town. After a few years of saving up, he bought a house of his own in Well Springs about five streets over on Washington Street. It's a cute little place – three bedrooms, two baths. Of course, the lawn always looks nice.

Christmas time around 2005 – he was twenty-two or twenty-three – he told me he was going out on his own. I didn't know what he meant. I asked if he was finally leaving Well Springs.

"No, no," he told me. "I think I'm going to start my own company."

"Oh my goodness," I said. "Are you sure? Do you know how to do that?"

"Yeah, I already filled out the paperwork and everything. I'm going to do it," he said.

"That's exciting! Are you still doing landscaping?"

"Yeah, it's what I know best."

"What are you going to call it? Cody's Landscaping?"

"No, no," he said. "Adams Landscaping Company."

"Adams?"

"Yeah, what do you think?"

"Why Adams?"

"Well, it's your family name," he said.

"But why not Jenkins Landscaping?"

"I don't know. Adams sounds better."

I told him I supported him and to ask me if he needed any help. He's really made a name for himself. His company started off with only a few regulars but it really became popular. Rightfully so. He does such a good job. It started out with only him, but then he hired a few more people. Then he started fixing up houses around town. Then people in the surrounding towns started reaching out. He's done quite well for himself. I think he really enjoys the restoration side of it — turning something ugly into something beautiful.

He loves his work a little too much, though. I always ask when he'll find a woman and start a family. He's thirty-five now. You wouldn't know how successful his company is by looking at his lifestyle. His house is nice and well-kept, but it's modest. There's no fancy truck or expensive decorations. He's got to have a lot of money in the bank. I don't know what he's saving up for, though. I hope he finds a girl and starts a family. He would be such a good father.

Why is it the people who would be the best parents are the ones who aren't having the kids?

**

Cody was the only one of the kids to stay in Well Springs. Tommy is a really successful attorney in Denton. Sam would have *loved* how he turned out. Tommy can be very headstrong and is the go-get-it type. Sam would be proud about Tommy winning the big case and the expensive lifestyle he lives. He tries to stay in touch with me, but he's so busy — he's got a wife and those children. Plus the career. I always tell him he's got to slow down. He needs to appreciate everything.

Nicole flew away to San Antonio pretty soon after she graduated. Her husband — boyfriend at the time — went to school at UT-San Antonio and she followed with him. They have a nice life too. She's got a couple of really sweet children. San Antonio is so far away, so we only see them once a year if I'm lucky. One year their van broke down in the middle of nowhere driving to Well Springs. This was before cell phones, so they were stuck there for hours before they got help. I think that really spooked her making the drive. Sometimes Cody and I will come visit them, but they're also so busy with life that I hate to feel like a bother. If I'm being honest, I think Nicole moved on and never really wanted to talk about Sam much. I would be surprised if she agrees to talk to you, just so you know.

Cassandra is – I don't know. I know one day she will figure everything out. I think Sam's death really affected her. During high school, she got caught up in the wrong crowd. She'd come home really drunk – if I was lucky – or high on who-knows-what. I have tried everything. I tried hard discipline. I tried open arms. I don't know. She told me it feels like she has this hole in her soul. That she doesn't know what to fill it with. I take her back over and over again, but she can't help herself. When she was in her early twenties, Cody paid to have her go to rehab in Odessa. It was expensive but it worked – at least for a little while. She stayed in Odessa and got a new job. Then I heard she got fired because she didn't show up anymore. She had these men she was seeing that weren't helping much. To be honest, I don't hear much from her anymore. She reaches out to Cody when she needs something. I would be surprised if you can get ahold of her.

It was only a few years ago – 2016 – when all of us were together again for Thanksgiving. Everybody under one roof at the old house. I was so excited that I couldn't help but be nervous. Tommy and Nikki brought their whole families and Cassie even looked healthy. I know she was trying. After all the food was on the table, Cody said grace:

"Dear Lord, we thank you for this wonderful meal we're about to enjoy. We thank you for all the blessings in our lives. Lord, we thank you that Tommy and his family could make it from Denton. We thank you for Nicole and her family for coming home. We thank you for Cassie making it here from Odessa. We thank you for mama, for raising this family right. We offer thanks for everything you've given this family. We ask our lives could reflect the glory you've shown us. We pray in the savior's name, amen."

"Amen," we all said.

"No prayer for dad, huh?" Tommy said.

"I suppose if dad had something to tell God, he could just tell him himself," Cody said, picking up the plate of turkey and passing it to Cassie.

"Has there been any update?" Tommy said.

"We can talk about that later if you want, but I think we should enjoy this meal mama put together," Cody said.

"Thank you, mama," Nikki said. "It looks delicious."

The topic thankfully changed to how things were going in San Antonio. To my knowledge, I don't know if Tommy ever brought up the case again after dinner.

**

I can't put into words how much I appreciate what Sheriff Cremble has done for us. Everything could have ruined our family. It could have ruined the town. There are a lot of ways it could have played out, but I think things turned out about as well as they could. I don't know how much will change after this comes out.

I hope you understand what he did for us. I hope you think you would have done the same.

Truthfully, I am a bit nervous to see what the town thinks when the truth comes out. Will they understand? Will they feel betrayed? I wonder if people will reach out with support like they did after Sam died? Tell us it's okay. They understand. Or will they gossip and talk about they're ashamed of us?

I honestly don't know.

A few days before I came to talk with you, I went to First Church of Well Springs in the middle of the day. I walked in and couldn't find anybody, so I sat in the pews and looked up at the cross. I thought, what was the right thing to do? To tell you what happened? Or keep living my lie?

"Well how are we doing today?" a booming voice came behind me. It was Pastor Wilheim.

"Hello Pastor," I said.

"What brings you into the church, Debra?"

"I've been thinking about stuff," I said as he sat down next to me.

"What have you been thinking about?"

"Pastor, would you mind praying for me?"

"Is there something wrong, Debra?" he asked, putting his hand on mine.

"I could use some prayer is all."

"Is everything all right? Is there anything you need to tell me?" he asked.

"I just could use some strength right now," I said.

"I see," he said.

"Do you mind praying for me?"

"Of course," he said and we both closed our eyes. "Lord God in heaven, you have told us, 'Come to me, all who are weary, and I will give you rest.' I pray for Debra, Lord, who needs your strength. Our humanity is of no use without the strength of your word, God. And I thank you *for* Debra. I thank you that you have blessed this town with her presence, Lord. We all have times of weakness. Times of doubt. Times of uncertainty. It is in these times that we find strength in you. I pray whatever is burdening Debra, whatever the source of that weight, I pray you help her through this. We understand all struggles in this world are fleeting. Storms pass. They come and go but your love is forever. The eternal nature of your kingdom is a comforting light in the darkness of this world. For if you are for us, Lord, who can be against us? I pray for

Debra, God, but I thank you for Debra. It is in your magnificent name we pray, amen."

"Amen," I said, wiping away the tears from my cheek.

"Is everyone okay, Debra? Is there anything you need to tell me?"

"No, Pastor," I said. "Thank you for your prayer."

Chapter Sixteen

Sheriff George Cremble

t woulda been Christmas '99, because I remember we was talking about all that Y2K nonsense – with the computers and whatnot. And I believe Helen Doyle was dealing with her medical condition at the time. My old man had been sick for most of the year. Coughing fits and fevers and the works. Spent quite a bit of time in the hospital because my mama made him. I think he's like a lotta us when it comes to our health – stubborn as a two-dollar mule. I asked him when the last time he went to the doctor and he'd respond asking when the last time I went to the doctor. Fair point. But he was in real rough shape in early December and there was a stretch there we thought it would be it. We had arrangements all made. But the tough son of a gun pulled through and there we was talking at Christmas.

"Things pretty quiet at work?" he asked me when it was just the two of us in the living room.

"As a mouse."

"Quiet can be good," he said, sipping his hot bourbon.

"Can be," I said. "I know some of the fellas wish there was a little more action."

"Action is a young man's game," he said.

"I suppose."

"How much you feel like you got left?" he asked.

"I don't know," I said. "Five years. Maybe ten. Sometimes it depends what day you ask me."

"Yeah, you've had a pretty good run."

"Twenty-six years," I said.

"Not quite thirty," he said with a smile.

"I'm sure I'll catch you one of these days."

"Hope you do. You glad you done it?"

"Be sheriff?"

"Yes sir. You glad you done it?"

"I don't know if I had a choice in the matter."

"Oh, come on now. Everybody got a choice. You wishing you did something else?"

"No, no. I'm glad I done it. Carried the name."

"Looks like the Cremble line for sheriffs is ending the day you retire," he said.

We only had girls, you know, and even the grandchildren – all girls. It was like the universe was saying it ain't want no more Crembles as sheriff in Well Springs. Maybe one of the granddaughters will grow up to be sheriff – show the universe you can't stop Cremble blood.

"Are *you* glad you done it?" I asked him.

"I think so," he said.

"You think?"

"Yeah, I think we done some good in our time," he said. "I know it didn't end on the most pleasant of terms – with what happened with

Charles. But I know whatever I done, I always had the best for Well Springs in my heart."

"I feel the same way," I said.

The thought crossed me to tell him about what really happened with Sam Jenkins. It really had. We was reminiscing and it was just the two of us. I coulda told him what I done with the Jenkins boy and seen what he woulda thought. Get his opinion while he was still with us, you know. Maybe he woulda told me to walk with my chin held high – that I done the right thing and it was best for the family to let it be. Or maybe he'd be ashamed of me. Ashamed I used the power of the badge to cover up a murder. Then he woulda gone to his grave thinking his boy ain't worth two licks, in terms of being a sheriff. Maybe he woulda felt the obligation to turn *me* in. How about that for a family Christmas?

I ain't say a word. I kept to myself and thought maybe next Christmas I'd let him know. Maybe I'd feel different then.

On December 29, 1999, Mama called the house and told Maggie what had happened. Sheriff William Cremble had himself a brain hemorrhage and died right there in his living room.

**

I stayed long after everybody left – I even told Maggie to go on home. I wanted a little alone time with my old man. She gave me a kiss on the cheek and then took the girls and grandbabies back to our house. There was a pile of flowers and pictures and little knick-knacks laying on his grave. It was a beautiful ceremony – lots of speakers and tears and laughter. But now I stood alone, looking at his tombstone.

Sheriff William W. Cremble

1917 – 1999

The Conscience of Well Springs

"How you doing there, Dad?" I asked. "I know you're up there in a better place, so I feel like a real piece of work being so sad about it. I know there's lots that I coulda said over the years. I hope you know how much I loved you. I hope you know how much I admired you. And not just 'cause you were my daddy. You was a great man. It says right there: 'The Conscience of Well Springs.' Maggie thought that one up. It's a good one.

"I know they talk about the Cremble Curse and whatnot. Hell, you know the curse I felt? Trying to outrun the shadow you left being sheriff. I thought about telling you this at Christmas. I mean it. I really did think about it.

"I know you wondered about the Jenkins case. Well, I need to tell you. I don't know why I never did tell you. Maybe I was scared about it. I was scared about what you might think. I always tried to do the job proud. I always took the job seriously because I know it was a part of the family – which meant the job I done as sheriff would always be a part of you.

"It wasn't no stranger, Sheriff. It wasn't no stranger.

"The boy killed him. The eldest. Cody. Shot him dead at night when he slept. Shot him over and over and over. I never seen something so nasty. Fred Doyle called me and so I went over to the Jenkins house and into the bedroom and there they was: Sam shot to hell lying dead in the bed. Debra was off in the corner. Cody stood at the foot of the bed with the gun in his hands. Can't believe something like this – in Well Springs.

"And you know what I done? Covered it up.

"I covered the whole doggone damn thing up. I told Debra and Cody I would take care of everything. We came up with the plan to say it was some stranger from outta town that was there to rob them. I even went to talk to Fred and got him sharing a story about something that ain't even happen. Got him testifying about a vehicle driving off that weren't even there.

"What was I supposed to do? I mean it. What was I supposed to do, Sheriff? Arrest a ten-year-old boy? Sam Jenkins was a real son of a bitch. Why should that boy spend the rest of his days behind bars for doing something nobody else had the guts to do? What would you have done? Let's say a child killed Charles instead of you that day? Would you uphold the law and arrest the child? Or let things be?

"Maybe things is black and white. Maybe. Maybe there's right and there's wrong and what Cody done was wrong and he needed to pay the price. Where does it end, though? I think we make compromises every day of our life. We know what we should do, but then there's what we actually do.

"I don't know.

"From the day it happened, I wondered what you woulda done. I wondered what you woulda thought about what I done. Would you approve? Never had the guts to say it though. I should have. Lord knows I should have. But I admired you so much that I couldn't handle if you thought I brought shame to the position. And if you do feel that way, I wanted to let you know I'm sorry. I'm sorry for what I had done to the job you held so dear.

"You was in the right, you know that? With what happened with Charles. He woulda killed me or you or both of us. He woulda killed you, Sheriff. It was your instinct. If I asked you if you meant to kill him, you woulda said you didn't *mean* to do anything. You just did it. I wonder how things woulda turned out if Charles ain't come at us like that. Maybe he finally settles down and lives a nice, God-fearing life. That means you ain't step down when you did. Maybe you keep being sheriff and you was in charge in '93 when the Jenkins murder went down.

"What would you have done?"

I looked around the cemetery and it was only me. I composed myself and looked back down at all of the flowers near the tombstone. Somebody had knitted this sheriff's badge. It had *Well Springs Police* on it and everything. I couldn't help but think he was the only one to deserve it. I told him I loved him one more time and headed back to my truck, but then I came across the Jenkins family. There they was, all lined up in a row. Henry. Loretta. Sam. Father, mother, son. I stopped at Sam's tombstone.

"How you doing, Sam?" I said. "I don't know if word spread up there yet, but my old man died recently. They buried him right over there. Bad stroke. I ain't gonna insult you, talking about how bad I got it. Sheriff Cremble was a good man. A good father. I'm sorry you got the upbringing you had. I know Henry ain't much of a kind-hearted man. I can't believe you put up with it all that time.

"I don't wanna sound morbid or nothing like that, but I wonder how much things woulda been different if you done to Henry what Cody done to you. I wonder if you woulda turned out different. Maybe my old man woulda had to deal with that – you killing Henry. Wouldn't that have been something? Then I woulda known what he woulda done in my situation.

"But you ain't do it. You ain't kill your old man. You decided to live with it and look what it turned you into. You know, you had a lot of chances, son. You ain't need to turn out like Henry. I warned you. Remember? When I came to your house and told you to straighten up. You had this great life Sam, and you couldn't handle it. I can't think of a man alive who wouldn't have loved the life you got – a beautiful wife and four darling children. Why couldn't you turn it around, Sam? If you woulda taken responsibility for your actions, Cody wouldn't have done that. Then I wouldn't need to live with what I done. We all coulda lived happily ever after if you just got your life together.

"But you couldn't do it. You wanted to create this giant mess for the rest of us and look where it got you. Buried here next to Henry.

"Maybe I shoulda done more. Maybe we all shoulda done more to get you straight. Maybe I shoulda brought you in. It ain't have to end like this – with you lying there.

"Your family's doing pretty good. I know Tommy idolizes you. Cody turned into a good young man. He ain't into football and all that, but he's got a good heart. He's gonna be a good man, you can just see it.

"What would you have wanted me to do? If you had known? Would you want me to arrest Cody? Put him behind bars? Pin it on Debra and send her away and leave the children without a parent? It'd ruin the family forever. Hell, you'd want Henry and Loretta to get the children?

"Or would you rather me do what I done? Cover it up for the good of the children? Let everybody just move on? I think I done the right thing, but I need you to know that I have felt the weight of it since the day it happened. Maybe it's you lingering around. But it's best. I mean it, Sam. I thought of *everything* and this was the way it had to be. I hope you can come to terms with it."

I nodded to Sam's tombstone before doing the same to Henry and Loretta's – no sense in being rude. I walked back to my truck and sat there for a little while. Thinking. It's a lot.

You know the funny deal about all this? The way the cemetery's set up, in order to get to my old man's grave, I gotta walk past Sam's.

**

I never talked to Debra about it, but I wonder if she thinks about it on Easter. Can't imagine she ain't think about it. I wonder if she's even able to think about Easter itself – about Jesus coming back from the dead and what-not. For a while there, no matter what Pastor Wilheim said up there, I ain't think about nothing other than Sam Jenkins.

You ask Debra about that?

I remember one year, when the pastor was preaching, I thought about the *symbolism* of it all. Easter and Sam. Death and life, you know? Maybe I was putting too much into it. But that's what Easter is all about ain't it? Being reborn from death. Conquering the grave, the man said.

The people those children became — except for maybe Cassie, bless her heart — I think everything turned out pretty okay.

Maybe Sam's death is what gave them all life. Maybe Sam's death set that family free. I know, I know. I'm stretching now. But what if I ain't? What if it really is the truth? It's one of those, what'd they call it, difficult truths? Difficult truths is still true.

Or maybe I'm trying to convince myself.

I'd say for a good ten years it consumed me on Easter. The family got together for a nice dinner and I'd smile my way through it, but I'd think 'bout what I'd seen that night — seeing Sam like that. Seeing what Cody done to him. I thought it'd be my curse till the end of time.

I can't pinpoint when things started to change and I began to think about that night less and less. Eventually, Easters would come and I'd think about Jesus again and what he'd done for me. Quite the sacrifice for a sinner like me. I enjoyed Easter dinners and time spent with family and friends. You always hear that expression about time being the ultimate healer, or something or another. Time heals all wounds, I believe. I suppose there's some truth to that.

Debra and the children eventually moved on with their lives. I was able to move on with mine. We never did catch "the burglar," but Well Springs moved on too. People stopped asking and worrying about it. Maybe some people still think about it and wonder what happened. That's why I wasn't too sure about doing this. Talking with you. Why bring something back up if everyone decided to move on? But maybe some wounds ain't deserve to heal.

It's one of those deals you ain't know how you'd feel unless it happened to you. Maybe you'd think you'd never forget about it. Maybe you'd think it would always be there. Be a part of you.

That's fair.

But you know what it reminds me about? I remember the day Sam got put in the ground, and they filled the hole back up. There was his grave, brimming with fresh dirt – a wretched shade of brown dirt.

You know what eventually happens?

Grass starts growing.

**

We had a couple of kids – teenagers – spray some real nasty stuff on the wall outside the library during the summer of 2009. It ain't even worth repeating. It wasn't nothing about the case – just some nasty stuff. When I was growing up, you had respect for your town. You had respect for your elders. These kids now, they got a mean streak and don't care much for Well Springs. Talking trash and skateboarding and what-have-you.

I felt it brewing for a while, but I talked to Maggie one night about hanging it up.

"Are you sure sweetheart?" she said, putting down her book.

"I think I am," I said.

"What will you do?"

"I don't know. The world, Maggie, I think it's passing me by."

"Why do you say that?"

"I don't know. Kids these days, they got no respect. Maybe sheriff is a young man's game. Why sit around when somebody else can do the job?"

"Well Springs without a Sheriff Cremble," she said.

"Believe me, I thought about that too," I said.

"Are you gonna have enough to keep busy?"

"I'm sure. I got projects around the house and we can see the grandkids. Go to their games and whatnot."

"Are you sure about this Georgie?"

"I think it's time."

I got to the station a little early the next day – feeling sentimental and all. We got pictures of the other Sheriff Crembles on the wall – Sheriff Wesley Cremble and Sheriff William Cremble. I knew after I retired, my kisser was going up there too. Maybe I wasn't the best of the Sheriff Crembles, but I was the longest serving. Thirty-six years. Nobody could take that away. There was bad nights, back after Cody killed Sam, that I thought about walking away. I felt like I ain't deserve the badge.

"You'll be up there one day, Sheriff, don't worry," a voice called behind me. It was Kyle Dunham, one of my men. He snapped me out of it.

"I'm only looking, Kyle," I said.

"You're here early," he said, putting his things down on the desk.

"Felt like coming in."

"One of the boys finally ratted out the others," he said. "Now we got names, so I'll probably swing by their houses today."

"That's good. I don't know about this generation."

"Oh, come on now, Sheriff. There's always some knuckleheads in every generation. It's human nature."

"I suppose. Did we get all the paint off the library?"

"I believe so."

"That's good. That's good. I don't know, Kyle. These teenagers."

"Boys will be boys, Sheriff."

During our morning meeting, I called everybody together and told thm I was stepping down. I told them I was an old man and an old man ain't cut out to be no sheriff. There was some gasps and a couple of obscene words whispered when I told them the news. They was so gracious though. They tried to talk me outta it – saying Well Springs needed a Sheriff Cremble. I told them the decision was final. I was gonna be calling the county commission and let them know I was stepping down – I wanted the team to know before I started sharing the news.

Word spread pretty quick, I'd say. It weren't even lunch before I started getting phone calls from people about town. Couldn't get any work done because it was one phone call after the next. People was so kind and had such nice things to say. At the end of the day, I put everything on my desk – badge, gun and so forth. Then I walked out.

The county put together an emergency meeting and asked me if I had any thoughts about who should take over the position. It was pretty clear Kyle Dunham should be the man – even a blind man could see it. Of course, he ended up getting it and he's done a heck of a job. He's got a beautiful wife and a couple of young children. The perfect family. I walked away knowing Well Springs was in good hands. After he got sworn in, I came into the station – felt a little odd walking in without wearing my uniform – and he had already settled in to the new desk.

"Sheriff Cremble, what brings you in? You have a change of heart and want the position back?" Sheriff Dunham said, meeting me with a handshake.

"Very funny," I said. "I wanted to stop by and make sure there ain't nothing you needed help with."

"Not at the moment," he said. "You see we put your picture up?"

I hadn't, but sure enough there I was. Lined up next to my daddy and granddaddy. It was something else seeing it up there. We stood there admiring it.

"They'd be proud," he said, patting me on the back.

"Well, I sure hope so," I said.

"You keeping busy?"

"Trying to, but here I am."

"Good point. I hope you know you are always welcome here. Anytime you want to stop by and chat or help me with anything. You always have a place here. Consider yourself Sheriff Emeritus."

"I sure appreciate that."

"I know I got a lot to learn, so any advice for a young fool?" he said.

"I'll tell you the same thing my old man told me: whatever you do, you make sure you do what's right."

"That's good advice."

"You're gonna be one hell of a Sheriff, Kyle. I know it."

"You're very kind, Sheriff," he said. "I guess now that I'm the one in charge, anything about the job I should know about?"

"How do you mean?"

"I don't know. Anything about the job you keep private from the other officers?"

"Like what?"

"Sensitive information or something?"

"You been watching too many movies, Kyle," I said.

"I was only messing around, Sheriff. I know this gig isn't like the movies. I hope my time is nice and quiet like yours."

"I don't know if my time was all that quiet," I said. "I wish you the best, son. I know you'll do what's best for this town."

**

In the movies and TV shows, when somebody is laying there dying, they always say something memorable and profound. It's all dramatic-like. They tell you everything you need to know: how much you mean to them, how much they enjoyed being with you, how much they loved you. It's a nice sentiment.

By the end, Maggie was in pretty rough shape. She got pretty bad pretty quick. She just laid in bed. I tried talking to her, but she ain't respond to nothing. If it weren't for the pulse, you'd believe she passed.

The lights were on, as they say, but nobody was home. This was a few years back. I'm glad I spent some years retired so we could enjoy what time we had left together. We traveled all over. We saw the grandchildren grow up. We had a lot of love in this house.

It was a Wednesday morning and I was sitting in my chair on her side of the bed.

"I hope I was a good man to you Margaret," I said. She ain't respond, of course. She just stared up at the ceiling. "I hope you felt loved. I couldn't have asked for a better wife. Truly. I can't begin to tell you how lucky I felt each and every day of my life. You supported me and maybe I never appreciated how much support you gave me. I know you loved me, darling.

"There is something I gotta tell you, though. Ain't no affair or nothing. I don't want you worrying about that. I will love you and only you until my last breath. But I had done something as sheriff and I don't know if you'd approve. I thought about telling you, but I ain't want you losing respect for me. I also ain't want you to feel complicit, so to speak.

"I know I told you back in the day it was a burglar that had gone and killed Sam Jenkins. And I spent the rest of my career chasing and looking for the person who killed him.

"Truth is, I knew who done it. I knew who done it since the night it happened. No. It weren't her. Some people thought it was, but she ain't the one. It was one of the boys. Cody. He woulda been about ten or so when he killed Sam. It was terrible, Margaret. Terrible. I never seen nothing like it. The boy shot him over and over again. Fred Doyle called me, as you remember. When I got there, it was just the four of us – myself, Cody, Debra and what was left of Sam.

"Can you imagine? A young boy standing there after killing his daddy. I couldn't believe it. And I helped cover it up. I was the one to come up with the phony baloney story about a burglar. I wanted it to go away. I don't know if I done the right thing. I don't know if you can understand me, but I felt I needed to tell you. I felt like you deserved to know the truth. Least when you're still here with me.

"Do you think I done the right thing? Why should the boy – he was just a boy! He didn't know no better. Sam Jenkins had every opportunity to make the most of what he had and he kept letting them down. Hitting her and drinking himself to death. What if Sam was the one to go too far? Wouldn't *that* be the tragedy? But then what good is a sheriff if he ain't uphold the law.

"Believe me, sweetheart: it was a tricky one. I hope you woulda told me I done the best I could. That enforcing the law woulda only caused more harm to this town – sending the boy away or sending the mama away. Then what?

"Deep down, I think I done the right thing. The town ended up healing and the Jenkins family turned out all right. Cody got himself a nice business and turned into a good young man. The others turned out good, for the most part. If Cody gets arrested, who knows how the family woulda turned out. Even so, I don't know why I spent my life feeling like I got away with something. If it was the right thing, why did I feel like I had to hide it from you?

"I don't know.

"It probably ain't right of me to tell you all this. If you ain't happy with me, that's fair. I hope you understand though. I wish I told you back when it happened. I shouldn't have hidden the truth from you. But I didn't wanna drag you into the muck.

"I know you ain't able to say nothing, but I'd give the king's ransom to hear you tell me you love me one more time. To tell me that you understand, and you still believe I done the right thing. That I can hold my head high and come to heaven myself and have my daddy and granddaddy tell me that I'd done good."

Of course, she ain't say nothing back because this ain't the movies. She kept staring at the ceiling. The next day, I woke up, took my shower, and got ready. I was heading off somewhere – don't remember where – when I went to kiss her on the forehead. I felt her neck like I always done before leaving and didn't feel nothing.

She was finally gone.

I can't help but feel telling her what I done is what killed her. Maybe that's me finally paying the price.

It was a beautiful funeral. Pastor Wilheim had a nice sermon and everybody had such lovely things to say about Maggie. It felt like the whole doggone town was inside the church. Our girls had come with their families and sat by my side, holding my hands. I told Pastor Wilheim I'd like to say a few words. I wrote up a short little speech and had it tucked into my pocket, but forgot to take it out when I got to the podium.

"I'd like to thank everyone for showing up here today. I know she woulda been tickled pink to see so many people. She loved this town. We loved this town. I can't imagine raising a family anywhere other than Well Springs. I can feel your love.

"I have been with Margaret for more than sixty years. That's an awful long time to keep a woman like her. She was the best person I ever known. A great wife and even better mother. Some of you may know this, but my daddy was sheriff before me. When I took over, it was a very emotional time. A lot going on, you know. I will never forget it. I stepped down off the stage to go sit next to her after taking the sheriff position. There she was – smiling and crying – when she rubbed back and said 'Sheriff Cremble.'

"I can imagine being a sheriff's wife can be a bit hard. I probably ain't spend as much time as I should have at home with her. There are things

I shoulda done. Things I shoulda said. I suppose I need to tell you all something, now that she's gone. Ain't no point in hiding it no more."

I could feel my hands shaking a bit and I looked out to the crowd. I looked at my babies and grandbabies. There was the Jenkinses – Debra and Cody. When I said that, Debra grabbed his hand. Lots of people was crying and wiping their eyes. There was Sheriff Dunham, standing there in uniform.

"Uh..." I started, and I could feel my voice start shaking. "I wanted to tell y'all I can't help but feel like I failed as a man. Being a sheriff, you know, there's a lot to it. I know it's been a long while, but I still think about how Sam Jenkins died on my watch. I told Maggie I'd find the man who done it. I looked in her eyes and told her I would protect this town. That I would find him. She believed me. Y'all believed me. She believed every word and I spent my life running away from the feeling that I let her down. That I let Well Springs down. I couldn't do it. I couldn't find the person who done it.

"I failed her. And I failed y'all."

"Sheriff, come on now," Pastor Wilheim said, coming up on stage. "I know I speak for everyone when I say how proud I am of the job you have done for Well Springs. You are a good man, Sheriff Cremble. Margaret was proud to be your wife. I could see it in the way she looked at you. We all could. You mustn't be so hard on yourself."

"I hope she woulda been proud of what I done," I softly said to myself.

**

I remember reading something about how when somebody dies, their spouse ain't stick around too much longer after that. Maybe it's 'cause they wanna get back to them. Maybe it's 'cause the body ain't find a reason to fight death no more. I was expecting I would kick the bucket pretty soon after Maggie went. I felt like I ain't have much to live for anymore. I would wake up and fiddle around the house. Kill enough time to make it to the next day and wonder if I'd see her after I went to bed.

But I kept waking up in the morning.

I know Maggie woulda grabbed me by the collar if she knew I was moping around. You know what changed my mood? I can't tell you how much I appreciate this: Sheriff Dunham came to my door one day. Part of me was a bit nervous, thinking word finally got out and he was coming to get me. Instead, he told he wanted me to have lunch with him every Monday and Friday.

I would tell him stories about back in the day and he'd tell me stories about what's going on now. He'd pick my brain and ask for advice on things. Maybe he was just being kind – humoring an old man. Maybe he meant it. I'll tell you what: those lunches are my favorite times of the week. Gives me something to look forward to.

I'm gonna miss those lunches.

But I suppose it's time for me to pay the piper. When you first came to me, asking to talk about everything with the Sam Jenkins case, I ain't know what to think. I don't know who told what. Maybe you was just looking into cold cases – the mystery of it all.

You're lucky I'm a tired old fool, you know that? I don't know if you talked to Cody or Debra. Or who you talked to. After you reached out, I went over to Cody's house. Knocked on the door and Debra answered.

"Debra, how are you?" I asked.

"I'm doing fine, Sheriff. How are you?"

"Oh, I don't know. I actually need to talk to Cody about something."

"I know you do," she said.

"You do?"

"I do. Come on in."

I walked into the living room and Cody was already sitting there on the sofa. He got up and shook my hand and asked if I wanted anything. I declined and we sat together there.

"Got an interesting call the other day," I said.

"That makes two of us."

"What'd they tell you?"

"They said they wanted to talk to me about my dad's death."

"Yeah."

"What do you think?" he asked.

"What do I think? Well, that's a good one. I told myself I would never tell a soul. And I hadn't."

"You haven't?" Cody asked.

"No sir. Well, I told Maggie but that was right before she passed."

"What do you think we should do?" he asked.

"Cody, I told you I would protect you and your mama until my dying day and if that's what you would like, then I will be happy to tell them I am not interested in talking about the case."

"I think you want to talk," he said.

"Come on, Cody," I said.

"I don't mean any ill will about it. I put you and my mama in a pretty bad spot. You had to spend a long time covering for me. That isn't right."

"Well, it was necessary, son."

"Maybe so. Do you think you would feel better if people knew the truth?"

"Oh, I don't know," I said.

"It's okay if the answer is yes, Sheriff. That's an awful big thing to hold onto. It isn't like they're going to send you away."

"You don't know that."

"Sheriff, please don't take it personal, but they aren't about to send a man of your age to prison for something like this."

297

"And what about you?" I said.

"What about me?

"They're gonna take you in."

"Maybe," Cody said.

"Debra, you wanna talk some sense into him?"

"Sheriff, he's a man now. He can make his own decisions," she said.

"Cody, you ain't gotta do this," I said.

"I'm still thinking about it."

"Have you thought much about it over the years?" I asked Cody. "Other than when they came and asked about it?"

"A little bit here and there. I've tried to keep myself busy so I wouldn't think about it. Besides, if they lock me up, it's not like I have a wife or kids or anything."

"What about your brother and sisters? What would they think?"

"Tommy would try and be the attorney to put me away," Cody laughed. "He'd try and get the death penalty."

"That ain't funny, Cody," I said.

"Sheriff, I was a boy. I didn't know any better."

"I know you ain't."

"Do you think we did the right thing?" he asked me.

"I do."

"Well, then we shouldn't have anything to worry about," he said. He got up and came to shake my hand. "Thank you, Sheriff."

"I wish you the best, son."

After I left his house, I drove back over to Debra's. I parked on the curb and stayed in the truck. She had painted the house a few years back, so it looks a little different from the day Sam was killed. I thought about all them children growing up there. I remember seeing them running all over the yard. I remember them hosting parties in the backyard in the summer when the children were older. Alotta love.

Then I thought about the image of Sam Jenkins – bloody and lifeless there in the bed. I thought about the screams from Debra and about Cody's face looking at me. Pure brutality.

Then I thought about driving over the station, walking over to Sheriff Dunham, and telling him I was the one who killed Sam Jenkins. That I killed him and covered it up. That I told Debra if she told a soul, I would pin it on her and send her away and give her children to Henry and Loretta. Then I thought about them taking my picture down off that wall in the station. That I weren't good enough to be up there with Sheriff Wesley Cremble and Sheriff William Cremble. Then I thought about my own girls – how it would ruin them. Their daddy, the lawman of Well Springs, was nothing more than a criminal himself. A killer.

I sat there in the truck for quite some time, just thinking. Wondering what mighta been. Then I thought about how pointless it is to wonder, you know? It happened and there ain't no do-overs and so forth. I turned on my truck, drove myself home, and sat down on the living room couch.

That's when I called you back.

Author's Note: Cody Jenkins declined multiple interview requests.

About the Author

Jesse Severson spent more than a decade as an award-winning journalist before leaving the industry to become a copywriter for a marketing/advertising agency. Born and raised in Portland, Oregon, he now lives in the Chicago suburbs with his wife. Cody is his first novel.

Made in the USA
Monee, IL
27 May 2023